Alouette, Michigan. Located high on the Upper Peninsula. Home to strong men, stalwart women and lots and lots of trees. If you come, bring your camera—you won't believe the number of stars in our skies or the color of our sunsets. And if you're lucky, you might just meet a cute critter or two. But remember: The U.P. is not like anywhere else. We even have our own language. Don't worry, though. It's easy to learn. Here are a couple of pointers:

YOOPER: resident of Michigan's Upper Peninsula (aka the U.P.)

FOURTH OF JULY: Yooper summer.

HOLY WAH!: Yooper exclamation.

TROLL: resident of Michigan's Lower Peninsula (below the Mackinac Bridge).

FINNISH TERMS:

MUMMU: grandmother

PIKKU: little (girl)

RIIESKA: half bread, half biscuit—all good

SISU: character, grit, spunk—Finnish-style

SAUNA: steam bath (aka Finnish religion)

VIHTA: switch made of birch branches

Dear Reader,

This book was a long time in coming. Ever since I began writing for Harlequin, I've intended to set a book in my hometown area, the Upper Peninsula of Michigan. But it had to be the right story, the right setting and the right characters....

Noah and Claire are it—big and bold and brave. And Bay House is it, so real to me on the cliff overlooking Lake Superior that I just might try to check in. As for the town of Alouette and the supporting cast—well, they're completely fictional, but also entirely familiar. I hope you recognize a little bit of your own hometown in them.

Please look for my forthcoming Superromance stories about the people of Alouette. If you'd like to know more, visit my new Web site at www.carriealexander.com, where you can get the inside scoop and secret family recipes for lumberjack cookies and *riieska*.

Forever a Yooper,

Carrie Alexander

Books by Carrie Alexander

HARLEQUIN SUPERROMANCE
1042—THE MAVERICK

HARLEQUIN DUETS
83—ONCE UPON A TIARA
   HENRY EVER AFTER

North Country Man
Carrie Alexander

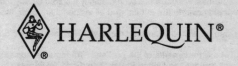

HARLEQUIN®

TORONTO • NEW YORK • LONDON
AMSTERDAM • PARIS • SYDNEY • HAMBURG
STOCKHOLM • ATHENS • TOKYO • MILAN • MADRID
PRAGUE • WARSAW • BUDAPEST • AUCKLAND

ISBN 0-373-71102-6

NORTH COUNTRY MAN

Copyright © 2002 by Carrie Antilla.

This edition published by arrangement with Harlequin Books S.A.

® and TM are trademarks of the publisher. Trademarks indicated with ® are registered in the United States Patent and Trademark Office, the Canadian Trade Marks Office and in other countries.

Visit us at www.eHarlequin.com

Printed in U.S.A.

CHAPTER ONE

"YEAH, I WANTED to get away from it all," Claire Levander said to herself as the rental car bumpety-bumped along the ridges of the lonely two-lane country road. The blacktop had buckled like cardboard left out in the rain. "But I didn't expect to be sent to the ends of the earth."

Suddenly a pickup truck with a gun rack in its rear window roared by on the left. Her lungs seized as she jerked the steering wheel to the right, then fought to control her instinctive need to get away. The truck was too close.

Claire didn't draw a proper breath until the vehicle had swung into the proper lane. The eggbeater rattle of its engine was shockingly loud with no other traffic around. She was accustomed to the efficient hum of the airport shuttles that were her normal mode of transportation to a new job.

Truthfully, it was the entire situation that had shaken her. Although she'd practically begged Drake for an easy assignment, she'd been thinking deluxe accommodations, not unrelenting rusticity. For her, country meant friendly folks, humble cottages, open farmland and a freeway to the city.

Not this—this barely civilized wilderness.

The pickup sped away, blatting stinky blue smoke from its tailpipe. The rust-eaten muffler drooped dangerously low, hanging on by a few wires.

Claire imagined that these backwoods roads were constantly littered with mufflers, tailpipes and oil pans. The country was supposed to be safe, but the odds of her getting stranded with car trouble out here in the boondocks were probably worse than being mugged on a subway.

"Drat that Drake. This is not what I need right now." Claire clenched her fingers on the wheel and slowly eased her rental car's tires away from the crumbling edge of the blacktop. She did not want to wind up in the ditch.

A dense, tangled forest met in a canopy over the narrow road, screening all but the ambient light of the setting sun. The snatches of sky visible through the interlaced treetops looked bruised—purple and dusky blue, faintly tinged with yellow. If she'd known her journey to the hinterlands would end like this, she'd have forgone her habit of arriving the day before a meeting and booked a morning flight. Instead, efficient as ever, she'd chosen to be early. To get the lay of the land.

Never had the phrase been so appropriate. Thus far, it was a wild, rugged, alarmingly unpopulated land. She'd driven a half hour from the airport before she'd reached a town of any consequence, then realized that she still had farther to go. Since Marquette, signs of civilization had diminished. There were no roadside conveniences. Little traffic. No habitation, either, except for the occasional driveways—if such overgrown paths could be called driveways—that led off through the woods.

"To the ends of the earth," Claire muttered, wishing she hadn't been quite so open with Drake about her dilemma.

Upon hearing the dubious results of Claire's annual physical, her boss had promised her a working vacation. "This one's a slam dunk, Claire. You'll love Upper Michigan," Drake the Snake had said, speaking with the usual forked tongue. "One breath of the fresh air will clear your lungs of city pollution. One walk through the woods will soothe that incipient ulcer. You'll have pure relaxation—no worries and no expectations. We've booked you directly into Bay House, so you'll be on the premises with almost nothing to do. Set your own pace on this one, hon." Drake had chuckled. "No, that's not so wise, is it? I want you to take it easy this time out. You've earned a gimme assignment."

Claire nodded. Why hadn't Drake sent her to Key West or Carmel-by-the-Sea, where she could have relaxed in luxury? Because he was a slithering reptile, that's why. For months now, he'd been raking in the accolades that were rightfully hers.

The sun had almost set. She frowned at the darkening road. Feeling vaguely like Livingstone hacking through the jungle, she switched the headlights to high beams and pressed on. It took more than a slimy boss and a little bit of wilderness to defeat Claire Levander.

Friends and acquaintances considered her job with the Bel Vista Hotel Corporation a paid vacation. They were dead wrong. She did advance acquisition work for the luxury bed-and-breakfast division, which meant she traveled around the U.S. and Canada and even the occasional foreign port, checking into tourist towns, checking out various charming inns and stately Victorians for potential profitability.

It had seemed like a plum assignment when she'd been awarded the position eighteen months ago. But the nomadic lifestyle, combined with the pressure of recommending acquisitions that could go from black ink to black hole with one unforeseen mechanical failure or plumbing disaster, had wreaked havoc with her nervous system. Even the company's doctor had advised her to scale back, and he was notoriously more corporate than caring.

To Claire's surprise, the prospect of slowing her climb to the top had been appealing, even when she tried to remember that it was traitorous to the goals she'd set for herself at sixteen. She'd been with Bel Vista since college, had worked her way up from the most junior of executive assistants. The long hours and hectic schedule had meant postponing her personal life, particularly the romantic side of it. Even her family obligations had suffered. She'd felt guilty about that, but she hadn't stopped to think that the stress would eventually become physical as well as emotional.

She'd grown up in a small, old-fashioned town where it had sometimes seemed that hairdresser or housewife were the only options for a female. Claire had set her sights…further. Not higher, really, just further.

Early on, she'd realized that a good education and career were her best routes out of Florence, Nebraska. She hadn't foreseen that she might grow to miss what she'd once been desperate to leave or that settling down did not always mean settling.

Unfortunately, *settling down* and *Bel Vista executive* were not synonymous expressions. She had four weeks of vacation coming, but Drake the Snake wasn't about to clear the way for her to take it. Her present assignment—an unpromising bed-and-breakfast in the dinky backwater town of Alouette, Michigan—was about as generous as Drake Wylie got.

Not even *he* seemed to expect her to come up with a business plan to buy Bay House cheap and turn it into a thriving Bel Vista operation. Meaning she had an entire week to do her research and produce a complimentary but ultimately negative report that would satisfy the fat-cat executive who'd proposed the idea in the first place.

That also gave her a week to decide which path her life should take. Tough luck for her that she'd have to do it in such an unsettling, bewildering land.

Claire let out a wry chuckle as she peered out the window at the dense forest. She wanted to find her way—not lose all direction.

Just when she'd seriously begun to wonder if she was the last person on earth, a roadside convenience store appeared up ahead. She slowed to look it over as she passed.

The Buck Stop.

Frankly, the place was a dump. Asphalt shingles, worn board siding plastered with faded advertisements. A neon beer sign in the window and one bare light-bulb over the crooked screen door. A nondescript car idled in the small gravel parking lot. Bel Vista's up-scale clientele would sooner go without their frappuccinos than shop at such a shabby joint—and that included the ones who'd read too much Hemingway and fancied themselves backwoods adventurers.

Claire sniffed. So much for civilization!

A minute later, she squinted at the odometer. Before setting off from the airport, she'd studied her map, laid out her route and calculated the mileage. Alouette, with a population of approximately sixteen hundred forsaken souls, wasn't far now. Electricity and hot water were probably the best she could hope for out of Bay House, but her spirits lifted anyway.

As she settled back in the car seat, a movement at the side of the road caught her eye.

Bear!

The large, furry shape shifted, blending into the shadows as she sped by, but there was no mistaking the small, gamboling creature at its heels. A cub. Fearfully glancing over her shoulder, Claire touched the brake. The underbrush, briefly lit by the car's taillights, had swallowed the hirsute pair. Slim silvery trunks stood out against the shadowy forest primeval.

"*Wild Kingdom,*" she whispered, struck by her reaction to the raw nature of it all. Her heart was racing, and blood sang in her ears like a timpani.

Only a second or two had passed, but she returned her attention to the road just in time to glimpse a pair of amber eyes glowing at her directly ahead. She slammed on the brakes as a tawny shape—a deer, she realized—flew across the hood as though it had sprouted wings. A thud shook the car.

Claire wrenched the wheel. The vehicle shot off the road, its rear end slewing. She thought she screamed, although the screeching sound that filled the car might have been the brakes. She'd jammed the pedal to the floorboard.

The dense forest closed around the car. Branches and twigs cracked on all sides. Overhanging boughs whisked the windshield like a perverse rural car wash. The auto slammed into something solid and came to a sudden shuddering halt, front end canted at an awkward downward angle.

Claire pushed herself off the steering wheel and cut the ignition. Her panting filled the terrible silence. "I'm fine, I'm fine," she said, feeling her face with shaking fingertips. No blood or broken bones. She released the seat belt. "Fine and dandy."

What about the deer? She remembered the awful thud. It might have been the sound of hooves on the hood. Then again, it might not. Her eyes burned; she squeezed them shut.

"Okay. First things first." She took a deep breath, trying to ease the tight, panicky feeling in her chest. With so much foliage pressed against the windows, the interior of the car was dark and close, almost claustrophobic. She had to get out. Assess the damage. Look for the deer.

The deer. Oh, please.

"Nothing to be afraid of," Claire said, falling back on the habit of talking through a difficult situation. It was a technique she'd used on her brother, Max, to get him to the dentist. And on her baby sister, Lyndsay, to distract her from window-rattling thunderstorms.

Once Claire was finally on her own, she'd found that the technique also worked on herself. She'd talked herself into leaving home for college and staying there even when times got tough. She'd talked herself through standing up for herself with Drake and demanding an overdue raise and promotion. Through the horrible night six months ago when word of her father's death had come while she'd been stranded by a snowstorm in a Vermont inn. The sheer helplessness of not being there for her family had been devastating. The only comfort she'd had was her own voice, repeating into the dark silence of the guest room, "They'll be okay, be okay, be okay...."

Claire was the oldest child in a family of eight, with one parent unreliable and the other consumed with earning a living. It had always been her job to make sure everything was okay. The house. Meals. Clothes. Appointments. School. And especially her siblings.

"But you're okay alone," she said firmly. She opened the door a crack, pushing experimentally at the smothering branches. They were flexible enough to bend out of the way. She poked a leg outside, followed by her head and shoulders. "The deer is okay, too. But I have to make sure."

Her brave voice was swallowed by the overwhelming silence of a north woods night. She stood, inhaling the clear cold air. The forest was all around her. The scent was impossible to describe—nothing like the little pine-tree air freshener that hung from the rearview mirror. She could only define it as green. Earthy. Alive. But it wasn't as quiet as she'd first thought. There were all sorts of sounds—rustling and chattering and an eerie creaking that accompanied each gust of the chilly breeze.

She swallowed nervously. "Nothing to be afraid of. Safe as houses." With a hollow chuckle at the inappropriate expression, she crunched through the brush to check out the front of the car. The bumper was jammed into a huge fallen log. A jagged chunk had been torn out of the mossy bark, revealing a gash of fresh orangy-yellow wood so punky the splinters crumbled at her touch.

A long shallow dent creased the auto's hood. She ran her hand along it and found a clump of hair caught in the grill. Coarse, reddish-brown hair, the silkier ends tipped in gold.

"But no blood," she said, her stomach dropping all the same. She'd never forgive herself if—

"Don't even think it. Just go and look."

Claire returned to the open car door and reached inside to flick off the headlights, which weren't illuminating much besides the fallen log. Still, the depth of the blackness increased by another degree. For a few moments, she was nearly blind. Then her eyes began to adjust. Eventually she realized that the moonlight was bright enough for her to readily see the way. Through the tangled underbrush, the road was visible— a black expanse reflecting the silvery moonlight.

She gathered the car keys, the heavy sweater she'd thrown on the passenger seat—it was mid-May, but colder than she'd expected—and her handbag. Her baggage and laptop computer were safely stowed in the trunk. She slammed the door shut and set the locks, briefly considering her cell phone. She could dial 911. But this probably didn't qualify as an emergency. If she found the deer injured, she'd call. Or she could backtrack a mile to the Buck Stop, probably doing her version of "whistling past the graveyard" the entire way. Someone there would know the procedure.

It wasn't until she'd hiked a short way along the narrow sand shoulder of the road that she remembered the mother bear and her cub. Dread filled her at the chance they could still be lurking nearby. She froze, fists jammed into the pockets of her sweater, wanting nothing so much as to cut and run. Lock herself inside the car. If it was stuck, she'd call AAA. If there was no AAA, she'd stay right there till morning light.

Logically, she knew that the bears were long gone. Wild animals didn't stick around to investigate car crashes. And there weren't grizzlies in Michigan. Even in the Rockies, where they did have them, the odds of a bear attacking a human were greatly exaggerated. On one of her first assignments after the promotion, she'd studied up on grizzlies for a thorough recommendation on a mountain ski lodge that was now a Bel Vista luxury inn frequented by the rich and famous. After all, having a celebrity eaten by a bear would be a publicity nightmare. As an employee, she was more expendable.

Claire tried to laugh. Didn't work. "No bears," she said out loud. She knew that the sound of a human voice should scare them away. "No bears," she repeated, raising the volume.

She took several steps. The noise was minimal in the soft sand, so she moved onto the blacktop, stomping her feet. "Here I am, Mama Bear, heading your way."

The road curved just ahead. She thought this was approximately where she saw the deer, though it was difficult to tell when the landscape was unrelenting forest. The evergreen trees all looked the same, thick and black-green. The deciduous trees were sparse, not yet fully leafed.

Claire spun in a circle, batting away an annoying bug, then shrugged. There was no obvious sign of the accident. No skid marks. Even the place where she'd crashed into the woods looked relatively undisturbed, as if the dense vegetation had swallowed the car whole. How could she possibly find an injured deer?

Talking all the while, she walked slowly through the long weeds that choked the roadside, using a piece of deadwood to poke at the underbrush. A small animal scurried away, too quick and sneaky for her to catch a glimpse.

She shuddered, wanting to believe that the deer had escaped unharmed. Wanting even more to be able to return to the rental car and reverse it onto the road.

And what the heck, while she was at it, why not turn around and drive back to the airport and pretend this was all a bad dream? Her health and optimism would return if she could simply go home to her family—never mind that her stress levels would be quadrupled by their clingy neediness.

Claire peered into the woods. A stand of slender gray poplars stood out against the conifers, striking a chord. This was where she'd seen the big mama bear, silhouetted for an instant against the pale trunks. She'd walked far enough. The deer *must* have bounded away, uninjured.

"Time to turn around," she murmured.

A funny feeling tickled her spine, creeping upward to prickle the hair at her nape. Apprehension.

Her eyes searched the forest. Was that a path?

She stepped closer. It *was* a path. Crowded by saplings and fresh young ferns, nearly overgrown except for a narrow trail that led deeper into the woods. An animal trail, she supposed. Deer and rabbits followed trails. Did bear?

"If they do, I surely won't." Claire swung around to leave, only to realize that something large and hulking was approaching through the woods. How she knew, she wasn't sure. Animal instinct, perhaps. The beast didn't make a lot of noise. Barely a rustling of leaves. But it was there. And it was between her and the car.

The bear.

Icy fear gripped her, rooting her feet in terror. She didn't dare break for the road, where she'd be openly visible. And she could not make herself plunge into the deep, dark woods. Instead she raised the stick she'd picked up, praying it was true that bears rarely attacked humans but ready to defend herself all the same.

The shadowy creature halted, obscured by a thicket of yellow sumac. The air crackled with their mutual awareness. Through the leafy screen, she detected a slight glint. Eyes. Watching eyes.

A sniffling sound, low to the ground, made every hair on Claire's body stand upright. Claws scraped across stone. The cub!

In a flash, she remembered her research. Mother bears were notoriously protective of their cubs. But running might provoke an attack. She should slowly back away. If she could get her feet to move.

The brush began to part.

Don't run, don't run, don't run.

A bloodcurdling yell might scare the bear away.

Claire opened her mouth. Out came a peep so pitiful it wouldn't frighten a rabbit.

Terrified, she dropped her handbag with a soft thud and put both hands on her measly weapon. One foot slid backward, then the other.

The bear lifted its furry head. God, it was huge. Nearly seven feet.

It made a chuffing sound.

Suddenly the cub burst from the bush and charged toward Claire, cavorting like a puppy. Claire yelped and fell, landing on her rump in the tall grass. Momentum sent her somersaulting backward, but she managed to regain her feet. The cub rolled with her, as if this were a game.

"Get away!" Claire turned and stumbled along the path, flailing her weapon from side to side. The cub was on her heels, making eager grunts and groans. It still wanted to play!

The night air seemed to shift, and she could feel the adult bear right behind her, large and hot and hulking. *Oh, please, Sweet Mary, mother of God—*

The bear reached past her shoulder and tugged at the flailing branch. Claire started to tug back out of sheer stubbornness, then realized how foolish, how futile—

For one instant, her mind blanked out. Then it clicked on again.

Bears didn't reach. They swiped. And they probably didn't tug. They snatched.

"Hey, Babe Ruth, want to turn over the weapon before you hit one out of the ballpark?" said a deep, resonant, masculine voice. Without a doubt, a *human* voice.

Claire let go of the branch. She turned, stiff and slow, her wobbly knee joints locked into place. "You're not a bear."

"Nope."

"I thought you were a bear." Her voice rasped like an old rusty hinge.

"Didn't mean to scare you, lady."

Lady? She was shaking in her shoes, fearing for her life, and this unkempt beast was calling her *lady*?

Even though the man wasn't a bear, he was an astonishing sight. Not seven feet, but close to six and a half, maybe. He was huge and muscular, bearded, with thick, shaggy hair that was dark underneath but golden brown on top. No wonder she'd mistaken him for a bear. The man had never made acquaintance with a razor in his life!

"Hello, Grizzly Adams," she said under her breath, not realizing she'd spoken until he tossed his head and laughed.

She took a step back.

His straightforward gaze swept her face. "You're not the first to say so."

Claire offered him a tentative smile, though she was not altogether comforted. He was a stranger, one who looked quite capable of tearing her from limb to limb. At five-eight and one hundred sixty pounds, she was no flyweight herself, but this man was huge all over, from his teeth to his immense chest and the broad hands gripped around the length of wood, right down to his gunboat feet, shod in a pair of tough leather boots with rawhide laces and thick lug soles.

Every instinct told her there was something not quite civilized about him. Perhaps it was his scent—wild and woodsy and musky, utterly foreign to her. Or perhaps it was his barbaric aura—as if he could wrestle a cougar and crunch bones between his teeth.

Claire shivered. She prided herself on her self-sufficiency and adaptability, but this encounter was too much even for her. The man was overwhelming.

Not to mention his sidekick, the bear cub. The little beast stood on its hind legs and batted at her thigh, snagging her trousers. She cried out, backing away.

DKNY separates weren't made for bear cub abuse. The lightweight wool would not hold up to even a playful clawing.

"Stop it, Scrap," said the man. He threw Claire's impromptu baseball bat into the brush, and the cub scrambled after it to investigate, grunting with pleasure as it worried at the undergrowth, rolling back and forth like a giddy toddler.

Claire scrubbed a hand over her face in disbelief. Nope, he was still there. Solid as a tree trunk. And watching her, his eyes predatory beneath a pair of thick brown brows. "What are you doing in the woods at night with a bear cub?" she asked, sounding accusatory rather than merely curious. Her nerves were on edge, and it showed.

"Out for a walk." Almost self-consciously, he touched a brown paper package that lay flat against his right side, tucked inside his belt.

Claire's insides went hollow. She thought of the paper-wrapped bottles her father and his cronies passed around the back room of the family gas station. Then she thought of the liquor signs in the window of the Buck Stop and drew herself up haughtily in defense. "I see." Her hands shook, so she tucked them into fists inside the cuffs of her sweater.

Between the night and the man's beard, she couldn't tell for sure, but she thought he smiled. Briefly. "Fact is, you're the one who's out of place," he said, his deep voice seeming as mild as he could make it. He squatted to pet the cub, who'd emerged from the brush dragging the stick.

Claire blinked. He'd crouched purposely, she thought. To minimize his size.

He knew she was afraid of him.

"You ran your car off the road?" he asked.

"Um, no..." She wasn't sure she wanted him to know the full extent of the situation. Her position was too vulnerable.

"I heard the crash." The cub tumbled head over heels, and he scratched its belly. It really was rather cute and cuddly, no bigger than an oversize teddy bear. "That's why I backtracked."

"I didn't run it off the road," she insisted. "It was your fault."

The fleeting smile again. "Mine?"

"I saw you on the side of the road. I thought you were a bear. You distracted me."

"That so?"

She swallowed thickly. "There was a deer—it might be injured."

He stood, stepping closer so he loomed over her. "You hit it?"

Claire fought not to back away from his sudden aggression. *Never show fear.* Having faced down corporate connivers and street toughs alike, she was not a weakling. She would not cower.

"I don't know for sure. It jumped—right over the car. But there was a thud. And it left a dent. That's why I was looking. I thought— I mean, I had to know..."

He let out a breath and backed off to a less invasive

distance. "If the deer jumped your car, it's probably all right. There's no sign of it?"

"N-no."

"Was the thud hard enough to rock the car?"

"Not really. More of a glancing blow. The car went off the road because I lost control after I slammed on the brakes. I wasn't going very fast in the first place."

"Then the deer will probably survive."

"Oh, thank heaven," Claire gushed. "I've been having Bambi trauma flashbacks. I'd probably cry if—" She felt her cheeks coloring. Now, why had she said that? Female emotions were not valued in the cutthroat corporate world; they probably weren't acceptable here, either.

She continued more briskly. "Tell me, is this sort of thing common in these parts? Do bear cubs substitute for domestic pets? Are the woods populated with Grizzly Adams look-alikes?" Her tone lightened. "Do deer fly?"

Do bearded, disreputable—yet strangely compelling—backwoods characters lurk in the bushes specifically to ambush spooked foreigners?

The man drew his eyebrows down, further screening his eyes. She had no clear idea of his face—it was obscured by the beard and the deep shadows. She almost wanted him to come closer again, just to see the shape of his lips. The color of his eyes.

Almost.

"Do wolves howl at the moon or the man in it?" he said, unexpectedly.

Her eyes widened. "Good question." She hesitated, but her wry sense of humor had kicked in. "Do sharks swim at midnight?" she countered.

"Ah. Do the stars twinkle at noon?"

"If a cell phone rings in the forest and no one's there to hear it, does it make a sound?"

He laughed. A nice, rumbling laugh. "I sure hope not, eh?" Again, he sobered quickly. Obviously he hadn't opened the liquor yet. "Did you bring one—a cell phone?" he asked. "Have you called Triple A?"

"So there is Triple A out here in the boonies?"

"Sure." He shifted from foot to foot. Considering his size, the movement was on a par with the tremors of an avalanche. "Jimmy Jarvi at the Five-Star Oil station takes Triple A calls. Might take him a while to reach you, is all."

"Yeah. Like what—a week?"

"I couldn't say. Never signed up for Triple A myself."

"Well, I'm not sure that I need the assistance. My car's running—"

"Do cars ever run wild?" he cut in, musing out loud, then seemed sheepish that he had. "Sorry."

A smile twitched the corners of Claire's mouth, but she purposely returned to the matter at hand. "I crashed into the bushes. Hit a log. If I can get the car onto the road, it should run—" her lips curved "—just fine."

"I'll give you a push."

She shoved her bangs out of her eyes and looked him up and down. His clothes—a faded chambray shirt and sturdy canvas pants—were worn but clean. Perhaps he wasn't as disreputable as all that. And he certainly looked like he could push a semitrailer out of a swamp. One-handed.

"Thank you," she said. Wings fluttered in her stomach. A disconcerting reaction, seeing as she'd decided he was safe despite the bottle tucked inside his belt. And her judgment was always sound. Always. "I would appreciate that."

He stepped into the long grass to let her go first. She glanced from the disturbing stranger to the playful cub, her sense of the absurd expanding proportionally. None of this was what she'd expected, but for some reason she couldn't wait to see what came next.

There were times in every woman's life when all she could do was roll with the punches.

Or the cub, as the case may be.

WITH THE TOE of his boot, Noah Saari gave Scrap a boost off the rotting log. The orphaned bear cub grunted with surprise and sat down hard on its round rump, confused by its abrupt removal from the center of action.

Noah leaned over the hood of the woman's sedan, keeping one eye on Scrap and the other on the spinning front wheels. "Goose it," he hollered over the sound of the engine, applying his muscle to the task of getting her car on the road.

The stranded city woman nodded, clenching her jaw as she gripped the wheel and brought her foot down on the gas pedal. She looked deadly serious yet still a little pale and wide-eyed. Noah smiled, oddly tickled by her reaction to him. He put his head down and pushed harder, his shoulder muscles bunching with the effort.

The wheels spun, eating through a thick layer of humus and pine needles before the car gave a lurch and began to roll backward. Too speedily. Branches snapped beneath the wheels. Noah gave a shout. "Hold up!"

He stepped over the log, one hand shading his eyes from the harsh glare of the headlights slicing through the undergrowth. The woman eased the car backward out of the brush slowly, her head swiveling to check for clearance. So she wasn't one of those completely self-centered clear-the-roads-I'm-coming-through city drivers.

Not even close.

Noah didn't blame her for the deer, even if she had been naive enough to mistake him for a bear. Plenty of lifelong Yoopers who knew to be on the lookout could be surprised by a fleet deer bounding from the brush. The creatures seemed to have no sense when it came to traffic, crossing right when a car came along, running the wrong way, freezing in the lights.

Stopping so abruptly might not have been the woman's initial intention, but he gave her credit for going back to look for an injured deer. Deluxe rental car, cell phone and high-heeled boots notwithstanding, she had more guts than your usual tourist. She'd even faced down a bear. That the bear had only been Scrap, who'd never met a stranger he wouldn't slobber over, was not the point.

The car turned onto the shoulder of the road and rolled to a stop. For a moment it idled, lights cutting a swath in the dark night. Noah thought she was going to take off with only a wave of thanks for his trouble. Normally he'd be just as happy for their contact to be as brief as possible, but with this woman... Well, he couldn't put his finger on what it was, but she had a way about her that had engaged his dormant interest.

It might have been the jut of her jaw and the tremble in her hands when she'd raised the club, ready to knock his block off. Maybe it was the perfectly smooth column of her throat and the strong pulse beating in the hollow at the base of it when she'd studied him with rounded eyes and a tilted chin. Or most likely it was the up-front femininity of her flagrantly curvy shape, undeniably sexy beneath the rich fabrics and tailored cut of her designer styles.

Then again, it could be a matter of simple deprivation. He'd been holed up in his cabin for so long the sight of a woman, especially one who smelled like lilacs in the spring, was a shock. Probably any woman—any but Wild Rose Robbin, the only female tough enough to take on the nighttime shift at the Buck Stop—would look as good to him.

The damsel in distress flicked off the headlights and stepped from the car. She didn't look like a typical skinny, scaredy-cat city woman any more than she acted like one, although beneath the polished veneer of a stylish haircut and manicured nails, a certain wariness—and weariness—showed in her face. But he could also see that her legs were long, her body strong. And that her breasts were full and round beneath the thick cable-knit sweater she'd buttoned all the way to her neck.

She said, "I guess that does it," as she walked toward him, leaving the engine running.

Running wild. Like Noah's appetite.

Her kind of satisfaction he didn't need. He'd been battling one of his cravings all evening, but only after he'd fed and watered and bandaged his menagerie had he finally given in and made the three-mile walk to the convenience store. Henry Jussila had been there, licking his chops over the liquor bottles. Wild Rose had watched the old lumberjack like a hawk, barely acknowledging Noah as he'd gotten what he needed and left her a couple of dollars. Wild Rose wasn't like the rest of the local busybodies; she didn't ask too many questions in the name of the small-town friendliness that had always felt more like gossip to Noah—even before he had something to hide.

"So..." The city woman crossed her arms over her chest like she was cold, though the weather was in the fifties. It had been a warm April, melting the snow by the first of May. You couldn't ask for more than that. "Thank you for the push."

Noah nodded. "No problem." For the first time in a long while, he wanted to say more. But after so many months living alone with no one to talk to but wild critters, it seemed that he'd lost his knack for conversation.

"You live around here? May I—" she took a quick, nervous breath "—offer you a ride?"

"Scrap's never ridden in a car."

Incredibly, her eyes got larger. "Oh, right. The bear."

"But if you're game," he said, only to tease her.

She swallowed. "Sure. Why not?" Scrap was in the bushes, sniffing at the rabbit trails. "I've never chauffeured a bear cub before. Should he misbehave, the car's only a rental."

Noah laughed, surprising himself with how good it felt to have something to laugh about. Strange that his amusement should come in such an unexpected package. "That's okay. You couldn't take a car like that where I'm going. I live in the woods, off the beaten path a ways."

She glanced toward the trail that led into the forest. Her eyes widened as if the path were as fraught with danger as the Chisholm trail. When she looked at him, her stare was direct but not uncomfortable. Ever since he'd come back to Alouette, battered, busted and burned, he'd endured enough curious stares to last him a lifetime.

She doesn't gape because she doesn't know, he reminded himself, running a hand over the lower half of his face. The beard was an obvious attempt at camouflage. A mistaken one. Even in his isolation, he'd heard enough of the rumors to realize it had only upped his curiosity factor with the townsfolk.

"Then you're an honest-to-goodness backwoods-man?" The twinkle of whimsy returned to her eyes. "Like the ones in *Tall Tales of the North Country*?" She shrugged. "I picked up a rather outlandish paper-back at the airport."

"I guess you could say that."

"I'm in awe." A wide smile transformed her some-what plain face. She had character and smarts—he'd seen that right off—but her natural smile and the quirky sense of humor that accompanied it made her seem less serious and more attractive. Almost pretty. He thought she needed reason to smile more often.

Like he had any right to give advice on the subject.

"Don't be. I'm not Paul Bunyan." Noah dropped his hand to his belt. Tourists tended to consider the natives of Upper Michigan quaint in an uneducated, unsophisticated way. He wasn't willing to be the source of their entertainment. All he wanted was to live his life as simply, decently and privately as possible.

Which didn't allow for women with wide eyes, wide smiles and wide, curvy, made-for-a-man's-hand hips.

Her eyes, having followed the direction of his low-ered hand, became dark and serious again. "Then I'm off." She spun on her heel and walked briskly to the car, all business. The way he'd thought he preferred it, right? "According to my map, I should be within a mile or two of Alouette. Is that right?"

"You're on track," he said, sorry for her departure

all the same. It was only his loneliness, he decided. There were better cures. For one, he could pay his folks a long-overdue visit as soon as they got back to town. Maybe even drop in on old friend or two. It might be time.

"Well…" She paused beside the door for a moment, seeming to search for a suitable expression of gratitude. "Thank you," she said, simple and sincere, a woman after his own heart. Which was strictly a manner of speaking, he reminded himself.

"Welcome." He sounded suitably gruff, even though he wanted to ask her name or her destination. It was safer not to. This way, they'd never meet again.

For the sake of his peace of mind, that was best.

She slid behind the wheel and he closed the door after her, the soft thunk overriding the moment when she might have said something more. Behind the glass, she blinked at him, her lips slightly parted. *Get going,* he made himself think so she would read the sentiment on his face and take him for no more than a grouchy backwoods hermit, a role he'd filled well for the past two years.

Her glance dropped again to his belt, and she turned resolutely away, putting the car in gear with a sure thrust of her hand. She peered over the hood, tapping the horn for warning. Scrap was still snuffling at the underbrush, so Noah gave her a wave to send her on her way.

She went, not looking back except for one quick flash of her eyes in the side mirror. They were blue, he saw, deeply blue as a spring-fed lake on a sunny day. His body stirred with renewed interest, but he tamped it down, telling himself the pretty color of her eyes didn't mean jack. Hell, he could look at the genuine thing fifty yards outside his cabin door. He sure didn't need to get tangled up with a woman because her eyes were clear-lake blue. Nor because her smile was soft and her heart was courageous and her body was the generous sort that could keep a man warm at night.

CHAPTER TWO

"THESE DIRECTIONS are ridiculous." Claire double-checked her notes before tossing them aside and edging the car toward what might—or might not—turn out to be Bayside Road. There were no road signs to speak of, but her instructions were to make a sharp right at the Berry Dairy ice-cream cone stand and continue up the hill till she came to the Neptune gateposts. "Whatever happened to street addresses?" she wondered, turning the wheel hand over hand.

Alouette was a nice little town, she'd give it that. Picture-postcard pretty in the daytime, she suspected, when spring sunshine would glance off the dancing waters to brighten the bayside business district of red-and-cream-colored brick and stone buildings.

But for now the town was dark and silent. At the marina, black-as-midnight waves slapped at the hulls of boats that had been battened down with sails tightly furled. Even so, it was surprisingly easy for Claire to imagine herself there, sipping coffee in a café that overlooked the harbor. Idling away her time. Doing nothing.

She sighed.

The road to Bay House rose steeply through another

thick pine forest. Interspersed with a few maples and birch, the trees densely carpeted the hillside, making the twining roadway seem insignificant in comparison. Claire was beginning to understand that this was a land where nature always overpowered humankind.

She was glad to see that paved driveways had been carved out of the wilderness. Lawns even—vast stretches of them, lit by old-fashioned globe street-lights. The handful of houses she glimpsed through the trees were more handsome and substantial than the humble frame bungalows she'd seen down below. She shifted behind the wheel. Given the upscale neighborhood, Bay House might yet turn out to be a prospect.

At the top of the hill she found the Neptune gate-posts—matching sea-god statuary set atop red stone bases gone green with moss and twined with vines. The connecting wrought-iron fence was clogged with a tangle of shrubbery and trees that obscured her view of the house. The gate, an elaborate construction running to rust, stood open, one side pulled halfway off its hinges and dipping lopsided into unmown grass.

"Here I yam," Claire announced as she always did, clicking to low beams as she drove through the gate. "All that I yam."

It was a silly saying that had become habit, one she'd begun with her first assignment for Bel Vista. She'd been sent to a ritzy Cliffwalk mansion in Newport be-cause the owners were going bankrupt and the property was available at a bargain-basement price, a "cheap" three mil or so. Coming from modest Midwestern be-ginnings as she had, she'd been awed and intimidated by the grandeur of how the other half—make that the upper two percent—lived. Although not all her subsequent assignments were as swank, reminding herself that she was worthy exactly as she was helped tame her butterflies.

At a glance she knew that Bay House, rising before her on a grassy knoll, was not so grand, though it was a mansion. The bed-and-breakfast was plentiful in size, made of red sandstone in the Victorian style with several wings, steep peaked dormers and even a turret, its witch-capped roof thrust high against the diamond-laden sky.

A pair of wrought-iron lampposts flanked the walkway, but they were not lighted. The only illumination provided for guests was the dull glow of a solitary fixture shining beside the front door. Saving on electricity?

Claire drove once around the circular driveway, then parked in a paved area alongside several other cars and a well-used pickup truck. She got out, making a mental note of the charming carriage house set back among the trees that bordered the neighboring property. Wondering about the commercial zoning ordinance, she peered through the branches, studying the house next door. A purring black sports car arrived, headlights briefly illuminating the home's immense white facade. A well-dressed but rumpled man in his mid-thirties lurched out of the car. Claire lifted a hand to wave—never too soon to be friendly with neighbors who might object about Bel Vista moving in—but he threw her a sour, slit-eyed glare and disappeared inside.

"Okay for you," she said, shrugging. She ducked inside the car to slip the keys from the ignition and reach for her purse.

Her palm landed flat on the passenger seat.

Where was her purse?

"Oh, no," she moaned under her breath, shooting from the car to check the back seat and trunk. A futile effort. She remembered dropping the purse when that Grizzly Adams character had emerged from the underbrush. Between the shock and distraction and her somersault with Scrap, she'd forgotten all about it.

Good going. What now?

She stared at Bay House, exasperated with herself. The building remained dark and quiet—no sign of a welcome. Well, then. She'd try checking in, and if they wouldn't take her at her word and demanded identification, she'd have to backtrack in search of the purse. In the meantime, it wasn't likely anyone would stumble across it on such a little-used road in a sparsely populated area.

"Hoo." Claire blew out a disgusted breath while hauling her baggage from the trunk. The prospect of facing the wilderness again was disheartening when all she wanted was civilization and its creature comforts.

No other creatures need apply, she silently added, thinking of her rescuer and his bear cub. She had plenty of decisions to make without a big, male, Sasquatch-like creature complicating matters. Even one who had rock-hard muscles and a whimsical sense of humor.

With a piece of luggage in each hand, her computer satchel slung over one shoulder and her carry-on over the other, Claire headed toward the house, automatically taking in its architectural details. Bay windows with leaded mullions, carved stone designs, copper gutters and drainpipes—all very impressive. The place was in dire need of upkeep, but the basic structure appeared sound. Heaven only knew what nasty surprises lurked within. She was experienced enough with reno budgets to know that hidden problems in an older building could double or triple the initial estimate.

A wide front porch stretched from the tower past a bay window. The front door had a knocker and a doorbell, but she tried the blackened brass knob and found it open.

The foyer was large, dim, stuffed with furniture. It looked more like a Victorian brothel than a hotel lobby, complete with swags and furbelows, fringed lamp shades, velvet settees and armchairs. Family pictures and dingy oil paintings crowded busy wallpaper. Claire blinked at the yellowed pattern. It was predominated by fairies and naked nymphs draped in gauze. Ugh.

"Hello?" She set down her suitcase and advanced through a jungle of ferns and other assorted foliage. "Hello?" she called again.

On her left, carved-wood double doors remained closed. On her right were glass doors that had been left open to a dining room. A wide, carpeted staircase loomed before her, but she continued past it to a row of closed doors in the narrowing hallway. She was about to knock on the one that bore a tarnished brass nameplate labeled Office when a long, wheezy snore came from the vicinity of the fern jungle.

Claire retraced her steps. Closer inspection revealed a pair of pajama-clad legs extending out of the greenery, the splayed feet clad in hand-knitted red socks riddled with holes. Poking from the largest was a fat pink toe.

Apparently this was Claire's evening to roust men from bushes. She peeled away the crisscrossed straps of her bags and dropped them to the carpet with a jarring thud. No response from the sleeper except another snore.

She inched closer. Lifted a palm frond for a better look. A tubby little man slumped in a chair, swaddled in a robe and a crocheted throw, his short, thick fingers clasped atop a chest that rose and fell with each congested breath. *Choork,* went the inhale with a fluttering of nostrils. *Choo,* came the whistling exhale, making his moist lower lip vibrate.

Claire's amusement showed in her tired smile. The man was elfin, with sticky-out ears, a round face and a funny button nose. Wispy white hair made a tonsure around his head.

Choork…

She cleared her throat. "Hello…sir? Could you please wake up?"

Choo…

"I'm dead tired," she said.

Choork…

She tickled the knob of his nose with the frond.

"Choo!" he said, eyes popping open. He sprang out of the chair.

Claire leaped backward, her hands flying up in defense.

"Wha—whu—who—" the little man said, cartwheeling his arms. The jungle rustled around him.

Claire took another step back. "I'm, uh, Claire Levander. You're expecting me? I have reservations?"

"Umf." The fellow grunted suspiciously, rocking back on his heels. "Howzat?" He rubbed a finger beneath his nose. Strands of hair floated around his head as he swayed forward onto the balls of his feet, blinking at Claire. The bare toe curled into the carpet. "Whozzat?"

"Claire Levander," she repeated, resisting the urge to steady the confused elf.

His eyes brightened as he continued rocking to and fro. "Ar-har, Miss Lavender."

"Levander." She pushed her bangs out of her eyes.

"Righto. Here we are." He'd rescued a registry book from its upside-down position on the carpet and was squinting at the crumpled pages. "You got a pen?"

She patted her pockets. "No. You see, I've lost my purse. But I can—"

The man slapped the book shut and dumped it on the chair. "Never mind that. I'll take you straight oopstairs."

"Oop?" she said, becoming as addled as her host.

He looked her up and down, his small blue eyes twinkling. "You'll want the bridal suite, eh?" His accent was thick—somewhere between Fargo and Canadian.

"I'm not on a honeymoon."

"No groom?" He frowned at the front door as if expecting one to burst through. "Okeydokey, that's prefect. I'll put you in Valentina's bridal suite."

"No! I mean, yes. I'm alone. That is, I'm—" Claire caught her lower lip between her teeth. She hadn't planned to reveal herself as a Bel Vista executive. Not yet. But the elf seemed confused about her reservations, and she did have business cards she could show him. She kept a slim sliver case of them in her purse, but there were extras in her computer satchel.

"Count on Toivo, Miss Lavender. He kin getcha one." The strange little man toddled off to grab one of her suitcases, then started carting it up the stairs.

One? One what? Did he mean a husband? And who was Toivo? The elf? Claire grabbed the other pieces of luggage, tucking the bags under her arms. "Wait. I don't want a groom. Just a room. A regular room will do fine. If you have newlyweds arriving…"

He huffed and puffed, mounting the wide, steep steps. "Nope. Newdywebs won't touch the bridal. They think it's bad luck."

Newdywebs? Claire stopped and shook her head. She had to be hearing things.

From below, there came a thud and then the creak of a door opening. Claire glanced over the banister. A young woman, leaning heavily on the doorknob, poked her tousled red head into the hallway. She looked up, blinking, saw Claire and said, "Stay out of the bridal suite," in a sleepy voice. "'S cursed."

Claire's skin felt pinpricked. "Pardon—?"

The door shut abruptly.

"Crazy rumor." The rosy man elf was standing at the top of the stairs, bobbing on the balls of his feet, waiting for Claire to decide. He beamed. "Best room in the house."

"Is there anything else available?"

"There are the attic rooms. Kinda small. Lootsa dust. You got elegies?"

After a beat, she said, "Allergies? Not so far as I know. But I'd really rather—" Nonsense, she thought, following the man. She didn't believe in luck, good or bad. You made your own future, and hers didn't include either a groom or a curse. "Okay. I'll take the bridal suite."

"We'll need the key. Em's always hiding it from Shari."

Claire's muscles went lax as she slumped against a wall papered in a glitzy but faded red and gold Chinese design that clashed terribly with the fairies below. Fatigue, complicated by confusion, was hitting her hard. She dropped her luggage. "You don't have a key?" She couldn't summon up the strength to ask about Em and Shari. The redhead, maybe? And what was that about a curse?

"It's around here somewheres."

Claire wove together a few of the tangled threads. "But if this is the only room available and you knew I was coming…"

"Ar-har, here it is!" After unsuccessfully rummaging through the contents of a narrow étagère, the elf had found the key at the bottom of an urn full of musty peacock feathers. He sneezed, scrubbed at his nose, then inserted the old-fashioned latchkey in a door at the end of the hall. "Voilà. The bridal suite, Miss Lavender." He disappeared inside to switch on the lights.

"Levander..." Claire's voice faded as she stepped into the room. The bridal suite was large and opulent yet serene, scrupulously dusted and polished from the facets of the crystal chandelier to the gleaming dark wood floor. A massive four-poster bed dominated the room. Its linens looked freshly bleached and starched, stark white and topped with a fancy crocheted spread as fragile as frost on a windowpane. A more colorful quilt was folded at the foot.

Her pajama-clad host was bringing in the luggage. Despite her exhaustion, Claire went to the glass doors that opened onto a small balcony with a spiked iron railing.

Oh, my.

The view was amazing. Beyond the wild mess of a backyard garden, a sheer cliff dropped away to the vast expanse of Lake Superior. The water glistened like obsidian beneath a glowing wedge of quarter moon. On the opposite side of the harbor, beyond more steep rocks and treetops, was the blinking beacon of a lighthouse.

Trying unsuccessfully to prop up heavy eyelids, she lingered to listen to the surf swish against the rocks, the sough of the wind in the pines. The natural rhythms were hypnotic. It wasn't long before her eyes had drifted shut. A little bit of peace settled inside her, like a smooth round pebble floating to the bottom of a murky pond. If she stayed at the inn long enough, Claire wondered dreamily, would the peacefulness spread like rings on the surface of the water? Would her muddy future come clear?

She gave herself another little shake and returned inside. "It's a beautiful view," she told her host, who was beaming at her, practically rubbing his hands with glee. "And a lovely room. I'll sign in properly tomorrow morn—"

"We don't stand on celery at Bay House," he said, moving to the door. "I'll tell Emmie to let you sleep as late as you like, Miss Lavender. Otherways she'll be in here at seven a.m. with a breakfast tray, trying to get a lookie-loo."

"I'd appreciate that, Mr...."

The elf's white hair swirled around his head when he nodded. "Toivo Whitaker. Me 'n' my sister Em own this place."

Claire's smile froze as he swung the door shut. That was unfortunate. Two elderly owners, apparently naive and good-hearted, and a run-down mansion set on a fabulous piece of waterfront acreage. On the surface, it seemed to be a perfect situation from Bel Vista's point of view—a juicy plum of property ripe for the plucking.

Already Claire suspected that she'd dread making this report. From what she'd seen so far, Bay House was unique, even magical, like an enchanted castle out of time.

Out of time? Oh, she hoped not.

Unfortunately, it was her job to deliver the verdict.

CLAIRE ROSE from the deep cottony down of sleep like a butterfly fluttering toward a sunbeam. A delicious warmth touched her face—sunlight, streaming through the balcony doors. Her lids trembled as she moved languidly beneath a crisp sheet that smelled like the outdoors. Gradually she grew aware of muffled voices in the hallway. Without coming fully awake, she concentrated to listen.

"She's not supposed to be in the bridal suite," said a woman, sounding cross. Her accent was similar to the elf's. "I told you to put her in the blue room."

"The couple from Canada are in the blue room." Toivo Whitaker, Claire thought sleepily. He was clearly befuddled, which was probably his regular state of affairs.

"They're in the green room, you silly old man."

"Then who's in the red room?"

"The fisherman from Minneapolis. I switched him because of the wasp nest. If you'd gotten the bug bomb like I asked…" The voices faded as Toivo and his sister moved along the hall.

Smiling, Claire rolled over and buried her face in the sweet-smelling pillowcase. She'd slept better than she had in months. It must have been her exhaustion, because the mattress was terribly soft and lumpy.

The sunshine and rhythmical sound of the waves rocked her in a cradle of somnolence. She was drifting toward sleep again when another person paused outside the door. "It's ain't fair," said a female voice, loud enough to be easily heard. *Thud.* Something had dropped to the carpet outside the door. *Bam.* The door rattled.

From a kick, Claire decided, wondering if she should get up. But the woman was moving away, mumbling as she went. ''Ain't fair, ain't fair, ain't fair…''

Claire frowned. How odd.

She remembered the sleepy redhead who'd muttered the warning about a curse. Toivo, who'd been downright scatterbrained about her reservation but had then insisted on the bridal suite with a curious glee.

Argh, what nonsense. Sheer fancy. There was no reason she shouldn't enjoy every comfort the room provided, especially if they were going to move her out as soon as she showed her face.

Claire sighed and rubbed her cheek against the pillowcase. Sun dried. Not many Bel Vista hotels could provide such a service.

The heavy footsteps returned, traipsing in the direction of the staircase. ''Ain't fair, ain't fair, ain't fair…''

A comfortable silence descended. *Shush, shush,* went the waves. *Shush, shush, shush…* Birds twittered in the sunshine. Somewhere in the hall, a grandfather clock ticked, steady and sonorous.

I yam what I yam and I yam here, Claire said silently, welcoming the pleasure that accompanied the familiar statement. *For good or for bad, I yam here.*

She slid an arm beneath the pillow, thoughts drifting to her encounter with the woodsman the way iron filings are drawn to a magnet. My, but he'd been large.

And so very masculine. She shivered, wondering how he'd look in the daylight.

There *was* her purse to retrieve.

She might see him again.

Did she want to?

As Claire weighed that question, an uncomfortable awareness slowly came over her. Her scalp began to prickle. As if…ugh, no. She shoved the creepy feeling away, but it returned.

It was as if someone was staring at her.

She opened one eye and squinted, scanned the room through her lashes. One look at the opposite wall and suddenly she was wide-awake, propped up on her elbows, her heart pounding wildly.

The bride! The curse!

It was only a painting, she realized, flushing at her ridiculous overreaction. Yet her distaste remained. From the far wall, a bride stared at her, looking cold and calm and severe in her snowy lace garments, as glacial as an iceberg. Claire recognized the French doors that were the bride's backdrop, propped open to the blue vista of the big lake and infinite sky. It should have been a lovely painting, the blond bride serene in her wedding raiment, and instead it was terrible. Forbidding. Chilling.

Cursed.

"Get a grip." Hugging herself, Claire climbed out of the high bed, her bare feet landing on one of the threadbare needlepoint rugs scattered over the hardwood floor. She reached for the sweater she'd carelessly tossed into her open suitcase when she'd changed for bed. The night before, she'd been too tired to notice the grouping of old family portraits that hung on the bridal suite's fireplace wall. And she'd slept fine. So why be bothered now?

"Psych out," she said. Scowling at the portrait in spite of her goose bumps, she slid the sweater on over her nightgown. The bride's cold blue stare had leached all the warmth from the room.

It's only the power of suggestion, Claire told herself, stepping over for a closer look. If she'd been told this was a blessed bridal suite, she'd still be in bed, relaxed to the core, lolling in the sunshine like a fat, lazy cat.

"No, I wouldn't." She stood before the marble mantel and lifted her chin to confront the coldhearted bride. "You're a frigid, deadening old witch, aren't you? I pity the man who married you. No wonder the room is cursed."

"The room's not cursed."

Claire swung around in surprise. She hadn't heard the door open.

"Eh, that Toivo." The short, round older woman who stood in the doorway with a breakfast tray had to be the elf's sister, Emmie. Although her eyes snapped with sharp intellect and her hair was a dark iron gray scraped into a severe braid, the two innkeepers were as alike as a matched pair of salt and pepper shakers.

"Tch, tch. I've told the old coot not to carry tales," Emmie Whitaker said with a peppery flare, stooping to retrieve the folded newspaper on the doorstep before advancing into the room. Mingled scents of hot coffee, fresh orange juice and a sweet, spicy cinnamon bun rose from the tray, making Claire's mouth water.

The innkeeper set the tray on a side table and fussily rearranged the decorative crocheted bedspread Claire had laid aside. "I'm Emmaline Alice Whitaker. Call me Emmie—everyone does." She poured a cup of coffee, added cream and two lumps of sugar without asking. "Bay House is my family home. Lived here all my life, along with Toivo. Our younger sister ran away to California. Been married three times, if you can imagine, and had a baby with each husband. I've never been married, myself. Looking after Toivo and Bay House is enough for any woman."

Claire inhaled the steam from the coffee before taking a grateful sip, nearly moaning with bliss. She'd drastically cut down, but the first shot of morning caffeine was an indulgence she couldn't deny herself. This coffee was heavenly—rich and strong and sweet.

Emmie's lips tucked into a tight, satisfied smile. "We're plain coffee drinkers at Bay House. It's the Finnish way. Don't be asking me for fancy teas or Italian espresso."

"I wouldn't dream of it."

The hostess nodded. "You'll be down soon for breakfast, Miss Lavender?"

Claire offered her hand. "It's Levander, actually. Claire Levander."

"Levander?" Emmie's hand was plump and strong. "Leave it to Toivo," she said, tsking again.

"Well, you see, I lost my purse, so I didn't check

in properly," Claire began. "I'll need to go and search for it first thing—"

"Goodness gracious. I'd send Toivo looking, but Lord knows what that goofball would come back with. Why don't you tell us all about it at breakfast? The usual suspects are waiting to meet you, Miss Levander."

Claire glanced at the sweet roll. It was the size of a softball, oozing with frosting. "Breakfast? Isn't this breakfast?"

Emmie clucked in disbelief. "Coffee and a roll? Goodness, no. My dear mama, bless her soul, would spin in her grave if I served such a miserly breakfast at Bay House." She paused at the door, casting a surreptitious glance toward the bridal portrait. "You get dressed and come right down. Never mind that silly talk of curses. It's pure balderdash."

Claire, warmed by coffee, was inclined to agree, even though she still felt the bride's stare like an icicle between the shoulder blades. She turned to look at the portrait. "Who is she?"

Emmie hesitated, smoothing the gingham-checked apron she wore over an orange fleece track suit. "Valentina Whitaker, younger sister to Ogden Whitaker, my great-grandfather, the lumber baron who built Bay House. Poor Valentina was gone long before Toivo and I were born to Mama Mae and Ogden Three."

"Gone?"

Emmie's round face crinkled into a hard knot like a dried apple. "Valentina Whitaker jumped off the cliff on her wedding night,'' she said through pursed lips, and firmly shut the door behind her.

Well, that cuts it, Claire thought cheerfully as she made her way downstairs fifteen minutes later, carrying a tray with a drained coffee cup and plate empty of all but crumbs and a few daubs of frosting. *I've been cursed—doomed to throw myself off a cliff on my wedding night.*

Oh, the horror, the horror!

She found several houseguests gathered in the dining room around a long, oval bird's-eye maple table. Their chatter grew silent when she entered.

''Good morning.'' Uneasy with their stares, she concentrated on the room, instead. Red stone walls and too many heavy wood furnishings gave it an oppressive feel. The bay window was shrouded by ivy on the outside and heavy brocade drapes on the inside, letting in little light. Trim back the ivy, take out the curtains and half the furniture, and it would be a charming room.

''Morning.'' Toivo piped from the head of the table. ''Did ya sleep good, Miss Lavender?''

''Wonderfully, thank you, Mr. Whitaker.''

He chuckled. ''No bad dreams?''

The pale blue gaze of the spare, middle-aged fellow at Toivo's left dropped to his plate. The petite redhead who'd warned Claire about the curse watched her with a mischievous pink rosebud of a smile. Two others, clearly tourists, looked up from their blueberry pancakes with pleasant, uninformed expressions.

''Only one,'' Claire said as she put the tray on a sideboard and took a seat at the table. She lowered her voice to a sepulchral level. "I dreamed I was falling. It was black and cold. I could hear waves breaking upon the rocks. But I kept falling." Ever so slowly she drew her napkin from the place setting, dragging out the suspense. "Falling," she intoned. "Endlessly fall-ing…"

The redhead's eyes had gone round. She was young—early twenties at most. "Falling?" she squeaked.

Toivo's moist bottom lip hung open. "B-but how—"

"For gosh sakes." Emmie Whitaker marched into the room with a platter full of pancakes. "Can't you tell that our new guest is pulling your legs?"

The young woman let out a thankful laugh. "Oh, you had me going! I thought the curse had taken a new form." She leaned across the table, holding a small, pale hand out to Claire. Her manner was forthright, but her grip was weak. "Cassia Keegan. I'm renting a room here in Bay House." She nodded toward the staircase. "Didn't mean to put a scare into you last night, but I thought you should know about—" she hunched her shoulders and dropped her voice in imi-tation of Claire "—the curse."

"Here we go again." Emmie scowled as she forked pancakes and sausages onto Claire's plate. "Let's not bother Miss Levander with that nonsense, please, Cas-sia."

"I'd like to hear the story," Claire said, stopping Emmie at two of each. The tourists, introduced as the Bickermanns from Canada, professed their interest.

Cassia's eyes danced. Compressing her lips, she looked expectantly at Emmie, waiting for the go-ahead.

"So there is a cur—a, uh, legend?" Claire prodded. "I saw the bride's portrait. It's…beautiful." In a Snow Queen sort of way.

The innkeeper tilted her head, weighing the word *legend* versus the less hospitable *curse*. Finally she gave the redheaded girl a cursory nod and departed for the kitchen.

Clearly, Cassia was eager to tell the tale. Bouncy auburn waves curled around her heart-shaped face as she glanced from face to face, building the suspense. Her expressive eyes were hazel shaded toward gold and tipped up at the corners like a cat's. A palpable energy coursed through her slender body when her gaze reached Claire.

Cassia inhaled, her cheeks pinkening with excitement. "If the prophecy of Valentina Whitaker is true," she announced with utter seriousness, "you will be married before the year is out."

Claire swallowed. Her fingers clamped reflexively on the lever of the syrup jug. "Pardon?"

Cassia chortled. "Yep. I did try to warn you, Claire. But there's nothing you can do now. It's Valentina's prophecy."

Gleefully, Toivo quoted, "'Sleep all night in the bridal room, Turn of year, thee shall have a groom.'"

"Or…" Cassia said.

"Turn of year you'll be a groom," said the quiet man at Toivo's elbow. "Won't catch me sleeping there." He wadded up his napkin and left rather hastily.

"Don't mind Bill's manners," Toivo said. "He's afraid Shari's got plans for him."

Claire was mopping up the syrup that had run over the lip of her plate. "Shari?"

"The maid, Shari Shirley. She works here part-time," Cassia explained. "You'll run into her soon enough, Claire. She's forever trying to spend the night in Valentina's room, but Emmie won't let her near it, even to clean."

"I see. And why was I so lucky to land there?"

Toivo's cheeks became ruddy. "A small mix-up on my part."

Dishes clashed in the kitchen. "Huh!" Emmie came out, drying her sudsy hands on a towel. You were supposed to be in the blue room, Miss Levander. Color-blind numbskull," she scolded Toivo, tapping his bald spot. She snatched away his plate as soon as he stuffed a last bite of pancakes into his mouth.

"You should put married couples in the bridal suite," one of the Canadians suggested.

"Oh, no," Cassia breathed.

"Goodness gracious, no," Emmie said.

"Why not?" Mrs. Bickermann asked.

Cassia shook her head. "It's part of the legend. 'Happily married, bill and coo, Pay the piper, sorrow's due.'"

"You can't believe that stuff." Claire looked at her sodden pancakes and decided she couldn't eat despite her usually healthy appetite.

"Absolutely not." Emmie turned on her heel and returned to the kitchen with her hands full of dishes, using a generously rounded hip to bump open the swinging door.

"It's happened," Cassia vowed. "Single women have married, and couples have split up." Her eyes glowed like those of a child telling ghost stories beside a campfire. "Why do you think Emmie keeps the door locked?"

"It wasn't locked last night after I moved in. I didn't have the key." Claire laughed nervously, wishing for another shot of caffeine to bolster her rocky reactions.

On cue, Emmie entered with another cup, fixed the way Claire liked it. She accepted it with thanks.

Emmie patted her apron pocket. "I'm keeping charge of the key from here on out." She shot a scowl at her oblivious brother. "Even when there's no reason to lock the barn door after the cow's got out."

Claire smiled into her coffee. "Does that make me the cow?"

"Goodness, no. It means that you may as well sleep in Valentina's room for the duration of your stay. No use moving you now."

Cassia waved a hand. "You're already cursed!"

"Now stop that, *pikku,*" Emmie scolded on her way to the kitchen. "You'll be frightening off our guests."

"No worry here," Claire said. "I can assure you that I have no plans for marriage. Besides, it's already May. There's no way I'll meet and marry my groom before the turn of the year. I don't move that fast." Was she protesting too much?

Cassia tossed her curls. "I almost envy you for getting the bridal suite. Almost." She flashed a playful grin. "Personally, I'm not ready to settle down. I've got to take a good sampling of all the available prospects first. Woof!"

Claire shared Cassia's laughter, appreciating the other woman's enthusiasm for the opposite sex even though Claire's reluctance was a matter of straightening out priorities, not picking and choosing. Her opportunities in that area had been limited. She'd decided early that dating within the company was too complicated. And since her life was the company…

Priority one, Claire thought. *Change that.*

It was a sad state of affairs when one's love life was so barren Valentina's prophecy had zero chance of working.

After chatting about their planned daytime activities and the Whitakers' open invitation to board game night, the Bickermanns left the table escorted by Toivo, who was giving them directions to the Gull Rock lighthouse.

Claire looked across the table at Cassia as the girl settled back, realizing for the first time that the redhead sat in a wheelchair. "There must be more to the Valentina legend?" she said, returning to the subject now that they were alone.

With a deft touch on the electric controls of her chair, Cassia wheeled herself closer. "Valentina Whitaker was supposed to be married in the spring of 1914, in the rose garden of Bay House. But her bridegroom never showed up for the wedding. Valentina waited in her bedroom—your bedroom—watching from the balcony as the guests came and went. She waited and watched all day and into the night. There was no word until midnight, when one of the men Ogden Whitaker had sent out searching returned with the news that Valentina's fiancé had eloped with another woman."

"Oh." A quicksilver chill spilled along Claire's spine.

"Yep. The story says that Valentina went schizo." Cassia's eyes widened. "She carried on like a lunatic, cursing her fiancé and his new bride to eternal misery, swearing that never again would an unmarried woman suffer in Bay House the way she had. Ogden and his wife tried to restrain her, but she ran outside in her wedding dress and threw herself off the cliff." The redhead dramatically flung back her head, her hands sweeping wide. "Since then, Valentina's room has become a Whitaker family legend!"

"Hmm. It's a stunning tale." Claire couldn't hide her skepticism.

"It's true. All true. Emmie has shown me the old photos of Valentina. There's even one of her groom— her intended groom."

"But the curse itself? It must be apocryphal."

"I don't know what that means, but it sure is some wild, wacky stuff!" Cassia paused, then leaned forward to continue in a whisper. "Emmie doesn't like to talk about it, even though the legend has lasted all these years. Everyone around knows that any single woman who sleeps the night in Valentina's room will marry soon after. It supposedly happened to lots of the Whitaker relations over the years, before Bay House was opened to the public. At least that's what I've heard.

Since then, Emmie usually refuses to book the room. But every once in a while, if the other rooms are full, or if Toivo gets left in charge…'' Cassia shrugged.

"I'm not going to worry about it."

"Don't you want to get married?"

Claire laughed off the question. Given her present quandary, she wasn't ready to commit to so much as an answer. "Not as the result of a curse!"

"Well, y'know, lots of women wouldn't call it a curse. Shari's been campaigning to stay overnight in Valentina's room for months. There was even a woman from Grosse Pointe who wanted to pay Emmie a thousand bucks for the opportunity!"

"Did she allow it?"

"Nope. Emmie said it wasn't right, that grooms couldn't be bought." Cassia hunched her shoulders. "I think it was because the lady from downstate was about fifty and as crazed as a rabid pit bull. She might have been the one to put a stop to the legend! Didn't matter that the Whitakers needed the money for a new furnace. Emmie's stubborn that way."

And Toivo, Claire thought, *is mischievous that way.* She set aside her cup and saucer, deciding to change the subject. "You said you rent a room, Cassia. I thought Bay House is strictly a bed-and-breakfast. How long have you been here?" Was it too intrusive to ask if she had a lease?

"Not too long," Cassia said. "I was totally dying to live on my own, away from my parents." She rolled her eyes, looking like a typical young adult impatient to assert her independence. "Bay House was the best

I could do. For now. Emmie's bossy, but not as bad as my mother, that's for sure.''

"Are there other long-term tenants?"

"Just Bill Maki. He has an attic room. And there's Roxy, the Whitakers' niece, but she lives in the garage apartment. No worries there. You couldn't pay Roxy to come near Valentina's room.''

As the two women talked, they moved toward the large but crowded front hall, Cassia's chair catching momentarily on the fringed edge of a Persian rug. "Where do Emmie and Toivo sleep?" Claire asked when Cassia waved her off from helping. She was trying to gauge the number of bedrooms.

"On the first floor, near me." Cassia pointed as she spoke. Her face was bright with interest and friendliness. "There's the front parlor—that's open to all the guests. Then the office, with Emmie's and Toivo's rooms behind it. Then me, then the garden room that opens to the back yard, and on the other side is the kitchen, the pantry and the back stairs.''

"How many bedrooms up?"

"Five altogether. The green, the yellow, the red and the blue.''

A veritable rainbow. "Plus the bridal suite."

"Yeah, the white room, I guess you'd say." Cassia giggled.

"There's no way I'm getting married when I don't even have a boyfriend," Claire murmured, momentarily unaware she'd spoken out loud. When she realized she had, she looked sheepishly at Cassia, who only smiled.

"Join the club, sister." They laughed.

"I have to go," Claire remembered. "I lost my purse…"

"How'd that happen?"

Claire shuddered. "I nearly hit a deer on the drive to Alouette. Just past that place—the Buck Stop? It was awful."

Cassia shrugged. "Heck, that happens all the time. The woods up here are thick with deer. You have to keep your eyes open, driving at night."

"I was kind of, um…distracted. My car ran off the road."

"But how'd you lose the purse?"

Toivo was coming in the front door. "I got out of the car," Claire said hurriedly. "Then there was this man—"

Cassia's brows arched. She bounced in her chair. "A man? Did you say a man?"

"What man?" said Toivo, hands tucked into the pair of red suspenders that held up his baggy work pants. "The curse is already working, eh?"

"No!" Claire hadn't meant to get into this, even though her curiosity was full to bursting. Not much choice now. "Last night I met a man in the woods. At first I thought he was a bear—it was rather dark, and he had a beard—but it turned out to be no big deal. He helped get my car back on the road, is all."

Cassia wheeled closer. "What was his name? Was he good-looking?"

"I didn't get his name. And between all his hair and all his—" *Muscle.* Her face was growing warm. "All the darkness, I mean.…"

"Ooh. A mystery man."

"No. Really. He was—" Claire didn't know why her heart was beating so fast. Why her palms were clammy. Why she couldn't calm the jitters in her belly. "He was just some backwoods character. Lives out of the way, I take it. He had a bear cub."

"That'd be Noah Saari," Toivo put in.

Cassia clasped her hands together. "Wow, Claire— you saw Noah Saari!"

"Noah?" Claire's tongue felt thick. "Is the name supposed to mean something to me?"

Toivo rocked on his heels, making the flyaway strands of hair waver about his bald pate. "Noah's a local fella. Did us proud, fighting that big forest fire out west a coupla years ago. Some of us, leastaways." The elfin face grew serious. "Came home a changed man. Different in the head, they say."

"Noah Saari's sort of a local legend." Cassia touched her steepled fingers to her chin, sighing lustfully. "He returned to Alouette as a hero, but ever since he's been living way out in the boonies. He hardly ever comes to town." She beamed at Claire. "And you met him! That's so cool!"

Claire's answering smile was weak. She'd done nothing but run her car off the road and attempt to outrun a bear, but here was Cassia, leaning closer, her expression one of awe.

"Did you get a good look at him?" the redhead asked, nearly breathless. "Did you get to—did you see—" She stopped and took a deep breath before asking, "Did you see his scars?"

CHAPTER THREE

"HIS SCARS?" Claire barely heard her echo. She was thinking about Noah Saari's face. Did he have scars? She couldn't say; there'd been too much beard. A little chill gripped her. *Scars.* The poor guy. Was that why he'd grown so much hair?

"Facial scars," Cassia said. "That's the rumor. I don't know if anyone has actually seen them."

"Myron has," Toivo said.

Cassia rolled her eyes. "Oh, Myron! You can't believe a word he says."

"Sure you can." Toivo hitched up his pants. "Myron was visiting the Saaris the day Noah came home after the fire. The boy hadn't grown a beard yet. Myron seen his face. Seen it clearly." Toivo nodded emphatically, rocking on his heels, all the motion making his round belly jiggle. "Myron says the scars were red. Infamed. Up the side of Noah's face, down into his collar. Mebbe they go right to his toes. They say his clothes got burnt right off him in the big blaze."

"You don't know that," Cassia protested. She shook her head at Claire. "He does *not* know. Myron Mykkanen is the biggest gossip in town. He tells a good story, but he exaggerates like crazy."

"Scars from head to toe," Toivo said. "That's what Myron says."

"Toivo's partner in crime," Cassia stage-whispered.

Claire swallowed. "Well, I didn't see any scars." Even to her own ears, she sounded unsure.

"What *did* you see?" Both Cassia and Toivo looked highly interested.

"Very little."

"Aw, c'mon." Cassia rubbed her delicate hands together. "How often do we hear of an honest-to-goodness Noah Saari sighting? He's been hiding away in that cabin ever since he came back to Alouette. The only person who sees him regularly is Wild Rose, who works at the Buck Stop, where Noah buys groceries. And she's not very talkative." Cassia sighed. "Won't give away a single fun detail, even when I beg and cajole."

Toivo joined in. "Noah's parents don't see him much, neither, not since he fixed up the cabin. Back when, the mayor and Sheriff Bob wanted to give Noah a medal, but he flat-out refused. Always was the quiet type."

"There was only *mention* of a medal, Toivo. Don't you remember the fuss that that Terry Lindstrom kicked up? The mayor wouldn't go against the Lindstroms," she advised Claire. "They're one of the founding families who live on the hill. That's their house, right next door."

"I can't see anything from my window but water and trees," Claire said, then remembered her glimpse of the neighboring house from the Bay House parking area. And the unfriendly man.

"Trust me," Cassia muttered darkly, "they're there. It's the big white house. The Lindstroms live there with their oldest son, Terry."

Toivo chuckled. "You're just holding a grudge because of the way the youngest boy used to tease you—"

"I'm not listening," Cassia sang, pressing the toggle on the controls of her chair and moving smoothly into the jungle of the foyer. "I'll talk to you later, Claire," she called over her shoulder. "I want the inside scoop!"

Claire gave a small wave. There was no inside scoop. She was, however, even more intrigued than before. This Noah fellow was a character, apparently. They didn't seem to think he was dangerous, though. She remembered her instinctive retreat when he'd loomed over her, seven intimidating feet—or so it had seemed—of muscle and hair and animal magnetism. She could picture white teeth and the way his hard eyes had softened with whimsy, but the rest was a blur. She'd been worried about being ravaged by a bear. Who knew she should have been looking for scars?

Claire slipped on the light jacket she'd brought downstairs. Even though it was a sunny spring day, she didn't intend to be caught underdressed again. At the front door, she stopped and looked at Toivo, who was watching her with interest. *Gossip,* she thought.

"I'm going to look for my purse." It wasn't that she was scared. The wise thing was to tell someone where she was going. Just in case. "On the road leading into town—I forget—"

"County road 525."

"Right. That one." She fixed her collar as she stepped onto the porch. "I'll be back shortly."

Toivo came to the door. "You won't see him. Not 'less he wants ya to."

Claire hurried away without looking back. No use explaining herself, even though the innkeeper's words followed her as she drove down the hill. Between Toivo and Cassia, the entire household would soon be thinking she'd gone looking for Noah Saari, mysterious man of the wilderness, when all she wanted was to retrieve her purse. Really. If Noah was a recluse, she wouldn't dream of barging in on him. He'd been kind to her, but they weren't friends. His life—and scars— was none of her business. She couldn't interfere.

Just because she was fascinated...

Just because she was cursed...

Claire made a scoffing sound as she reached the bottom of the hill and slowed to make her turn. The story of Valentina was no more than a colorful fable to tell the guests. The Bel Vista publicity department would eat it up. They might even market it. Valentina soaps, candles, sachets. Valentina postcards. Cliff-side tours. Maybe even a Valentina reenactment every year on the fateful wedding date.

It would be awful. But they'd make money. And so would the town. Emmie and Toivo would be well paid for the marketing rights to their family name, if they had the foresight not to sell them along with the house.

Would they? The question gnawed at Claire, a good sign that she was already too involved in these people's lives. She was supposed to swoop in, gather information, make a report and then leave the negotiations to the corporation. No need to start worrying about the aftermath.

Her gut cramped. *Oh, dear.* Some executive she made.

Deliberately, she focused her thoughts on the town. It was much as she'd envisioned last night—quaint and picturesque, the old brick buildings softened by spring flowers and the bursting foliage of mature trees. A number of businesses had opened their doors, but the downtown area wasn't very busy aside from the occasional pedestrian and a few cars and other vehicles crisscrossing the intersection. Alouette businesspeople would likely welcome the increased tourist traffic of an aggressively marketed B and B inn. It wasn't only the Whitakers she should think about. If she recommended that Bel Vista buy Bay House, it could turn out to be a boon to the town as a whole.

Uh-huh. So why did that feel like a justification?

She didn't relax until she reached the desolate county road. The soothing quiet and the fresh green promise of spring spoke to her. In the dark, the forest had seemed foreboding. Now it was bright and alive…but all the same.

She drove slowly, looking for familiar landmarks. A tree was a tree was a tree. Coming from the opposite direction made it even more difficult to tell them apart.

She continued on to the Buck Stop, planning to turn

and retrace her route. When she pulled into the sparse gravel parking lot, bumping across ruts worn into the dirt, she saw a woman lounging beside the crooked screen door, smoking a cigarette beneath a Live Bait sign. Would that be Wild Rose Robbin? The one Noah saw regularly? She was about medium height, a lighter weight than Claire but built sturdily. A strong woman. Or maybe that was the attitude she projected, even though half her face was hidden behind an unruly mop of dark hair.

Claire parked. She shut off the engine, then hesitated, wondering how she should approach the stranger, who was looking at her unfamiliar car with some suspicion.

The woman took a deep drag, dropped her cigarette and snubbed it out beneath her heel. Instead of leaving it, she stooped and picked up the crushed butt, exhaling twin plumes of smoke through her nostrils. She ambled toward the car. "Can I help you?"

Claire rolled down her window. "Maybe. Are you, um, Rose?"

The woman cocked her head to one side. "Wild Rose, yup." She scraped back her tousled jet-black hair, revealing a face that was not as old and ravaged as Claire had expected. As if an employee had to be as run-down as the business—Claire scolded herself.

Wild Rose had a hard face, though. Her expression was sober and reserved, and her narrowed dark eyes had the weariness of one who'd seen it all. And maybe done it all, too.

Claire gulped. "I was wondering…do you know Noah Saari?"

Wild Rose's shrug was neither a confirmation nor a denial.

"I met him last night," Claire said, uncomfortable with the other woman's scrutiny. She'd dressed casually this morning, in pants, a sweater and the trim suede jacket, but she was still bandbox perfect in comparison to Wild Rose's disheveled hair, loose plaid shirt and scruffy, threadbare jeans. Rose's boots were like Noah's, built for rugged use, whereas Claire had on a pair of expensive black leather ankle boots with stacked high heels. You wouldn't know to look at her that she'd grown up in T-shirts, shorts and flip-flops. In her years away from Florence, she'd forgotten—purposely, she supposed—how to dress for the country.

Wild Rose hadn't responded.

"He helped me get my car out of the ditch," Claire prompted.

"Mmm."

"I, uh, thought maybe you'd seen him this morning. He might have mentioned me? It seems I lost my purse, and I was hoping…." Claire let her voice trail off. She didn't know what she was hoping. That Noah had found her purse and dropped it off at the Buck Stop, or that he'd been so awed by their meeting that he'd emerged from his lengthy hibernation to seek her out?

"Noah doesn't come by that often."

"But he *was* here last night." Claire remembered the small brown paper parcel tucked inside his belt.

Wild Rose's mouth pursed. "He had a craving."

Thoughtful, Claire drew her teeth across her bottom lip. She really did not need to get involved in *that*. Her father hadn't been a drunk or anything, but he'd tippled frequently enough that it had contributed toward his all-around laziness. Sam Levander's name had been on the sign, but it was his no-nonsense wife who'd run the family's thriving gas station and repair shop, leaving Claire to manage domestic duties.

"Does he live close by?"

Wild Rose folded her arms, one hand cupped around the cigarette butt. "Why're you asking?"

"I'm Claire Levander, from Chicago. Here on… business. I'm staying at Bay House. I ask because I lost my purse, as I said, and I thought possibly Noah had found it."

"He'll return it if he did."

"He doesn't know who I am."

"Does now."

"Oh." Claire blinked. "All right. Thank you." She didn't move.

"Anything else?" Wild Rose prompted.

"I'm—no." She could hardly ask this taciturn woman about Noah's past. Or his scars. "Thank you," she repeated. "I'll be on my way."

Wild Rose nodded. She walked away, tossing the butt into a rusty trash can beside the door, then turning to look as another car pulled into the parking lot, spitting gravel as it braked hard. Wild Rose's expression twisted and she fled inside, letting the screen door bang shut behind her.

Claire watched as the fair-complected man she recognized as the Whitakers' next-door neighbor emerged from the black BMW. Lindstrom was the name. He glanced at her and she smiled, almost reflexively, feeling wary. He looked presentable enough, expensively dressed and good-looking in a conventional, slightly flabby way. Home in Chicago, her friends would have probably voted that this one was more her type than Noah Saari. But there was a sour air about the man that made her uneasy. As if he'd gone soft and rotten at the core.

Lindstrom stopped, leaning casually against his car while he evaluated Claire. She sat up a little straighter. "Hi."

He nodded.

She was determined not to make another overture.

"You're a guest at Bay House?" he finally said.

"That's right."

"I'm Terry Lindstrom." Not boasting, but smug.

She wanted to say, "So?" Not a good idea. "Claire Levander."

"Staying long?"

"About a week." Out of the corner of her eye, she saw movement behind the screen door. Wild Rose was watching.

Lindstrom slouched, both he and the gleaming auto looking out of place outside the Buck Stop. "If you want to escape the Whitakers to have a good time, give me a call."

Hmph. Claire started her car. "Thank you, but I'm looking forward to staying in with the Whitakers. I hear they're big on Scrabble." She drove away with her head high, hoping that would be the last of Terry Lind-strom. Wild Rose was probably quite capable of dealing with his sullen attitude, although it was hard to imagine why the man would be slumming at the dilapidated store.

Claire cruised slowly along the road. There was no reason she couldn't find her purse—or Noah—on her own. It couldn't be that difficult. If she had to, she'd prowl through the underbrush until she found the path into the woods.

Minutes later, that's what she'd come to. Either the trees had grown leafier since last night or she was hopelessly unobservant, but she wasn't able to distinguish the right location until she'd parked and walked along the roadside. Eventually she discovered the log she'd run into, spotting the fresh yellow gash in the trunk through a gap of broken branches. From there, she was able to retrace her steps—more like a panicked zigzag if she remembered correctly—until she stumbled onto the overgrown trail.

Still no purse. She waded through the grass, looking for it, then stopped, setting her hands on her hips as she squinted into the woods. What now? If Noah had picked up the purse, he obviously hadn't brought it to Wild Rose's store. And she wasn't sure, but hadn't he made a comment about not owning a car? Or was that her assumption, because of his remote living quarters and simple lifestyle? She wasn't accustomed to men who took nighttime strolls through the forest with a bear cub at their heels. It didn't fit that such an anachronism would own a car.

What would it hurt to take a short walk into the woods, as long as she stuck to the trail, such as it was? Possibly she'd been getting her leg pulled, and Noah's house was just beyond the trees, fully furnished, with all conveniences and a four-wheel-drive SUV parked in the garage.

Claire started off. She relaxed by degrees, slowing her stride to enjoy the twitter of birds in the sun-flecked trees. It was so pleasant, in fact, she walked farther than she'd intended, not ready to stop.

Realizing how much she'd missed the country, she began mentally toting up her years away. She'd been living in the city since she'd left for college at twenty, a year later than she'd planned because of family and money problems. Eleven years. Whew. She'd changed a lot in that time. And given up more than she'd intended.

But there still had to be a lot of Florence, Nebraska, left in her, right? Her old hometown was decidedly rural, lots of farmland and flat, open plains. Her favorite place had been a willow grove that surrounded a pond near their house. After one of the twins had fallen in and nearly drowned, she was extra-vigilant about keeping her brothers and sisters away, herding them toward the safety of the public beach, instead. They'd walked or pedaled their hand-me-down bikes, the two youngest riding on the handlebars, forming a crowd wherever they went. It had been a good childhood, even though she'd had to be more of a mother than a sister.

Claire stopped, ostensibly to check her watch. The

hollow, tight feeling inside her wasn't only job stress—
it was longing. Homesickness. After all these years
away from home, she was turning sentimental.

Could she have a midlife crisis at thirty-one? Wasn't
that too young? Maybe her dissatisfaction was a standard case of biological urges. Three of her siblings
were married; she had four nephews with another baby
on the way. Claire, the unmarried ''career girl,'' was
considered the odd one out for staying in the city on
her own.

Maybe she was.

''Don't do that to yourself,'' she said, her gaze skim-
ming the treetops. ''Remember, I yam what I yam.''

She laughed, even though she knew she was in denial. The company doctor had warned her that in a year
she'd be back in his office with an ulcer if she didn't
slow her pace and start living her life instead of working it.

She'd come to the top of a rise. The dense vegetation
had thinned out, but so had the path. She wasn't sure
which way to go. A slope led downward into a stand
of long-needled pine. A wetlands area was to the east,
marked by barren gray trunks that poked up from the
marsh like dead soldiers. There was no sign of a cabin.

''Play it smart,'' she told herself. ''Time to turn
back. You'll get lost if you don't.''

Tufts of feathery grass waved in the breeze. The
scent of the pines was intoxicating. Alluring. Claire
filled her lungs as she walked toward them. She'd probably come a mile, maybe more, so why give up now?

She was only going to look to see if the path picked up again.

The evergreens closed around her, hushing the world and creating a space as quiet and reverent as a confessional. The wands of long, smooth needles brushed like cool silk on her face and hands. She followed a narrow opening through the trees, drawn deeper as the incline steepened.

She sensed open space beyond the dense pines. There it was—a sliver of blue. Her anticipation leaped.

A rabbit darting from beneath a branch distracted her. She put her right foot down on a stone poking from the bed of pine needles. Her ankle turned, and suddenly she was falling, grabbing at a branch tacky with sap as her backside hit the soft earth. She slid a little way on the dry carpet of needles, the evergreen boughs closing over her head.

Ouch. Fire shot from her ankle. She lay flat on her back for a moment, then brushed away an overreaching branch and pushed to a sitting position. Her twisted ankle ached fiercely as she pulled it toward herself, fingers feeling across the leather boots and then poking tentatively inside. No broken bones. She could move her foot, even though it hurt when she tried. Better not to unzip the boot, she decided. The tight fit might give her ankle enough support so she could walk out of there.

"What an idiot." She heaved a sigh, looking heavenward, disgusted with herself. So much for her rural know-how. At least she wasn't lost. *That* would take the cake.

She'd have to stand eventually, but first she rested, idly picking dry pine needles off her sticky palm. The wind soughed through the tree branches, making them rustle. A far-off crow cawed complaints. Her ankle throbbed in agreement.

There'd been that flash of blue. Water, maybe. She could see only trees from her vantage point, but where there was water, there might be a cabin.

"Noah's cabin could be closer than the road," she said, distracting herself with conversation while she turned onto her knees. "He's going to think I'm a hopeless bumbler." She set her left foot down. "A babe in the woods, needing rescue twice in twenty-four hours."

She surged upward, most of her weight shifted to the left. Pain sizzled through her ankle when her right foot brushed the ground. She lifted it immediately, clutching branches, balancing like a flamingo amid the pines.

"Well." She panted as the pain subsided to an ache. "This is bad."

She couldn't hop down the slope. And sliding on her bottom seemed so...ignominious. She groaned at the thought. One innocent walk through the woods, and there went her reputation as a savvy, competent, independent woman.

Wasn't that the way? Just when she had it all figured out....

Who was she kidding? She hadn't figured anything out. For the past decade, she *thought* she had, but when she should have been enjoying her success, she was lamenting it, instead.

Very carefully, she rested her foot on the ground. Not *too* bad. The pain might subside if she could manage a few steps. "Work through it," she said, going for encouragement even though it sounded more like irony. She needed one of the rah-rah trainers from her gym, the gym she'd paid big bucks to join but didn't attend nearly often enough because women in spandex were prone to say things like, "Work though the pain."

Gritting her teeth, she took one funny little hop step. *Agony.*

She did it again anyway. *More agony.* Again. *Hot pain.* Again. *Hotter, burning pain.*

"Yeesh." She lurched, losing her balance on the incline. Suddenly she was down again. Tumbling. Rolling. With a *whump* that took her breath away, she came up against a fallen tree. Her ankle was flaming, but the burn felt almost good because at least she was *off* the damn thing.

After a minute, she rose to her elbows, aware through the fog of hurt that she'd cleared the pine grove. A layer of thick, mulchy leaves shifted beneath her as she pulled herself up, clinging to the fallen tree. Dry splinters broke off, dusting her jacket and hands.

She barely noticed, pushing higher to straddle the trunk. The view was stunning. A forest valley had opened before her, the endless rug of green broken only by a jagged stripe of bright blue water. A lake. The slope she'd tumbled down steepened to a bluff maybe ten feet in front of her. Gray and pink-striped rocks thrust from the ground, hazardous going even if she didn't have a rotten aching wound for an ankle.

Still… "It's beautiful." Ignoring her aches and pains for the moment, she made sounds of appreciation while searching the distant shoreline of the lake. There were too many trees to get a clear view, but at last she spotted a wisp of rising smoke. She squinted, picking out a slanted shingle roof and a patch of gray logs. If that was Noah's cabin, it fit so well into the landscape it was almost camouflaged.

Relief flooded her, then seeped away as she calculated the distance. A quarter of a mile, at least. Probably more. Over impossible terrain.

The cabin might as well have been on the moon.

"Pooh. I'll make a crutch." She'd done that for her brother Jesse once, when they'd been playing war in the back yard. She was Florence Nightingale, Jesse was a paratrooper with a busted leg—they hadn't worried about historical correctness—and a branch from the old ash tree had been his crutch.

She scanned the ground nearby. Lots of fruitless blueberry bushes, but no pieces of deadwood long enough to be a crutch. "Should have kept the bat," she said with a dry chuckle, remembering her plan to knock Noah's block off. Who knew wood would be so important to her survival in this wild land?

"Forest, forest, everywhere, and not a branch to…lean on." She shifted on the log, brushing off her jacket, smoothing her hair and tucking what she could behind her ears. "No need to look like a bag lady," she said, glancing at the horizon where a few thick rain clouds hung low in the sky. "Yet."

Ha! Stranded without a cell phone and a lipstick. The modern woman's nightmare.

She sighed, running out of cheerful chatter. This was a predicament, no two ways about it.

"Are you finished?"

A shock went through her at the unexpected voice. It was almost enough to bring her to her feet, but she quickly gave that up and sank onto the log. Her heart hammered like a woodpecker at a hollow tree as she searched the area around her. "Who—who is it? Where are you hiding?" She clutched the log, remembering Cassia and Toivo's description of the mysterious recluse.

She was *not* afraid of him—only wary.

Noah stepped into the clearing. "Sorry, ma'am. Didn't mean to startle you."

She stared without thinking. "You almost gave me a heart attack. Did you have to sneak up on me?"

"I wasn't sneaking. You were too involved to notice me." His brows arched. "Having a fine conversation with yourself."

Her cheeks warmed. "I thought I was alone."

"So did I."

She blinked. He was dressed as he'd been last night, maybe even the same clothes, although there *was* something different. It might have been seeing him in the daylight, but…

Oh, she thought. Of course. His face was more open, and it wasn't because of the sunshine. "You cut your beard."

Noah's hand went to his chin. "Trimmed it, yeah."

Bashfully, he turned his head to one side, sending his gaze across the green valley. Clearly, he wasn't accustomed to much attention.

She thought of the scars but didn't want to be obvious about looking for them. Sensing his discomfort—or possibly her own—she turned her face aside, too, giving both of them a little breathing room.

It didn't matter that she wasn't looking directly at him. He was *there*. There like no other man could be. So intrinsic to this place she couldn't even say she was all that surprised by his arrival, except for its suddenness. He belonged here. Somehow, she'd known she'd come across him…hoped it, even.

What she hadn't considered was that he might not want her here. Hermits tended to be antisocial.

"Is this your land?" she asked, sliding a quick glance over him before gesturing at the valley. "I've been admiring it."

Noah came closer. With his size, he could have shaken the earth when he walked. But he didn't. He moved as easily and naturally as the wind or trees or the wild creatures. By comparison, Claire felt awkwardly out of place.

"I have the deed to a forty. Forty acres, that is. On the lake."

"Then that's your cabin?"

"It is."

"Please excuse me for barging in—"

"No need. As long as you're not harming the land or disturbing the animals, you're welcome."

She smiled sheepishly. "Nope. I only harm myself."

At Noah's questioning look, she reached toward her boot. "Stupid me. I fell and twisted my ankle."

"Then you're not sitting here only to admire the view." With a throaty chuckle that was almost a tangible thing, the way it made her feel, Noah went down on one knee in front of her. Gently, he elevated her foot so her heel rested on his thigh. Her pulse sped up as she absorbed his nearness, which seemed personal, somehow, even though he was being very decorous.

He felt her ankle. She bit down on her teeth, speaking between them. "It's pretty bad." When he went to unzip her boot, she winced and said, "Noah, don't—"

He glanced up. "You know my name."

"Yes. It was mentioned."

He grimaced but didn't look away. "I can imagine what you heard."

"Well, don't worry. I took it with a grain of salt." She was riveted by the richness of his chocolate-brown eyes. Last night, they'd seemed fiercely black, but they weren't. They were nice eyes. Warm, even. And here she'd been certain that all hermits had piercing eyes like Heidi's Alm Uncle.

Noah had unzipped the boot without her noticing and carefully peeled back the leather. His fingers reached inside her sock, gently probing her tender, swollen flesh. It hurt a little, but he kept his eyes fixed on hers, and she couldn't manage to form so much as an *ow*.

He frowned. "It's not broken, but you can't walk on a sprain this bad."

"I found that out." She gestured. "I was going to make a crutch."

"That might work, except that it's all downhill to my cabin. Rough going."

"Your cabin."

"I can bandage you there. I even have ice." While he spoke, he was smoothing the cuff of her sock then zipping the boot shut. He kept her foot propped on his thigh, one hand lingering on her leg, the other cupping her heel. "These boots weren't made for walking."

She checked his face. Yep, the whimsy was back—the corners of his eyes had crinkled. "I confess," she said. "I'm no Nancy Sinatra." Her smile spread. "My boots may not be practical, but they're highly fashionable."

"In the woods, practical will do you more good."

"I'm not usually in the woods."

"I can tell that." He looked a question at her.

"My purse," she explained. "I dropped it last night, where we met, and so I came back to—"

To satisfy my curiosity. Her voice died. She sucked in a shallow breath, suddenly aware of his face beyond his eyes. There were no scars that she could see, but between his collar and the beard, she couldn't be sure.

"I found it last night, after you left."

"Oh. Good." She didn't care about her purse.

"I planned to return it." He looked down. Shifted her leg onto the log, keeping her ankle elevated.

"Do you have medical training?" she asked, struck by the deftness of his touch but mostly trying to distract him from her bungled scrutiny of his face. She wished they'd never told her about the scars! She hadn't cared before and wouldn't now if the idea hadn't been put in her head. Unfortunately, it was like not thinking of pink elephants.

"Yeah, some, but it doesn't take a degree to put a pressure bandage on a sprained ankle." He'd turned gruff, putting her foot aside and standing abruptly.

"I suppose." She hesitated a moment, then sat up a bit straighter and stuck out her hand. "We haven't introduced ourselves. I'm Claire Levander, damsel in distress."

He shook her hand—firmly, briefly. "Noah Saari. Nobody's hero."

She peered at him, squinting against the bright light. He was a massive silhouette against the sun; she couldn't see his face. By his shrug, he regretted the last two words. If she hadn't been told of his reticence, she might have been put off, thinking he meant he didn't care to rescue *her.*

"I wouldn't say that." She kept her tone pleasant but removed. "Look what you've done for me."

He seemed at a loss.

She wanted to explain that she'd already been told of his firefighting exploits, but because of the other rumors, that would cause more awkwardness than it relieved. "You're quite the champion, as far as I'm concerned. I appreciate your help." He didn't respond, so she went on. "And if you will bring me my purse and the cell phone is still inside, I'll probably be impelled to gush embarrassingly over you."

She thought he might have smiled. "That won't be necessary."

He came toward her, swooping in like an eagle with

outspread wings. Before she fully comprehended his intent, he had lifted her off the log and was carrying her toward the valley, skirting the pine grove as he traveled down the hill at a diagonal. His stride was long and sure, his hold on her extremely...competent.

Yes, competent.

Not stirringly romantic.

She had made a sound of surprise when he picked her up. Beyond that, she was speechless. Her arms had gone automatically around his neck. When she glanced toward the bluff, her grip tightened, a burst of fear squeezing words out of her frozen throat. "Noah—you can't—"

"There's a trail. It's not as steep as it looks."

"But—" She flushed. "I'm too heavy."

He glanced into her face. "Says who?" His arms curved around her back and thighs. One large hand gripped her rump. And she'd thought her twisted ankle burned!

"Stands to reason," she murmured, narrowing her view to his collar and throat. Below the newly trimmed dark gold beard, his Adam's apple bobbed.

He hefted her a little higher and kept walking.

She almost gasped at the sensuous flex of muscles in his chest. Their closeness was far too intimate. The warmth of his body seeped into hers. And she could smell him again, such a musky, strangely arousing scent she had to fight not to lay her head on his shoulder and take a deep whiff of his neck.

His breathing deepened. She closed her eyes, honing in on the pattern, her awareness of him stirring from physical instinct to something deeper. "Um, at least you can put me down for a while. Get your breath back."

"Best to keep going." He didn't seem overly strained. "It's a question of momentum."

"Please be careful," she said, opening and then closing her eyes when she saw the rocks, with a few scraggly jack pines growing between them. The dirt path zigzagged through the rough terrain. Pebbles crunched beneath Noah's heels.

"Almost at the bottom," he soothed, giving her backside an unconscious—or not—squeeze.

She had to swallow twice to stifle a hysterical giggle. "It really would have been easier to bring the cell phone to me." She finally managed to speak.

"But I couldn't leave you there alone."

Hero, she thought.

The ground began to even out as the rocks gave way to grass. Claire exhaled, opening her eyes again. Bushes sprouted, dotted with red berries. White flowering trees grew here and there, and then they were among the evergreens again. Beneath the lush boughs, the temperature cooled considerably—except where she was in contact with Noah. He was perspiring. And she was sweating out every moment of the contact.

He slowed, hefting her again.

"Please," she said, self-conscious of her weight. His arms must be aching. "Put me down. We're on flat ground."

"For a minute." He set her down very carefully, keeping hold of her even when she was standing on one foot. He sucked in a deep breath, then exhaled, his arm never leaving her waist.

"I'm mortified," Claire said.

"Why?" Noah was truly curious.

"You have to admit…" She blushed. "This doesn't happen except in movies. I feel silly. And—and…" She wouldn't be so fragmented if he'd stop touching her. "I'm what is discreetly called a big girl."

"I'm big, too," he said. "Is that bad?"

She blinked. At least he hadn't found it necessary to deny her size or give her false compliments. Fortunately, she wasn't overly sensitive on the subject, even though she intended to drop a few pounds as soon as someone invented a chocolate diet.

"Depends who you're asking," she said.

Noah's expression shifted. "Yeah."

They weren't talking about her anymore. "Big, strong men are admired."

"If they fulfill the role without failure."

Oh? "I suppose. We all suffer from expectations that can be difficult to meet." *No fat chicks. Brawn equals courage.*

Without warning, Noah swept her into his arms again. "We could find a crutch now," she said, but he didn't respond, just kept walking through the forest.

"This is easier," he said, not looking at her.

"How far?" She swallowed. Her heart had leap-frogged into her throat. Being carried by Noah was much too intimate to be prolonged.

"Not far."

A man of few words. "I'm never going to walk out of here on my own. Do you have a car or truck?"

"Not readily available."

"A motorbike? Four-wheeler? ATV?"

"I have a canoe."

"That's no use." She frowned, thinking about it. "You are *not* portaging me like Cleopatra on a litter."

Noah chuckled. "Don't worry. We'll get you fixed up."

"We?" Was there a Mrs. Bunyan?

"Me and Scrap."

"Where is Scrap?"

"Grounded for bad behavior. He got into the chicken coop this morning."

"Ew."

"No carnage except for a few ruffled feathers. I caught him in time. He just wanted to play, anyway. Bears are omnivores, but their diet mainly consists of vegetation."

"Nuts and berries?" Claire rested her chin on Noah's shoulder. The trees were flying by, and he didn't seem burdened at all. If it wasn't for her butt hanging out in the breeze, this would have been almost nice. Noah's stride was steady and smooth except for the occasional small jostle or bump when the ground was uneven. His upper body was solid against her. He was robust. Even *mighty*. There weren't many men who qualified as that, these days.

"Grubs and worms, too," he said.

"Ugh." Her gaze slid sideways. There *was* a scar. Alongside the back of his ear, across his neck, disappearing into his collar. Not bad. Slightly raised and pinker than the rest of his sun-weathered skin. Nothing to be self-conscious about...unless his beard hid worse.

Noah glanced at her and slowed. She looked quickly away, beyond his shoulder to the path they'd taken through the pine forest. The trees were so plentiful and tall, she couldn't see the bluff where he'd found her.

His hand slid upward, across her bottom to her waist, as he lowered her to the ground. She slithered, still pressed against him. Their faces were within inches for a moment, so close she could feel his breath and count his lashes. Instead of putting her arms out for balance as her foot touched the ground, she kept her arms looped around his neck. With a little encouragement...

Noah's hands remained at her waist to steady her, but he took a step back to put more distance between them. Her hands slipped to his chest, then dropped. She closed her eyes in mortification. *Good God. What was she trying to do?* The man might be a hermit, but he hadn't asked for female companionship.

"We're here," Noah said in a deep, rough voice. "This is my cabin."

CHAPTER FOUR

CLAIRE TURNED.

First she saw the lake, a deeper blue than the sky, almost green in the depths, with the shaggy sentinels of white pines towering above it. Then the cabin, mere steps from the shoreline.

Noah's home fit the surroundings perfectly. Built of fieldstone and round logs, the cabin was small and tidy, with storybook paned windows and a tin-roofed porch tucked beneath the eaves. The steep, shingled roof was layered with rusty pine needles that had fallen from the shrouding branches of nearby trees. A wisp of smoke drifted from the stone chimney.

"How lovely," she said.

Noah squinted one eye. "Lovely?"

"Homey, then."

"Yeah, I like it."

She turned and smiled. "Me, too."

He looked at her for a minute through serious eyes, then offered his arm. "Let's get you inside."

She hopped, leaning on him, becoming aware of certain sounds beyond the lapping of the water and the trees creaking in the wind. "I hear chickens," she said, cocking her head at the faint squabble and cluck. "But what's that other sound?'' Growly grunts and a metallic rattle, coming from somewhere behind the cabin among the trees.

''Scrap's penned up, but he knows we're here. He's agitating for release.'' Noah transferred her hand to a wood railing, made of a natural uncut branch that had been sanded and polished. Three wide plank steps led to the porch, each of them a uniquely shaped slab with rough bark edges. He put his hands on her waist and started to lift her bodily to the next step.

''Why don't I sit here?'' She hop-turned, boosting herself to plant her behind on the floor of the porch. ''It's such a beautiful day. I can enjoy the view.''

She couldn't say why she was suddenly wary of going inside. Maybe it was knowing that Noah had swept her into his arms and carried her off despite her mild resistance. She didn't think his intentions were less than noble, not for a minute, but all the same...

The situation was already intimate enough. And she *was* at his mercy, so to speak.

Not a bad place to be, whispered a voice inside her.

Noah said he'd be back in a minute. She clasped her hands around her knees, turning her head to watch him disappear inside through a screen door. He left the inner door standing open. She saw part of a wood floor and the rounded edge of a large rag rug. Otherwise, the interior was dark. Noah's bulky shape moved back and forth, making clanking noises. A wood stove, she thought, catching a whiff of smoke. Next he was hacking at something on a table. She leaned closer to gaze through the mesh, her shoulders hunched around her ears, then realized that Noah's head had lifted. He was looking at her.

She whipped around, embarrassed to be caught snooping, even though, for a man who was nearly a legend, Noah didn't appear to be overly guarded about his privacy. He'd invited her inside, after all. And he might easily have left her on the hill to fend for herself.

Or not, she mused. He seemed to be a natural care-giver.

A movement beneath one of the trees caught her eye. She watched with mild alarm as a fat animal waddled from under a branch, snuffling at the ground. A por-cupine, she realized after a tense moment, never having seen one up close before. She slid back a few inches.

The porcupine raised its head to look at her, small pink nose wiggling. The bristles on its body, which had been lying smooth, rose slightly.

Careful not to make any sudden movements, Claire set the heel of her good foot on the porch floor and shoved off, scooting backward toward the screen door. "Noah?" She peered into the cabin, but he didn't seem to be around. "There's an animal out here...."

The porcupine must have decided she was harmless. It ambled closer, putting its small front feet on the first step. Did porcupines shoot their quills? Did they bite? Not wanting to find out, she stomped her boot. "Shoo."

Suddenly the animal seemed to double in size, every quill on its round little body standing at full attention. Uh-oh. She'd made it mad.

But the porcupine wasn't looking at her. It had let

go of the step to huddle on the ground, a ball of bristly daggers. Claire understood why when Scrap appeared, galloping around the corner of the house. He saw the porcupine an instant before he ran into it and skidded to a stop, his back end riding up behind him as his claws dug into the dirt. The cub's astonishment was so comical, Claire laughed.

"Aw, hell," Noah said behind her. "Not again." The screen door nudged her.

"Oops. Sorry." She inched away to give him room to open the door. "Is the porcupine dangerous?"

Noah came out with a bundle of first-aid supplies. He set them down near Claire. "Only to those who don't give her a wide berth. The porky's a frequent visitor, so I call her Trouble. Trouble for Scrap, anyhow. I've pulled quills out of him three times so far. Nose, paw and rump."

"Looks like he's finally learned his lesson." Despite his obvious whisker-wiggling interest, the cub was staying away from the porcupine.

Noah strode over and held the squirming Scrap against his legs. After a moment, the porcupine saw it was safe and slowly waddled toward the shelter of the trees. Noah took a handful of puppy kibble from his pocket and gave it to the cub to keep him momentarily occupied.

He returned to the porch, taking in Claire's position against the cabin wall. "Did that little porky scare ya?"

Might as well admit it. "Sort of. I'm no Saint Francis of Assisi, like you." She rose partway and clambered to the steps. "Do porcupines shoot their quills?"

"Old wives' tale." Noah sat beside her and gathered the supplies, which weren't much—ice, a couple of cloths, bandages and a tube of topical ointment. "As long as you don't try to cuddle up with her, you're safe from Trouble."

"Next time I'll know." As if there'd be a next time. She didn't run into porcupines on Michigan Avenue, unless she counted the occasional bristly hairstyle left over from the punk generation.

"Give me your foot," Noah said, even as he placed it on his lap. He unzipped her boot. "This might hurt."

Except for minor twinges, it didn't. He eased off the boot and removed her sock carefully. He pushed up the hem of her pants. She shivered a little when his fingertips touched her calf.

"Not bad," he said.

She wondered what his definition of *bad* was. Her ankle was puffy—twice its size, just like the porcupine.

"Can you move your foot?"

She gritted her teeth and wiggled it from side to side. Her heel dug into Noah's thigh. "Hurts," she admitted.

"Okay." His hands soothed her.

She wondered if he knew he was doing it or if his gentle manner was inborn. She swallowed dryly. "If you would get my purse, I can call…"

"Who are you going to call?"

She made a weak stab at Noah-style whimsy. "Ghostbusters?"

His eyes glinted. "I might be a scary ogre, but the only ghosts here are mine." Her mouth opened; he went on hurriedly before she could speak. "We can call for transportation after you've rested. I don't want you moving yet. First step with a sprained ankle is to keep it iced and elevated.'' While he spoke, he put together a homemade ice pack—jagged ice chunks bundled into a clean linen cloth. ''Best I can do,'' he said, catching her frown.

''Why is your ice so—'' she waved a hand ''—so un-cubelike?''

''I don't have electricity. Just a little fridge that runs on propane and an old-fashioned ice chest. When I want ice, I chip some off.'' He placed the ice pack against her ankle, then wound a pressure bandage around the awkward bundle to hold it in place.

''I've stepped back in time.'' She winced at the intense cold. ''So, you have no television, no computer, no telephone, obviously.''

''I have a radio.''

''Don't you get lonely?''

He shook his head. ''Not with the menagerie around.''

''The menagerie?''

''No, you have to keep your foot up,'' he said when she tried to lift it off his lap. His palm curved around her heel, holding it still. The sole of her foot was pressed against his midsection. ''I'll show you the menagerie later. The pens are out back.'' He cocked his head toward the cabin. ''I take care of wild animals that have been injured. Mostly ones I find in the woods, but once in a while someone will bring me a bird with a broken wing or an orphaned fawn.''

''Oh.'' Then he wasn't a complete recluse. She

leaned against one of the peeled, polished tree trunks that supported the porch roof. "Is that how you make your living?"

"No. I don't get paid."

She smiled. *Out of the goodness of his heart.* "Noah's ark, is it?"

'I suppose so."

"What about Scrap?" The bear cub had devoured the dog food and was scrabbling beneath the trees, sniffing and grunting over the porcupine's trail.

"Scrap's mother was illegally killed by out-of-season hunters some weeks ago. I found the carcass days later. One of her cubs was already dead, but I rescued Scrap. He was just a little bitty scrap of fur at the time, all skin and bones. He's growing fast. I won't be keeping him too long—only for the summer. The less time he spends with me, the better chance he'll have of surviving in the wild."

Claire crossed her arms to suppress a shudder. "That's sad."

Noah shrugged. "It's life and death."

She bit her lip. He wasn't as detached as that...not if he had ghosts. "What other animals are you keeping?"

"Not too many right now. There's an owl with a broken wing, a possum with a mystery ailment, a raccoon. And a fox—" He frowned. "The fox is worrying me. He has a gash in his belly from a run-in with a wolf or wildcat. I brought him to a vet for stitches, so he should recover. But he won't eat. I'm not even sure he's drinking."

"What can you do?"

"Nothing. Leave him alone and hope for the best. Some wild animals are like that. They'll die in captivity."

"Couldn't you just...set it free?"

"I may have to, even though the stitches should come out first."

"Can I see it?"

"That's probably not a good idea. The less the fox is bothered, the better. I've got him in a small secluded pen right now, away from the others. Scrap, especially."

Claire wagged her head. "Noah's ark," she repeated fondly.

"Not quite," he said. "I've been lacking a woman."

Her brows shot up her forehead. *Did he say that?*

Noah had been mindlessly tracing small patterns on her skin above the swollen ankle. She'd taken that for a habitual soothing-the-wild-beast thing, until...*well.* At the sudden change of mood, his fingertips had stilled.

"Till now?" she croaked. Her mouth was an arid wasteland.

He laughed softly and leaned against the porch post. "Don't worry, Claire. I'm not intending to keep you." He patted her leg in a fatherly way. "At least, not for long."

Her stomach was flipping with excitement, not fear. She gave a shaky laugh. "You seem to have a talent for rescue."

His eyes darkened. "I can't save everyone." A beat of silence. "I mean every*thing*."

She said, "Of course not," rather cautiously, already attuned to his touchiness on the subject. She'd have to ask Cassia what the rest of the story was, since Noah obviously didn't consider himself a hero despite his firefighting exploits. "No one could."

He didn't respond. The silence lengthened until Scrap came over to investigate Claire's foot. He wanted to tug on the end of the bandage, but Noah batted the cub away.

Claire held out her hand. Scrap nuzzled her, his nose moist and wiggly against her palm. "Can I pet him?"

Noah nodded. "This once. I try to limit his contact to humans, but he's an incorrigible snoop."

The bear's fur was coarse, but softer underneath. His ears flitted against her arm, and he rubbed his hard head into her thigh, butting her until she laughed. "Rambunctious creature. Reminds me of my own menagerie."

"Yeah?"

"Five brothers and sisters. I'm the oldest."

"Big family."

"Eight of us, living in a three-bedroom house. There were times I would have welcomed isolating the kids into separate pens."

"Hmm. Where are they now?"

Noah's fingertips were brushing over her calf again. She closed her eyes, savoring the caress that was sweetly seductive whether or not he meant it to be. It had been a while since she'd been with a man who made her so aware of her body and its unmet needs.

She opened her eyes. "Um…" What were they talking about? Oh, yes, her family. She wasn't sure that Noah was interested, but the topic was safer than thoughts of languid caresses beneath the pines and mating up two-by-two to enter the ark.

"Maggie is the second oldest, nearly as bossy as me. Then there's Jesse and Josh, the energetic twins, and Max, the overachiever. Lyndsay's the baby, pretty as a picture. They all live within two hundred miles of our hometown in Nebraska, except for Jesse, who's in the Navy, and Max, who's still in school getting an advanced degree."

She glanced at Noah. He was looking at the lake, but he murmured, "Go on. Tell me about them."

She closed her eyes again. "Well, I have four nephews. Two are Maggie's kids, two are Josh's. Lyndsay's expecting. We're sort of hoping for a girl."

After a moment of thought, Claire sighed. "Lyndsay's only twenty-two. Still a newlywed. She was pregnant when she got married, which wouldn't have happened if *I'd* been around to watch out for her, but she seems happy enough. She and Greg are living with my mom until they—" Claire stopped. "I don't know why I'm telling you this."

"Because I asked?"

"You were being polite. You have no reason to care."

"But you do. That's pretty clear."

"Of course I do. They're my family."

"Then you're not one of those driven, self-important types who only focus on their job?"

Claire wiggled her toes. Her ankle was pleasantly numb. "I can be that, too, and still love my family." She brushed bits of leaves and pine needles off the front of her jacket. "It's just that I don't necessarily want to be in charge of them again. It was hard to break away, but I've been on my own since I was twenty. I've gotten used to my independence." She leaned her head against the porch post. "What about you? How does your family feel about you living way out here all alone without human contact?"

"I'm not without human contact."

Her gaze dropped to his hand on her leg. He was mighty fine at human contact. "Without amenities, then. What would you do in an emergency?"

"I'd take care of myself."

Claire looked at him through her lashes. Was that why he was alone? Because he wanted to be responsible for *only* himself, regardless of a natural affinity for rescue and recovery?

"You're doing a good job taking care of me."

Noah's shoulders shifted. "A sprained ankle isn't life or death." He set her foot on the floorboards of the porch.

She regretted the loss of unity; they were two separate people again—strangers, really. But it was better that way, wasn't it? "What about your family? They live in town?"

"Yes, but they're on vacation right now." He paused; she waited. "There's only my mother and father. No siblings. Dad's a bit of an outdoorsman, so he understands why I live here. Mom worries, like moms do. She always has.''

"Are you close to them?"

"Close enough."

The conversation had run down. For a few minutes, they sat in silence, looking over the lake. The charcoal clouds that had been clustered at the horizon had dissipated into cotton-batting puffs, palest gray against the bold blue. She wouldn't have to trek to Bay House in the rain. If she'd be traveling at all, that was.

"I should make a call," she said, then realized a puddle had formed beneath her foot. There was a big wet patch on Noah's canvas pants, too.

"First let's get this ice pack off." Noah did away with it in a few brisk motions, shaking the shrunken ice shards onto the grass. Scrap rushed over to investigate.

"How does it feel?" Noah dried her ankle and foot with a small towel.

"Comfortably numb."

"I'm going to rub on the ointment and wrap it now. Tell me if it feels too tight." He quickly dispensed with the ointment, then took a clean, dry bandage and wound it around her ankle, working very efficiently. No sign of attraction now, if there'd ever been—aside from her imagination. "How's that?"

"Good. Fine."

"Think you can stand?"

She was game. "Let's see."

He put his hands beneath her arms and hoisted her

up. She wobbled, then steadied herself, one hand clutching Noah's sleeve. "I am going to take a step," she announced, letting go. The wrapped ankle seemed stronger with the support. She was able to hobble across the porch, but was glad to find a twig bench near the door to sit on. She tried not to collapse heavily into it, even though her ankle was throbbing. "Not bad, huh?" she said brightly.

Noah looked at her eyes, not her fake smile. "You can't walk."

"Not so well," she admitted. "The bandage helps, but it really is a bad sprain. If you'll give me my phone, I can call—call…" She faltered.

"A taxi?"

"'Spose not. I'll call Bay House. This nice lady named Emmie Whitaker owns it. She'll know who to send. Luckily I programmed the number into my phone before I arrived."

"I know who Emmie is." Noah got the damp cloths—after a brief tug with Scrap—and went inside. Two seconds later, he came out with Claire's purse. "I was going to return this as soon as I figured out where you were staying."

"Never doubted it." She took the leather bag. "Thank you." She unzipped it and peered inside, not having to rummage because the contents were always in their place. Her wallet, sunglasses and a few personal items in one pocket, her business cards, PDA and backup date book in the other. The cell phone had its own little zippered pocket. "You should get one of these for emergencies," she said to Noah, flipping the stylish little phone open. There was a signal, thank goodness. She wouldn't be stranded.

"Ringing," she told Noah, who stood before her with his arms crossed. His brows were pulled together into a frown.

"Bay House," a voice said through a crackling noise.

"Hello!" Claire spoke loudly. "Who is this?"

More crackling. All she heard was something that sounded like "Shar-shursh."

"This is Claire Levander. *Levander!* I'm a guest. I've run into trouble—" The signal was too weak and staticky for her to be sure she was being understood. She shook the phone—a useless gesture. "I need help!"

A woman's tinny voice came through. "I'm sorry. We have no rooms available at this time."

"I know that. I'm already registered."

More static. "There's nothing in the book—"

"This is Claire Levander. I didn't sign the book. Ask Toivo Whitaker. Or Emmie. Tell them I called! This isn't an emergency, but I'm at Noah Saari's cabin and I need—oh, dammit." She held the phone away from her ear as a rushing sound drowned out her words.

"Bad connection?" Noah said.

She ended the call, then tried again, but she'd lost the signal entirely. "I'm not sure who answered, but she didn't get the message to send help. Maybe if I move into an open area, the signal will be—"

Noah told her to her sit down as soon as he saw that putting weight on her foot made her wince. "I'll make the call,'' he offered. Gratefully, she showed him which buttons to push. He walked toward the lake, trying the cell phone several times, but it was clear he'd been unsuccessful. He came back and offered her the phone. "Maybe your battery is dead?"

"No, I always keep it charged. I think being in a valley is the problem. Hills frequently cause interference.''

"I'll climb to the top of the bluff and try again. After lunch.'' Noah held out his hand.

She placed hers into it, her qualms about being alone with him inside the cabin all but forgotten. "I'm making such trouble for you.'' She smiled. "Just like the porky.''

"No trouble. It's kind of nice—different—having a visitor.'' He helped her limp into the cabin, keeping Scrap out with a nudge of the side of his boot.

"Oh,'' Claire said, looking around. "This is wonderful. Rustic, but very comfortable. I could sell Bel Vista on cabins like this any day of the week. Of course, they'd need all the amenities. Our guests want only the *illusion* of roughing it.'' She saw Noah's quizzical look, then realized what she'd said. Uh-oh. "I, ah, I work for the Bel Vista Hotel Corporation.''

"You're in town on business, then, not vacation? Don't tell me Bel Vista is thinking of putting up a hotel in Alouette.''

"Oh, no, of course not.'' She laughed nervously, hoping he wouldn't ask what her purpose was. She didn't want to lie, and she wouldn't, even if that caused complications in the deal for Bay House.

Thankfully, Noah's next question was, "Do you like grilled cheese?"

Claire sighed. "Yes."

"Go ahead and sit down. This won't take long."

"I want to help." She reached for one of the chairs positioned around a long, narrow dining table.

He put a loaf of bread, butter and cheese on the table. "You can butter the bread."

The cabin was a little warm, so she took off her jacket and folded it over the back of the chair before easing herself onto the seat. The bread was homemade; she cut thick slices with a large serrated knife. While she buttered them, she looked around the cabin, taking it in beyond the first glance. It was one large room, with an open loft space above that likely contained Noah's bed. A big black cast-iron woodstove sat in the center of the room, with the table nearby. The kitchen area—a short length of cabinet, a small fridge and a washbasin with a pump—was tucked beneath the loft floor. Shelves lined one entire wall, a good portion of the space filled with books. An interesting twig chair, a sorry-looking plaid couch and a massive armchair were positioned near the front windows to take advantage of the lake view.

The charm was in the details. Every piece of wood in the place was a pleasure to see—amber log walls, wide plank floors, lustrous, polished oak shelves and tables. Claire slid a hand across the rounded edge of the table. Like satin. Luxurious to the touch.

A rolltop desk was set against one wall. The cubbyholes were filled with interesting treasures—smooth stones, pine cones, feathers, even a set of small deer antlers. Old-fashioned oil lamps were placed around the room, and there was an honest-to-goodness chandelier overhead, fitted with candles instead of bulbs.

Claire's butter knife slowed while she examined it. "Your chandelier is made of wood. Carved wood! And the crystals are pieces of clear quartz. Are the colored pieces sea glass? That's incredible." She goggled at the fixture, which would have been too grand for the humble cabin if it hadn't been made of natural materials, aside from the curlicues of copper wire that had been used to attach the dangling bits. "It's stunning," she said. "A true work of art."

"Too fancy for me," Noah said, but he looked pleased. "But it'll sell."

"Who made it?"

He bent over the woodstove, stirring the embers. "Well...I did."

"You did?" She was momentarily flummoxed; he seemed too large and rugged for such delicate work. Then she remembered his deft fingers and gentle touch. "And all the other woodwork?"

"That, too."

"My gosh, Noah. You're an artisan. Do you sell your work?"

"Yeah, in town. At a little shop called North Country Crafts. I bring them a truckload of twig furniture a couple of times a year. The specialty pieces take too long to produce. If I get a commission, I do the fine carving during the winter."

She picked up the knife. There was more to Noah

Saari than met the eye. She felt lucky to have stumbled into him, even lucky to have sprained her ankle. Otherwise, she wouldn't have known. She'd have believed the rumors that made him out to be a wild man of the woods.

He was watching her somewhat warily. Not accustomed to revealing himself, she presumed.

"I won't blab about what I've seen here," she said. "But..."

She almost faltered. He was looking bearish again.

"It seems that you do have human contact—" *limited, like Scrap's* "—but do you realize that you're something of a...well, a tall tale in town? The Hermit of the Deep North Woods?" She went on despite his glower. "After what I was told, I was actually a little wary of you."

"So why didn't you stay away?"

She shrugged. "Because I'm a foolish city girl who prizes my purse above my life?"

Noah came over and lifted the sandwiches into a cast iron frying pan. He set it on the stove. "I'm a hermit. I'm even a grouch. But did you really think your life was in danger?"

After a moment, she smiled. "No. I'd already met you."

For an instant, his eyes met hers, and she saw emotion there, sensed his need for companionship. Before the bond could deepen, he turned away, going to the kitchen area to take plates and glasses from the open shelves. "My menu is limited. You can have water, coffee or powdered milk with lunch."

"Water," she requested after a short hesitation. So much was left unsaid, but that, it seemed, was how Noah wanted it.

They kept busy for the next few minutes. After Noah primed the pump and filled the basin, Claire hobbled to the sink to wash up. The water was cold but refreshing. He washed, too, and they laughingly shared either end of a hand towel. Her glance went to his face, then skipped away. She was not imagining the feeling between them.

The grilled sandwiches were perfect—melted cheese, crisp edges, real butter. As part of her new health regimen, Claire was supposed to be watching her diet. She rationalized that the morning's exercise made up for the way she inhaled the delicious sandwich.

Scrap had appeared, sniffing the air. He scraped at the mesh of the screen door, begging to come inside. Claire would have offered him the last bite of her sandwich, but Noah was adamant. He explained that he was careful about his various animals' diets, and the only time he took them into the house was during blizzards or below-zero temperatures, or when their condition required constant attention.

He had discipline, Claire thought. Whereas she'd gone softhearted at Scrap's piteous groans, even though she knew all about telling youngsters no and meaning it.

"How's the ankle doing?" Noah asked as he cleared the table.

"Good," she said. "As long as I don't walk on it."

She sighed. "This is something of a pickle, isn't it? I can't walk out, I can't even *call* out, but no one can drive in, either. Or is there a road I don't know about? How do you get your furniture out?"

"I haul it by hand about a mile west of here, where there's an old logging road that's passable."

She wrinkled her nose. "Want to haul me there, too?"

"That's your best chance of getting out of here today."

Her laugh was half-choked. "I wasn't serious, Noah!"

"The only other thing I can think of is to have someone drive in with an ATV...."

She buried her face in her hands. "Good Lord. What a production. After Toivo gets wind of this, I'll be the talk of the town. That's the last thing I need."

Noah stood beside the table with his hands hooked over the back of a chair. Between her fingers, Claire noticed that his knuckles had gone white. Odd.

"There's another option," he said cautiously.

She dropped her hands. "Oh?"

"By tomorrow, your ankle could be a lot better. I wouldn't recommend a three-mile walk, but I could help you to the logging road. From there, it wouldn't be much trouble for me to retrieve your car. Or even arrange a ride back to Bay House."

She'd fixated on one word of his proposition. "Tomorrow?"

He'd turned faintly pink around the edges of his

beard. "Tomorrow, yes. You'd have to stay the night here at my cabin."

She hesitated. Sure, she'd gotten over her nervousness about coming inside his cabin, but staying the night was an entirely different proposal. Particularly in one room.

She looked up, remembering the loft. Well…

He followed her glance. "I'd offer you the bed upstairs, except the ladder's probably too much for you. The couch is old, but comfortable. And you'd be near the door—in case you had to run, screaming, from my unwanted advances."

Claire's eyes grew round. She gripped the edge of the table.

He made a sheepish smile. "Sorry. Bad joke."

Her exhale was all shuddery. "I'm not sure. I…" She looked around the cabin, grasping for reasons to stay. No, to *go*. Reasons to go. But what?

A crumpled brown paper bag on a table beside the easy chair snagged her attention. The bottle from last night? It was lying on its side. Already empty? Was she entirely wrong about Noah's character?

"Thank you for the offer," she began, rising from her chair, keeping her gaze slanted away from his face as her doubts doubled. How could she trust him one hundred percent? She didn't, she wouldn't—not enough to stay the night. If she had to, she'd call the local firefighters to come and rescue her. Even though the thought was cringe-inducing.

"I really do appreciate all your kindnesses," she continued, putting all her effort into not lurching as she sidled as casually as possible toward the door. "But I simply can't—"

She couldn't help it. Her eyes went once more to the paper-wrapped bottle of booze.

Except it wasn't a bottle. Now that she was looking from another angle, she could see where some of the contents had spilled out onto the table. Colored candies. Red and green and brown. The torn edge of a familiar yellow package poked from the top of the bag.

The object of Noah's craving was a one-pound package of peanut M&M's?

Claire's relief showed in a huge, goofy smile. A sweet tooth was something she could identify with. She swiveled on her good foot, arms out for balance. Noah was waiting for her to finish.

She gulped, searching for words. "I simply can't, um, abide the idea of being so much trouble to you. But there doesn't seem to be any other option. If you're *sure* you want me to stay?"

"You're welcome to." His voice came out all gruff and grumbly, but she'd learned to recognize the real emotion behind it.

She threaded her fingers together, tingling with a strange sort of excitement. "Thank you, Noah. It's a generous offer. One I gratefully accept."

CHAPTER FIVE

"A WASHTUB?" Claire looked at Noah as if he was crazy.

"Yup." He set the large galvanized tin tub on the floor near the woodstove. "It's nearly as good as a regular bathtub and weighs next to nothing. I can move it around to wherever I need it." He wouldn't tell her that, other than himself, the last occupant had been Scrap, after his run-in with a skunk. "You learn the value of a portable washtub real fast after you've hauled water for a few baths."

Claire covered her mouth with her hand. Her eyes were dancing. "It's so old-fashioned. Almost cinematic. I picture a cowboy in red skivvies and a hat, chewing on a cigar, submerged up to his soiled bandanna…"

"With a saloon gal dumping hot water from a pitcher." Noah winked at Claire. "I'd doff the skivvies if I were you."

Her gaze flew toward his, then away. Every time he had her pegged, she reacted in a way he didn't expect. She was practical, but she'd been wandering around the woods in high-heeled boots. She was cautious, but seeking him out had been either impulsive or downright daring. The biggest shocker was that, despite being so wary of him, she'd accepted the invitation to stay overnight with an eager smile that had made his heart skip a beat.

"You can wash them out and leave them by the stove to dry so you'll have clean underthings to wear tomorrow," he continued, faintly astounded to find himself talking about her delicate unmentionables in a matter-of-fact way. He'd been without female contact for too long. Wild Rose didn't count; she was as blunt as a man.

He wondered if Claire was a plain white cotton girl or the type who indulged in satin and lace, as if she had to prove she was still a woman in spite of the high-powered career. Since she seemed so well grounded, his guess was that she'd know brains and a career only enhanced her womanhood. No need for satin and lace to make up for imagined deficiencies. Which was a shame. With her curves, she'd look choice.

He'd always liked women with a strong work ethic and an equally strong sense of independence. Was that why he found Claire so appealing? Well, the curves didn't hurt, either.

Lizabee had been like that—focused on the job during work hours, playful after the bell rang, but always all woman, all the time.

Thinking of Lizabee didn't disturb Noah as much these days, but he turned away from Claire all the same. He was used to hiding his feelings. And even though his heart had mended, he wasn't looking for a replacement for the woman he'd lost. Maybe someday.

"Um, good idea," Claire said hesitantly. The air between them had gone prickly with mutual awareness. "If you're sure this isn't too much trouble…"

"The warm water will be good for the swelling in your ankle. Especially if you alternate. I'll put out a second basin so you can soak your foot in cool water, too."

He brushed aside her offer to help. She sat at the table and watched while he stoked the stove and heated big kettles of water, dumping one after the other into the tin washtub. The cabin began to get humid, so he opened a window, letting in the chilly early evening air.

Claire scooted over to peer into the steaming tub. "Do you go through this much trouble every time you take a bath?"

"Since I take only two baths a year, it's not a problem," he said. "Once at Christmas and once in the spring."

She gaped at him, not certain if he was teasing.

He lifted a hank of hair to scratch his head. "I've made friends with my lice."

After a moment of shocked silence, she blurted out a laugh.

"Had you going," he said.

"I didn't believe it for a minute!"

"Only thirty seconds." He added another gallon of water to the tub. He'd already put in twice as much as he'd normally use, but he wanted Claire to be comfortable.

They'd whiled away the afternoon on the porch, entertained by Scrap's antics as they compared humble beginnings—surprisingly similar—and work histories that couldn't be more different. Claire had started out as an executive assistant after college and had stayed with the same company all this time. Noah had tried a year of college, but couldn't take the confinement. Since then, he'd jumped from place to place and job to job as he pleased—almost always choosing outdoor work when he could get it. He'd planted trees and worked construction, then picked crops, hired on to haying crews and wintered over as a ranch hand, slowly working his way west.

Claire had asked questions, but he'd stopped short of telling her about his years as a smoke jumper. He could see in her eyes that she already knew. In a town the size of Alouette, it didn't take long for rumors to reach even a newcomer's ears.

He was mightily impressed that she'd sought him out, even so.

After he'd deflected that area of interest, she'd asked about day-to-day life at the cabin, baffled over how he could survive without modern conveniences. He explained about oil lamps and propane, then sent her off to an encounter with the composting toilet. She got along all right with his walking stick, so they'd ended up at his garden, a big patch of earth he'd cleared and surrounded by high wire fences to keep out the deer and other nocturnal poachers. There was still the danger of frost, and would be throughout May, so he hadn't planted yet. Claire had happily tottered about, helping him prepare the soil.

Back at the cabin, she'd assured him that a bath wasn't necessary even though he'd seen her wince when she'd caught a glimpse of herself in the small mirror he'd hung above the washbasin. He remembered how Lizabee had liked her baths. Hell, he'd even joined her a time or two. He couldn't offer Claire fragrant candles or bath salts. The dented tin tub and privacy would have to do.

"Honestly," he told Claire, having teased her enough, "I take a real bath once a week whether I need it or not. Sponge baths and saunas do the rest of the time. Summer is easy. I jump in the lake."

"Saunas? You have a sauna?" She pronounced it the wrong way.

"*Sow-na,*" he said, "not *saw-na.* Trust me, I'm Finnish."

She looked dubious. "Okay. But we call it a *saw-na* in a hundred or so Bel Vista hotels."

"And now you know better." He pointed out one of the front windows. "See the small hut down by the lake? That's the sauna. It's tradition to plunge into the lake or roll naked in the snow between sweats." He thumped his chest. "Keeps the heart pumping."

"Naked in the snow?" She shivered. "Brr. You're putting me on again."

He laughed, betting that Claire would love it if she ever tried it. She might not be the kind of person who jumped in feet first, but she wasn't a shrinking violet, either. "It's true."

She hobbled to the window. "Where is this sauna? I don't see it." She put a hand to the panes.

"It's built into the steepest part of the bank. You can just see the chimney and tin roof between the pines." He took her hand and pointed with it.

"Ah." She sounded short of breath. "I see it now, thanks."

He let go, amazed by the way his lungs were seizing up. Not worse than they did when he was diving bare-ass naked into the snow, but bad enough to get him thinking about how long it had been since he'd touched a woman's soft skin. That explained why he was as randy as a buck in mating season. It wasn't Claire, specifically.

Or was it? There was something about having her standing near, and sensing how, with a small shift backward, she'd fit against him, snug and soft and very, very…right.

Maybe it *was* Claire, specifically.

He cleared his throat, stepping away from her and the unaccustomed thoughts. "I'll give you some privacy." The screen door wheezed as he opened it. "Yell if you need me. I'll be out back, tending to the animals." He left faster than was dignified, but what the hell. It was better than letting her see how she'd affected him.

He shook himself like a dog when he got outside. Time to remember that he'd sworn off women. He didn't intend to get burned a second time.

NOAH HAD FED and watered the various injured creatures and was shutting Scrap into his pen for the night when Claire's worried voice carried past the swaying branches. "Noah?"

He jammed the latch on his thumb, spat out a curse and hotfooted it to the cabin. Thick smoke had risen from the chimney into the evening sky, gray against the deep blue. Nothing to panic over.

"Noah?" Claire's tone had escalated, but she was keeping calm. "There seems to be a lot of smoke—"

Smoke…fire… Adrenaline lightning-bolted through him. He burst into the cabin as she was clambering out of the washtub, a towel clutched to her front. In one glance, he saw a lot of bare leg and rounded white buttock and *then* the charcoal smoke that was pouring from the squat woodstove.

Claire doubled over, coughing. He was at her side in an instant, folding her into his arms and guiding her to the door. She huddled against him, uncovering her mouth to grab at the drooping towel and sucking in another lungful of smoky air in the process.

He hustled her out of the cabin despite her gimpy ankle. She fumbled with the towel, obviously embarrassed. "Now's not the time to worry about covering your backside," he said. But he ripped off his shirt and threw it over her hunched shoulders.

He left her to run inside, assessing the situation as he dunked a hand towel in the bathwater and tied the cloth over the lower half of his face. Another billow of smoke belched from the stove when he opened the door of the firebox to gauge the blaze. He touched the hot stovepipe. It wasn't a chimney fire, thank God. With a poker, he knocked down what remained of the crackling fire, anyway. Most likely a downdraft had backed the smoke into the room. Relatively harmless, except for scaring Claire and stinking up the cabin.

He adjusted the damper and grabbed a small rag rug off the floor to wave at the smoke. He kicked the back door open and raised all the windows, then stopped to glance around the room. Claire would want her clothes. Except for the damp underwear that hung off the edge of the tub, her garments lay folded in a neat pile on one of the chairs. He gathered them along with a wool blanket from the back of the couch.

Claire had moved farther away from the cabin. She'd put on his shirt and buttoned it up to the collar. The striped towel was wrapped around her hips like a skirt. She clutched at it as she shifted from one bare foot to the other, throwing uneasy glances at the darkened forest.

"How's the cough?" Noah offered her the clothes.

She clasped them to her chest. "Not too bad." Her voice was slightly raspy. "What happened? Is there a fire?"

"Nope, it was nothing serious. The wind picked up, and that caused a downdraft in the chimney." He drew the blanket around her, tucking it in.

"Oh. Thank heaven. For a minute there, I thought I was cursed—" A startled expression crossed her face. "I mean, I thought I'd become Calamity Jane or something."

"It wasn't your fault. Just one of the hazards of heating with wood, I'm afraid."

She narrowed her eyes. "Then it wasn't a ploy to see me naked?"

He grinned. "Nope. Anyway, I couldn't see anything through the smoke."

She cocked her head. Moisture from her wet hair glistened on her cheek. "Liar." Her toes curled into the patchy grass. "You big fat liar."

"I forgot your boots. Hold on." He returned to the cabin, which was still hazy. Realizing she probably couldn't flex her ankle enough to fit into her boots, he grabbed the first footwear at hand.

She stared at the pair of extra-large boots he held out. "Good Lord. What are those? Sasquatch's rain boots?"

"We call them swampers. They should fit." He knelt and helped her step into them, his palm slipping to her smooth, firm calf as he lifted one foot. The towel parted a little as she bent her knee, offering him a glimpse of the inside of one shadowed thigh.

She ducked her head, looking at herself. "Oh, dear, aren't I a sight to behold?"

"High style, north woods version, aside from the towel."

"Damp towels aren't in fashion this year?"

"Long johns are warmer."

She shivered beneath the blanket.

He stood and wrapped his arms around her. For the warmth.

She gave the smallest of sighs and burrowed into him, her cheek pressed to his quilted undershirt. For the warmth.

He stroked her back. "Were you scared?"

"Some. Were you?"

How did she know? The exaggerated stories that still flew around town? Had she expected him to have a full-fledged freak-out over a little excess smoke?

"Nah," he said. The air in the cabin was probably breathable by now. He should take Claire inside before she caught a chill. But this was pleasant, standing by the wind-ruffled lake with a soft, warm woman in his arms. Tiny stars were popping out against the dark sky, making the heavens glitter. The birch and poplar trees swayed, their new leaves as shimmery as spangles on a fancy skirt. Peace—not simply solitude—seemed within his grasp. Never would he have suspected it should come to him accompanied by a city woman.

Claire drew back, tilting her face away from his. She was pale in the moonlight, damp spiky lashes framing eyes that had deepened like the lake. Her lips parted. They were full and moist and impossibly kissable.

Impossible. His hands slid to her shoulders, gripping too tight. She was a woman, not a wild thing. And she wasn't struggling.

That was him.

He cleared his throat. "You should be inside. You're shivering."

"Am I?"

Was *that* him, too?

He closed his eyes, inhaling the commingling scents—smoke, pine, water, woman...

"I'm not going to kiss you," he said. But his hands

slid inside the blanket, dropping to her hips, keeping her close.

Her eyes widened. "I don't remember asking you to." But she swayed toward him, close enough that he could feel the soft puff of her breath against his throat. It was warm.

Her arms, crossed over the clothing clutched to her chest, prevented full contact. Even so, her hips were inviting beneath his splayed palms. His shirt bagged on her. He sensed the emptiness where her back arched. Bare skin, so accessible, was mere inches away. A sound of frustration tore at his throat. He was almost overcome by his want, his need, his denial.

He would not kiss her.

Kissing her would be opening a door better left closed. One that he'd closed—and locked—two years ago. Never mind his recovery and his mended heart.

Instead he patted her behind. Stepped away. "Let's go inside. No sense standing out here in the wind."

She gulped audibly, fumbling with the clothing she'd wadded in her clenched hands. "Um." The blanket swung off one shoulder. She dropped a sock, bent to retrieve it, then bobbed up with nervous energy. "Right." She shook wet, stringy hair out of her eyes. "Yes, indeed. Inside we go."

Inside? The dampened towel clung to her round rump in a distracting way. Noah's thoughts veered in the wrong direction, taking a sharp turn toward lust. *Inside her. Where it was warm and liquid and welcoming...*

She was pure temptation. But he was adamant, accustomed to going without creature comforts.

He would not kiss her.

THE SMOKE was as dense as a curtain. He floated down into it, lost before he touched ground. He couldn't see. Stinging pain attacked his eyes, regardless of the goggles. The sound of his breathing filled his ears, short, raspy pants—already desperate…panicky…

Noah rolled to his side, submerged in sleep, knowing he was dreaming but not able to stop the images. He shoved the covers away. Sweat drenched his body.

The crackling sounds! He hated them. Like a hulking monster creeping through the woods, stopping frequently to lift its head and roar. First the hot, fetid breath, and then the rush of flames, searing the world to a crisp.

His chest drew tight enough to hurt. He groaned, throwing his head from side to side. Wake up. Wake up!

Voices. Vaguely human shapes blundered through the thick smoke, calling out to him, then disappearing. He ran. Stumbled. Ran harder, the burning monster at his heels, singeing the clothes on his back. "Noah… Noah…" Was that Martin's voice? "Noah…" Rick's? Go back, Rick. "Noah…" Oh, God, not Lizabee!

Noah came awake with a wrench, the roar and terror and screams filling his ears. His confused mind cried out in despair before he remembered. *Not Lizabee.* The monster hadn't touched Lizabee.

His heart galloped. Sweat trickled at his temples, along his jaw. He gripped the edge of the mattress, waiting for the horror to subside.

Breathe. He was home, in the north woods. The air was clean, fresh and pure, even if it was tinged with wood smoke.

Lizabee and Martin and Rick weren't with him. They never would be again.

He was alone, as he wanted.

Alone forever.

It was a long while before Noah realized that the thought hadn't given him any comfort. After the fire had taken Martin and Rick and the others, he'd believed only solitude would keep him safe. There was no running from the tearing grief and guilt, but to be alone meant he was responsible for no one but himself. It was a simplified solution, but it had worked for him for two years. Down deep, he'd known he probably wouldn't go on this way forever. Time would heal him. Solitude would become loneliness. For now, though...

He sat on the edge of the bed, running a hand over the scars on his neck and upper chest while he waited for his pulse to slow and his head to clear. He knew what people said; he'd suffered the open curiosity when he'd returned to Alouette. After a week of it, he'd moved to the cabin, an old logger's wreck, and had begun the work to make it livable. The longer he stayed out of the public eye, the harder it was to go back. The easier his retreat from society...and certain accusations.

There were nights he believed them. He woke shriveled with fear and knew he was a coward. *Nobody's hero.*

He stood and moved to the loft railing. An eerie pink light filled the cabin. For one instant, the smallest split second, alarm leaped in his heart. When he'd been a smoke jumper, the rosy light in the sky had come from fire encroaching on the horizon.

Here, where he was safe and alone, there was a different kind of fire in the sky.

His gaze dropped to the figure stretched out on his couch. *And a different woman.*

"Claire Levander." Even saying her name to himself lightened his heart.

She made an agitated sound and turned restlessly onto her back. The flickering light from the window touched her face, making her cheeks glow with a faint, soft rainbow of color. Noah watched her for a long minute before deciding the opportunity wasn't to be missed. Claire must see this.

He dragged a pair of jeans up his legs and found his discarded shirt, the one Claire had worn through dinner, her breasts shifting beneath the flannel whenever she moved, driving him plumb crazy with inappropriate ideas. His joke about her running from his advances hadn't been as far-fetched as he'd intended. Except that he wasn't altogether convinced she'd run, given the option. There was a look in her eyes when she turned them on him…an awareness that drove him as wild as the thought of holding her naked breasts in his hands, lowering his mouth…

Maybe it wasn't a good idea to wake her up.

Didn't matter. He was going to do it anyway. And try to keep his hands to himself.

He climbed down the ladder and padded barefooted across the room. He opened the door, moving quietly so she wouldn't be startled. The light outside was amazing—he stayed on the porch for a moment to admire the spectacle.

Movement from inside. Claire's sleep-softened voice said, "Noah? Are you okay?"

He went to her. She was rubbing her eyes, asking questions. "Shh," he said. "Don't talk. Just come with me."

She pushed the blankets aside and slipped her legs over the side of the couch. "Whattizit—"

"Shh." He took her hand. He'd given her a T-shirt to wear to bed. She'd left her legs bare but pulled a pair of his thick woolen socks over her cold feet. Her sleek bob was ruffled like the feathers of a screech owl. "Count yourself lucky. This is something special. Not everyone gets to see it."

He led her to the porch. Although her progress was halting, she was able to put weight on her ankle. Her hand tightened on his with each step. She needed his support. Once they were at the threshold, he stopped and brushed her eyes with his fingertips, closing the lids. "Don't look yet." He slipped behind her and urged her to the edge of the porch, positioning her with his hands on her shoulders. "Chin up," he whispered, putting his mouth near her ear. "Now look."

CLAIRE OPENED her eyes. She gasped.

Colored streamers of light filled the sky. They flickered and undulated, fading then reappearing, changing shape like the dancing flames of a bonfire. Pale green and rosy pink predominated, but there were also gossamer streaks of blue and purple, amber and orange and white, painted as soft and liquid as watercolors, from the horizon to the dizzying heights above their heads.

She stared, awestruck.

"The northern lights," Noah whispered.

"I can't—" No other words came. The spectacle was too vast, too beautiful for words. She shook her head. Noah squeezed her shoulders in silent communication.

They stayed like that for a long while. Claire tilted her head back, absorbed by the painted sky. The colors grew, spreading into vast ripples, then flickered out, only to reappear in another form. Again and again and again. Infinite, otherworldly beauty.

Aurora borealis. The phenomenon was mesmerizing. She lost herself in it.

"Steady," Noah said when she wavered on her feet, dizzy from the endless variety of color and motion. He wound his arms around her from behind. She leaned into him, her hands moving to rest atop his crisscrossed arms. Even better. She was secure.

"Are they always like this?"

"Not so bright. This is unusually colorful. I've seen the lights often, especially in spring, but usually they're white or a pale eerie green."

She murmured with appreciation. "There's no end...."

"They can go on for hours."

Ribbons of a deep red-pink streaked up from the horizon. The sky pulsated, saturated with the vivid display. Claire gasped, then flung a hand at it as if she were a supreme being with a paintbrush. "The sky's on fire."

"Fox fires," Noah said.

She glanced at him questioningly.

His eyes lowered to hers, the whites glistening in the moonlight, the irises black except for the dancing rainbow reflections. "In Finland, the aurorae are known as fox fires. It's a folk legend."

"Tell me." Her lips felt soft, full.

He dropped a gentle kiss on them, then paused, obviously struggling before giving in to kiss her again. She felt as though she was rising to meet his mouth, every inch of her focused on the wonderful sensations it created. As his tongue delved between her lips, ribbons of pleasure wound around her, silken but strong. Colors danced beneath her lids. She was alight, glowing from the inside out. And it was bliss.

After Noah had kissed her thoroughly, within an inch of permanent breathlessness, he squeezed her, then relaxed his hold, nudging her with his chin so she turned to look at the sky again. Her immense wonder over the northern lights was one thing, but satisfaction rose inside her, too, like water filling a well. It was depthless and pure, as if this was exactly where she belonged.

Fanciful, but then why did she feel Noah's voice in

her bones? "The northern lights are called *revontuli* in Finland," he said. "Translates to 'fires of a fox.' Folklore says the arctic fox starts fires in the sky with a sweep of his tail."

"Mmm. I like that."

"More romantic than the truth—charging electrons colliding with atoms of gas."

She laughed softly. "Yes, I prefer the fairy tale."

"There are others, but the Finnish version is the one I like best. I heard it from my *mummu*—grandmother."

"That's right, you're Finnish." He looked the part, too, like some great burly blond god who could trek through the snow and ice for days on end.

"Around here, many of us are."

"That explains the ethnic names I can't pronounce."

"Saari? That's easy."

She poked an elbow at him. "No apology necessary." She felt light as air, in her head and in her heart.

Noah chuckled. "All right. We'll set aside the Finns for now. Norse mythology tells of a burning bridge that arches across the sky, which the gods travel from Heaven to Earth. Some Native Americans tribes believed the spectacle was the light of lanterns carried by spirits seeking the souls of dead hunters. Romans called the aurora borealis *blood rain*. To the Chinese it's *candle dragon*." He paused. "I'm talking too much."

"No, it's fascinating." Claire's gaze followed as a luminous green curtain was drawn across the sky. "We should make up our own name." She strung words together. "Light…color. Sky…wind…fire. Moon and stars and creatures from Mars…"

"Fire wind," Noah said.

"Star fire."

"That would be a meteor."

She crinkled her nose. "Then...wind light."

"Not skylight?"

"You should have a skylight in your cabin. You could lie in bed and watch this all night long."

"This is nice enough. All that I could ask for. I like being outside, feeling the wind on my face."

"The chill on your toes."

He hugged her closer. "Are you cold?"

"Not a bit." She searched for a way to put her awe into words but had to settle for saying, "It's wonderful."

After that, she was quiet. Words were too small. They could communicate without them, she realized after a while, sensing Noah's reactions, even his thoughts, as they stood together in eloquent silence. The mood had been all wrong when she'd wakened, fractious and confused, as if she'd dreamed a horrible dream she couldn't remember. Whatever had been was gone. In the presence of such celestial radiance, they were humbled and elevated. The warmth of their intertwined bodies, the feeling that vibrated between them, his bedrock character and unquestionable compassion—all of it became entwined with the display of dancing, shimmering lights. She knew there would never be another night as perfect as this one.

Noah had given her an incredible gift. The radiance was inside her. She would remember this forever.

CHAPTER SIX

THE NEXT MORNING, Claire was self-conscious. Noah, too. It was hard to distinguish his natural reserve from the kind of sentient embarrassment she felt. There had been something magical between them as they'd watched the northern lights, but in daylight, uncertainty had returned.

Noah had a mysterious, apparently tragic past. Hero or not, she didn't know. He wasn't talking. The scars she didn't care about. At some point the previous night, she'd realized that his shirt had been half unbuttoned, revealing a hairy chest and several burn scars that ran from his left ear down the side of his throat onto his chest. They weren't bad at all. And she was *not* going to ask him about them.

Questions might lead straight to her. He'd already asked again about her job with Bel Vista and why she'd come to Alouette, but she'd managed to skim over the subject. The company preferred her to be discreet about their interest in a property. Her personal code was that she would not deceive anyone, but she didn't have to broadcast her intentions, either.

She suspected Noah wouldn't be in favor of Bel Vista taking over Bay House. From their conversation over a country breakfast of fresh-laid eggs and toast, she'd learned that he was a conservationist, tree-hugging type. It stood to reason that any man who lived in a remote cabin without social contact was going to resist change and progress. Add the fact that he apparently knew the Whitakers quite well....

She could tell him that Bay House would be updated and promoted, not ruined. Except she wasn't positive of that herself. History was a fragile thing. A fine line had to be drawn between restoration and gimmicky ostentation. It was a line Bel Vista had crossed in the past, turning a rustic ski lodge into a decadent hot-tubbing playground, a fine old San Francisco hotel into a gaudy display of crystal, marble and gold.

Besides, she would be gone in a week. Her memory of watching the northern lights with a remarkable man would not alter or diminish. But it *would* remain separate from the rest of her life.

Noah Saari wasn't reality.

Not hers. And maybe not even his own, because clearly he wasn't ready to deal with whatever had made him retreat from society.

Claire sighed as she hobbled out to sit on the steps. Her well-developed mothering instinct was trying to kick in. A good part of her wanted to heal Noah. The gritty, ambitious side—the part of her that had been bent on college and an important career in spite of her strong family ties—wanted otherwise. Leaving before her feelings got too complicated was the smart option.

She squinted at the sunshine glancing off the lake. Not necessarily the healthiest one, though.

Scrap charged around the corner of the house. Noah came next, holding a length of wood. He'd been in his workshop out back, fashioning her a crutch for the walk to civilization. She'd offered to call for help, but he'd decided that it was easiest for him to go get her car and rendezvous with her at the logging road.

He stamped the tip of the crude crutch on the top step. "What do you think? This should give you more support than my walking stick." He'd found a branch with a natural notch and had added a crosspiece to the top.

"Looks good. I should do fine. My ankle is feeling much better." She nudged her boots with her toe. "But I still can't get my boot on."

Noah frowned. "You shouldn't be wearing heels, anyway." He grabbed Scrap by the scruff when the bear tried to attack the boots. Claire took them into her lap. Yes, they were useless here, but she'd be wearing them again in the city, and she didn't want bear scratches marring the leather. Not even as a remembrance.

"Then shoes are going to be a problem," she said.

Noah's brows went up.

"Oh, no. I'm not wearing your swampers again. They wouldn't stay on my feet for ten yards."

"You can wear a triple thickness of socks."

"How about *only* a triple thickness of socks?"

"Nope. Ground's too wet in the spring. You need the swampers."

She rolled her eyes in defeat. "I'm so glad none of my friends are here to see this."

Noah went into the cabin and came out with the rubber boots and some socks. "You could start a new fashion."

She eyed his leather boots, faded jeans, chamois vest and red-and-black buffalo-plaid shirt. "Lumberjack chic."

"Sure, but I'm no lumberjack. I do have an ax and a chainsaw, but I don't cut very many trees down."

"No? What about your woodworking projects?"

"I use dead wood whenever possible." He waved at the forest. She knew by experience how thick, tangled and brushy it was, with enough split or uprooted trees and branches to provide Noah for a decade. "There's a large supply. For the twig furniture, I harvest willow branches. For birch-bark pieces, I look for downed trees. Peeling the bark off a live birch would kill it."

"Another area of my miseducation." Claire had pulled on the socks and boots and used the crutch to stand. "This has been a learning experience for me. I owe you one." Her glance darted over Noah's face. When there was enough conversation to fill the air, they were okay. It was the silences that made pesky carnal thoughts crowd out her reasonable decision to leave things on a friendly basis. "If you're ever in Chicago…"

"You'll show me how to hail a cab?"

She smiled. "I imagine you could manage that on your own." She scanned the glittering lake, the towering pines. It was beautiful, but desolate. So…big. She was an insignificant and fragile being here, not like in the city, where she knew her place and how to keep it.

She could take care of herself there. Here, she was literally a babe in the woods. "What I wouldn't give for a cab right now."

Noah shrugged.

"Why don't you keep some sort of motorized vehicle? If only for emergencies. What if you cut off a thumb or broke your neck?"

"Then I wouldn't be driving, would I?"

She hated to think of leaving him here alone—and lonely—even more than she was concerned with appearing too clingy and motherly. "Noah. It's not safe. And it's not natural. Humans are herd animals."

His eyes sought hers, silently asking why she cared. Or maybe that was her imagination. "I do have a snowmobile for the winter."

"The winter!" she said. "You must be completely snowed in for months on end. How can you stand it?"

His gaze dropped to her mouth. *Not* her imagination. "I'm starting to wonder."

A blush was climbing up her throat. She coughed. "Even hermits need—" *oh, no, don't be sappy enough to say love* "—companionship."

Noah hesitated for a beat too long. "I have Scrap."

"Only for the summer, you said."

"There's always another animal or bird that needs TLC."

"What about when you need it?"

He regarded her steadily. The thought of all the ways she could lavish him with tender loving care made her insides quiver.

Enough. She turned away and hopped down the

steps on her good foot. "I'm sorry. None of my business. Let's see how this crutch works, okay?" She tucked it under her arm and walked around the patch of sparse grass that passed for a front lawn. Her ankle gave off protesting twinges, but it wasn't bad. She'd make it to the road Noah had told her about.

Scrap scampered after her, pawing at the rough-hewn crutch. She wanted to pet the cub, but he was so rambunctious she was afraid that with any encouragement he'd barrel into her and send her sprawling. "Are we going to take Scrap?"

"We'd better not," said Noah. "I'll go put him away."

"I'll come with you." She hadn't been introduced to the other animals yet.

The animals were kept behind Noah's workshop, which was a simple frame building made of old rough-sawn boards. She peeked inside. Worktables, piles of twigs, scrap wood, a stove, then a number of hand tools hung in precise order on a peg board. The place smelled of sawdust and beeswax and varnish. Much nicer than the oily aroma of the back room of her parents' gas station.

The cages were outside, tucked onto shelves on the back wall, well sheltered by balsam fir—what she thought of as Christmas trees. Scrap scrambled up the trunk of a sugar maple, his brown nose twitching at his separate fenced-in enclosure. Noah had explained that ideally the cub would be sequestered with no human contact, but he didn't have the proper facilities. Nor the hard-heartedness to ignore Scrap's loneliness, she suspected, even though that meant it would be a challenge to reintroduce the bear to the wild. There was a chance, Noah said, that Scrap would be sent to a wilderness park, instead.

"Here's the owl," Noah said, keeping his voice low. "I call her Minx because she's a snippy, sassy little creature."

Claire peered into the cage. A small owl was perched on a branch that had been affixed inside, one bandaged wing hanging at an awkward angle. Its brown feathers were puffed up in defense. Round yellow eyes watched her warily.

"It's so small." The owl was agitated. Good wing flapping, it retreated to a shadowy corner, claws skittering over the wood-sided box. "What kind is it?"

"Common screech owl." Noah gave the bird fresh water and closed the door. "Eats grubs, worms and field mice. I'll be releasing Minx in a few weeks."

Claire squeaked. "Mice?"

"Sorry, but that's the way it is."

"Law of the jungle. I'm just glad it was you who found me—not some other carnivore."

He laughed. "You were never in danger."

"Aren't there wolves here?"

"Yes, and bobcats. But it would have been extremely unlikely that they'd have come upon you."

"I don't know…I did run into a bear, didn't I?"

"Scrap's harmless."

She smiled. "Scrap's not the bear I meant."

Noah opened another cage. "This is Rocky. My raccoon mischief maker. She's been trying to invade the cabin ever since I moved here. Thinks she's a pet, y'see."

"What happened to her?" The raccoon was a curious, bright-eyed creature with a thick coat of fur and a black mask. It tried to climb up Noah's arm as soon as he reached inside, and he had to pry it away, being careful of the back leg that was splinted and bandaged.

"I don't know. I found her huddled under the porch, nursing a hurt leg. She might have fallen or pinched her leg among the rocks." He held the plump raccoon against his chest. "Want to pet her?"

Tentatively, Claire stroked the thick brown fur. The raccoon's striped tail curled toward her hand. "I thought you didn't want them to become domesticated."

"Rocky's a hopeless case. She already likes me too much."

"Hmm. I know the feeling."

Noah grinned. "Actually, I'm not sure if it's me or the meals."

"The way to a female's heart…"

"Mealybugs and raw liver?" he said with an amused lilt.

"Maybe next time."

Noah put Rocky into the cage and secured the door. The raccoon pressed her little black nose against the wire mesh, making forlorn sounds. Claire identified.

"Rocky's almost healed. I've been holding on to her only because she's less of a pest with a splint on her leg. She'll go in a day or two. Not that she'll leave the area."

"This has been fascinating." Claire poked a finger at Rocky through the mesh. "Did you have special training to learn how to care for them?"

"I took a class, years ago. But most of it I learned on my own. I am a licensed rehabilitator. It's one of those don't-do-this-at-home gigs."

Claire peeped at an opossum who was huddled at the back of a cage, suffering a stomach ailment of some sort, according to Noah. He'd adopted a wait-and-see method with the possum. "What's this one's name?" she asked, having figured out that it would have one.

"Reader."

"Reader?"

He stroked his beard. "Well, when I found her, she was practically dead. I had to keep her in the cabin twenty-four seven, trying to get nourishment into her with an eyedropper. I took to reading out loud to keep awake, with poor little Reader curled up in a towel beside the oil lamp."

She gazed fondly at Noah. "I am so impressed."

He shook his head. "It's nothing."

Just like he's nobody's hero, she thought, but didn't press the point. "Can I see the fox?"

Noah raked a hand through his golden-brown hair, his forehead furrowed with concern. "You really shouldn't," he said. "The fox is my touchiest case."

She didn't want to push him on this, either, so she nodded, even though ever since he'd told her of the Finnish folk tale about fox fire, she'd hoped to get at least a glimpse of the elusive creature.

Noah echoed her earlier statement. "Maybe next time?"

"Sure."

But there might be no next time. Didn't he know that?

IT WAS MIDAFTERNOON by the time Claire arrived at Bay House. The walk through the woods hadn't been easy, even though her ankle was much better. The terrain was uneven, so every step had to be carefully chosen. Progress was slow. Eventually the strain was too much, and the sprained ankle began to throb. When Noah realized that, he picked her up and carried her—only for the last bit, but she felt awkward about it. And more than a little impressed by his heroics. Again.

He left her sitting on a bank beside the narrow track of the forgotten logger's road while he went to retrieve her car, moving ten times as fast without the burden of her. She'd barely had time to catch her breath—and think about how to say goodbye—before he was back, nosing the car between the trees. He had to go a little farther to find a clearing to turn around, and she was standing when he returned, pulled together with her jacket buttoned and her smoky hair smoothed and her romantic wishes all tucked in.

Saying goodbye wasn't a problem, after all. Noah gave her directions, got her settled behind the wheel, slammed the door and thumped his fist against the roof for good measure. She started the car, intending to roll the window down and say a final word of appreciation and summation—it was going to be some magnificent word—but he'd already faded into the trees.

One wave and he was gone.

She stared hard at the place where he'd been, detecting only the slight sway of an evergreen branch. After a moment, she climbed out of the car, found one of the large pinecones that littered the ground around the tree, then got behind the wheel and drove away. A pinecone wasn't much of a memento, but it and the scratches on her designer boots were all she'd apparently have.

She didn't know why she was left feeling so… *wanting*. Maybe it was the suspicion that Noah would have treated any weak, injured creature who crossed his path the same way, when she needed more than that. She wanted to be more to him than Rocky or Scrap or the mystery fox who, with one swipe of his tail, had made the sky burn with color and her heart sing with sweet, wild love.

"Oh, stop it," she told herself as she drove away. "He's a hermit, not a suitor. No matter what Valentina says."

Her reception at Bay House had more consequence. Cassia Keegan was waiting on the porch in her wheelchair. She raised the call as soon as Claire drove through the Neptune gateposts and up to the sandstone inn.

Emmie and Toivo Whitaker were at the door to greet Claire by the time she got there, exclaiming over her limp and the make-do crutch. Emmie forced Claire to sit at once in one of the purple velvet foyer chairs, smack-dab beneath an overgrown spider plant with dangling shoots that tickled her nose. Toivo brought her a small tufted "oddman" so she could prop up her foot.

"My goodness." Emmie set her hands on her hips and looked Claire over. "What happened to you, young lady?"

"You didn't get any of my message?"

Emmie's plump face creased. "Shari Shirley told us that a woman named Clevandish had called, looking for reservations. She couldn't make hide nor hair of it—the line was bad."

"That was me. On a cell phone."

Emmie nodded. "When Shari said that the caller had gotten a room at Noah Saari's cabin instead, Cassia and I put our heads together and figured out that it must be you. Then Toivo came home with tales about your car being spotted parked on 525. We've all been wondering what happened."

"I'm sorry for causing you worry," Claire said. "My cell phone wasn't working properly so I couldn't tell if my message got through. I had no other way of reaching you."

"Ach, that's all right. We figured out that you were being kept warm and safe and that we'd see you soon."

Cassia wheeled closer. Her eyes were huge with awe. "Did you really spend the night at Noah's cabin? What was he like? How did he treat you?"

Claire demurred. She trusted Cassia and Emmie to be somewhat discreet, but Toivo was also listening, taking in every word. He'd have no compunction about repeating her story, and probably get it all wrong in the bargain. She'd rather her stay with Noah was not mangled and disseminated like so much fodder for the mill.

But she had to tell them something. "You'll remember that I went to find the purse I'd dropped the night before. Well, it turned out Noah had already picked it up. So I walked to his cabin. But on the way, I fell and sprained my ankle." She pointed to her propped-up foot as if this was show-and-tell.

Emmie made sounds of sympathy. "Why on earth are you wearing swampers?"

"Gigantic ones," Cassia said. She looked at Claire and winked.

Claire bit her lip to keep from giggling. She knew what Cassia was thinking of. Big feet, big hands, big…man.

"I couldn't fit into my own boots because of the swelling. Noah let me wear his." Aha. She still had his boots! As good an excuse to see him again as any— if she wanted to.

"Let's get these off while you go on with your story." Emmie began untying the boot on Claire's bad foot. "Make yourself useful, Toivo, you gaping old goat. Do the other one."

"What happened then?" Cassia asked, positioning her chair so Toivo could kneel at Claire's left foot. She circled the innkeepers and came up on Claire's right, pushing aside the palm fronds. "You still made it to Noah's cabin?"

"No, he found me in the woods and, um, brought me there himself."

Cassia exhaled. "Oh. Wow."

Toivo had untied the boot. It was so oversize Claire gave a wiggle and it dropped off her foot. Emmie was being more careful, loosening the cord slowly and easing the other boot off. She peeled away the thick woolen socks—Noah's socks, too!—and clucked like a mother hen over her houseguest's bandaged ankle. "I can fix that right up for you, Claire. Or would you rather see a doctor?"

"No, thanks. That's not necessary. Noah took very good care of me. I'll keep off it for the rest of today, and tomorrow I should be almost back to normal. I've dealt with sprained ankles before." She shrugged. "Five active brothers and sisters."

Cassia lifted the hem of Claire's pants to examine the injury. "Noah took care of you?"

Claire nodded, her heart going warm and tender at the thought. She had to stop that.

"Wow," Cassia said. "What was he like?"

"Very gentlemanly and kind."

"Did you see the—" Cassia gestured at her face. "You know."

"He has a beard. If there are scars, they're not very noticeable."

"Huh." Toivo was obviously disappointed. "Boy, oh, man, Myron's been exasperating again."

"And exaggerating, too," Cassia said drolly. "I told you so, didn't I?"

"Toivo, how many times have I warned you? You

mustn't go around repeating that man's tall tales." Emmie gathered the swampers and socks and put them inside a closet that had been hidden by the houseplant jungle.

"Noah Saari is just like any other man," Claire said firmly, hoping to put an end to that line of questioning. At least for the moment, she added to herself, catching sight of Cassia's save-it-for-girl-talk double-eyebrow arch. "I really am so sorry for worrying you. Noah's cabin was too far from the road for me to walk out yesterday. I managed better today, using the crutch he made for me." She placed a hand on the crude device.

"You'll get splinters," said Emmie, looking it over. "Toivo, take that out back and hack it up for firewood."

"No, please!" Claire tucked it under her arm as she struggled to her feet. "I may still need it."

Emmie patted her arm. "Not to worry. I'll find you a nice new one as a replacement."

"I have a pair of metal crutches in my room," Cassia volunteered. At Claire's questioning look, she made a self-deprecating face. "Yes, I can walk. Or try to, anyhow. But it's not a pretty sight."

"Nonsense," Emmie said, huffing. "You do very well."

Cassia wagged her head. "Whatever!"

With the focus off her, Claire thought it was a good time to make her departure. She hobbled to the staircase, saying, "I need a long, hot soak in the bathtub, so if you'll excuse me…"

Emmie gave Toivo a nudge. "Don't just stand there

like a bump on a log. Help the lady up the stairs." To Claire, she called, "I'll bring up an ice pack, a fresh bandage and a lunch tray after your bath."

Toivo hovered at Claire's side while she took the steps one at a time. "That sounds wonderful, thank you," she told Emmie, relieved she'd gotten away with a bare-bones explanation for her absence. The Whitakers were being genuinely solicitous and caring, and the promise of food and hot water on tap was bliss. So why did she wish she'd been able to stay longer at Noah's cabin?

"Come back down after you've had a rest," Cassia said. "I have nothing to do and I could use some company." She looked up the staircase at Claire, making a sad puppy-dog face that might have been pitiful if not for the sparkle of mischief that couldn't be doused from her eyes. Her irrepressible cheer made Claire smile and agree that she would see Cassia later. There was an age gap between them, but it couldn't hurt to confide in someone. Cassia could substitute as a little sister.

And she probably knew more about Noah's past than she'd revealed so far.

Toivo stood by as Claire opened the door to the bridal suite. He was looking at her with his elfin face all scrunched up. "Do I need to give that man a talking-to?"

Claire's hand froze on the knob. "What?"

"A man like that, he hasn't been near a woman in months. He's bound to be—" Toivo's face got ruddy, but he plowed on. "You say the word, Miss Lavender, and I'll take care of him.'' He held up his fists like a prizefighter.

Santa's elf versus Grizzly Adams? Claire blinked furiously, trying not to betray the sheer absurdity of the match. "Oh, no, really. Noah's behavior was exemplary.'' *Darn it.* "I slept on the couch. Quite alone.'' That should put any rumors to rest!

Toivo bobbed and feinted. "Ya sure?''

She gave his fists several pats as she gently lowered them. "I appreciate you looking out for me. You're a dear man.''

The innkeeper beamed. "We treat every guest special at Bay House.''

Which was one of the homey touches that would be lost if Bel Vista took over operations.

I can't think about that now. Claire murmured more thanks, refused Toivo's offers—newspapers, extra blankets, a round of Scrabble—and escaped into her room. She collapsed on the bed with a grateful sigh. Valentina Whitaker, Miss Icy Eyes, watched from the opposite wall.

"Not a word out of you,'' Claire said.

Thankfully, none of the Bay House busybodies had connected her supposed impending marriage to her encounter with Noah. Only she knew he was the first man who'd made her heart pitter-patter since…well, since what seemed like forever. She'd better keep it that way, too.

Except…

Noah was so far removed from her usual prospects it was laughable. She usually went out with well-off

Terry Lindstrom types—men in business suits who seemed to like her well enough until the conversation eventually worked its way around to how looks weren't important but they did prefer a woman with blond hair and an athletic figure...or a woman who could adjust her schedule to theirs and didn't mind last-minute cancellations...or one who agreed that sex on a first date was a great way to get to know each other.

Noah's priorities were more to her taste. Aside from the hermit thing.

Yeah, there was the hermit thing to consider!

Claire tried to put him out of her mind as she took a long, luxurious bath—no smoke, no fire, no Noah—changed to comfortable sweats and lay in bed surrounded by plump feather pillows as Emmie bustled about applying ice packs that didn't leak and thankfully not asking too many questions. The innkeeper shot a few curious looks at her guest, but when Claire didn't volunteer answers, Emmie was too polite to pry.

Claire eagerly ate her late lunch, leaving only the tray and a few stray crumbs, then decided to take a short nap. When she woke sometime later, roused by loud thumping sounds from the floor above, the sky had darkened to a heavy cobalt blue. A few raindrops pattered against the glass of the French doors. She checked her travel clock and saw that she'd slept for three hours.

The thumping continued, accompanied by creaking footsteps. By the sound of it, someone was moving in or out upstairs. Claire made a mental note to investigate the cost of squeak-fixing and soundproofing.

Yawning, she swung her legs off the bed, flexing her right foot to test the ankle. It had stiffened after the walk, but the long rest had restored some function. Walking almost normally, she took a turn around the room before stopping at the glass doors to gaze at Lake Superior. Beneath the drizzling sky, the water was a choppy gray. A heavy fog had gathered near the cliffs, obscuring the steep drop. It almost looked as though a person could walk over the rocks and just keep on going, straight out to the water.

Claire's senses twitched. She turned slowly, using her bad foot as fulcrum. Valentina again, staring daggers. A less loving bride-to-be Claire couldn't imagine.

"No wonder your fiancé ran away." Claire hauled her suitcase out of the closet to rummage for a pair of sneakers. She really should unpack properly, but at the moment all she wanted was to make tracks out of the room. "You probably make *everyone* want to run away," she told Valentina from the door. "I'll have to speak to Emmie about turning you toward the wall. That expression is not very hospitable."

Laughing at herself, Claire went downstairs with the lunch tray. Although the door to Cassia's room was open, the redhead wasn't inside. There was evidence of a recent meal on the dining room table, but no diners. Claire was beginning to wonder where everyone had gone when a burst of laughter came from the next room.

She pushed through the swinging doors into an immense kitchen. Toivo and Bill Maki were seated at a small table, hastily finishing what was probably seconds on dessert. A young woman with a girl-next-door look was lounging against the refrigerator, picking at her nails. Cassia was across the room, drying a blue-and-white china plate Emmie had just laid in her lap.

Emmie was at the sink washing dishes. "About time," she said when Claire approached from behind. "Put them over here." She pressed a hand to her bosom when she saw who'd set the lunch tray down. "My heavenly stars. I thought you were Shari with the rest of the supper dishes. Where did she get to?"

"She may be upstairs. At least I think so. Someone was clumping around in the attic."

"Again!" Emmie shot a quick look at the others in the room. "Roxy, will you go up and roust her?"

"Ugh." The ponytailed blond thrust her hands into the pockets of her overalls. "You know Shari and I don't get along."

"Bill—"

Bill put down his plate, abandoning the last few bites of pie. "Not me." He moved swiftly toward the back door, swiping a hat from a peg on the wall. "I'm not going near that woman." He disappeared into the rain.

Emmie stopped her brother, who had his hand on the doorknob. "You do it, Toivo. She's probably up there searching for the key. You're the one who told her I'd hidden it on another floor."

Toivo wiped his mouth with the back of a sleeve. "Aw, Emmie…"

"Go on."

Shoulders slumped, he heaved a heavy sigh to show

his supreme sacrifice and slowly ambled from the kitchen.

Claire was curious. She had yet to set eyes on the maid, Shari Shirley, but the woman wasn't exactly quiet as she went about her work. "What is this about the key?"

"I told you." Cassia carefully added the dried plate to a small stack of them on an adjacent countertop. Emmie placed another wet one in her lap, which was covered by a linen towel. "Shari is fixated on Valentina's bridal suite." As she spoke, the fragile redhead blotted the surface of the plate with a wadded cloth, rotating it in her lap. She didn't seem to have full use of her hands, but her method was effective. "She's been trying to get into it for—well, ever since I've been here, and that's almost two months."

"It's been longer than that. I've been here nearly half a year, and I've had to foil Shari more times than I can remember." The young woman in overalls nodded at Claire. "I'm Roxy Whitaker, the Bay House handygirl."

"Claire Levander. Bay House guest."

Roxy smirked. "I hear Toivo put you in the bridal suite." She darted a glance at Emmie, who was scrubbing and splashing with an aggrieved air. "By *mistake*, of course."

Cassia chortled. "I hope you don't run into Shari in the middle of the night, Claire. She's liable to bonk you over the head and stick you in a closet, bound and gagged, so she can take your place in bed."

Emmie protested. "Now you're being ridiculous."

"I wouldn't put it past her," Roxy said.

"Shari wants a husband," Cassia told Claire.

Roxy grinned. "So do you."

Cassia tossed her hair. "Who says? I never said I wanted to settle down. I just want a boyfriend. I don't need Valentina's curse—*prophecy*—for that."

"It's a curse, all right," Roxy muttered. She took the last plate from Cassia, added it to the stack and put them away in a cupboard. "Of course, I don't actually believe it."

Cassia sent Claire a knowing look. "Then why don't *you* go and sleep in the bridal suite, Rox?"

"You girls," Emmie said, exasperated with the teasing. "Roxy's fine where she is. The bridal suite isn't a game. You'll give Claire the wrong idea with all this silly talk."

Claire picked up the dessert plates from the table. "Then the legend is exaggerated?"

"I wouldn't say that." Emmie took the plates from Claire. "Thank you, dear. But you're a guest. You don't have to help."

"I don't mind."

"Would you like me to warm a plate for you? We've all had supper, but there are plenty of leftovers. You were sleeping so peacefully, I didn't want to disturb you."

"Emmie—isn't Bay House a bed-and-breakfast? I don't expect you to feed me three meals a day. In fact, I owe you for lunch."

Emmie flapped a hand. "Phooey. Soup and a salad?

That was nothing. Meals are included for my boarders, so it's no trouble to add another place to the table.''

A little less hospitality and more bottom-line thinking was in order. Claire smiled, making light of it even though she was interested in how the business—if you could call it a business and not an open house—was run. "But I'm a big girl. Feeding me could cut into your profits."

Emmie looked her up and down. "Not too big. You've got a nice shape. Healthy." She smoothed her apron over her zaftig figure with a preening satisfaction that surprised Claire. She had assumed Emmie was strictly the egoless homebody type whose emotional needs were met by mothering all those around her. "Men appreciate us gals with vroom-vroom curves."

Cassia opened the neck of her blouse and looked inside. "So that's the problem. All I have are itty-bitty speed bumps!"

The women laughed. They continued the banter while finishing the dishes and cleaning up the kitchen. Claire declined the leftovers, saying she wasn't hungry yet. She insisted Emmie was to write a bill for all meals provided. In that case, the innkeeper told Claire, she should feel free to fix herself a snack any time she wanted. Satisfied she'd had the last word, Emmie went off in search of Shari and Toivo.

"I'm going to watch a movie in my room," Cassia said. "Who wants to join me?"

Roxy weighed the invitation. "Vin Diesel?" she asked hopefully.

Cassia shook her head.

"Give me Hugh Jackman, at least."

"Would you settle for Emilio Estevez?"

Roxy gagged. "I'd rather stick a needle in my eye than see *The Breakfast Club* one more time." She headed for the door. "Ask me again when you start watching grown-up movies."

Cassia looked at Claire after Roxy had run through the rain to her garage apartment. "I suppose you only watch foreign films about red balloons and circus freaks."

Claire held back her smile and said in a deadpan voice, "What do you think I am—a neo maxi zoom dweebie?"

Cassia gasped. "That's a Judd Nelson quote from *The Breakfast Club*. I thought I was the only adult who loves that movie."

"Are you kidding? I adore the entire genre. From *Ferris Bueller's Day Off* to *St. Elmo's Fire*. I *am* Mare Winningham. In college, I had an unrequited crush on a guitar player who looked like a blond Rob Lowe. I'd have given him my virginity, but he never asked."

Cassia made a funny face. "I've always felt a little bit like Molly Ringwald in *Sixteen Candles*."

"Ah, there's a classic," Claire said, nodding. "Long Duck Dong and his 'sexy, new style American girl-friend.'" She eyed Cassia. "Do you really have *The Breakfast Club*?"

"It's my favorite, even though I could never identify with Molly's character in that one. Too goody-goody."

"But she *wanted* to break out."

"With Bender? Ew!"

"He had the bad-boy thing going on." Claire tilted her head. "Hmm. Molly's character was named Claire, you know. Do you remember the line about Claire being a fat girl's name? I was always horribly certain Bender was talking about me." She became thoughtful, remembering how, despite the name, she'd identified most of all with Molly as Andie in *Pretty in Pink*. The poor girl who aspired to better things.

Claire brushed off the momentary blast from the past. "Do you have *Say Anything*?"

"Hot tamale! Lloyd Dobler can blast a boom box at me any time he wants."

"Oh, yeah." Claire held her arms overhead and danced around the kitchen.

"You know when Bender teases Claire about her lunch? 'You won't let a boy's tongue in your mouth but you'll eat sushi.' That totally cracked me up. Way before I knew what it was like to have…sushi." Cassia giggled at herself. "You can tell I've watched too many movies, huh? But I'm not ashamed to say that I have the entire John Hughes repertoire in my video collection." She raised her brows. "Interested?"

"Do you have *Some Kind of Wonderful* and *Pretty in Pink*?"

"Wouldn't be caught dead without 'em."

"Then you're on."

CHAPTER SEVEN

CLAIRE AND CASSIA watched spellbound as Duckie told Andie she should leave the prom to go after Blair. The rich-kid poor-girl couple met in a rather unglamorous parking lot and kissed to the strains of a forgettable hit song from the eighties.

"Oh," Cassia said, stretching, "that was satisfying."

"Did you think so? I always hope the ending will change and she'll decide that Duckie is the guy she loves. He was the one who really was there for her."

"But he was so goofy. 'Course, Andrew McCarthy doesn't do it for me, either. Too bland and safe. I like a guy with a little edge to him."

Claire sighed. "I used to watch these movies on video while I was in college, wondering why my relationships ended with a whimper instead of a crescendo of 'Don't You Forget About Me.' Still, don't you love a happy ending?"

Cassia was stretched out on her bed, surrounded by pillows. As the credits rolled, she leaned over to reach for the remote control. "Not exactly. My heart may melt when Molly gets her birthday kiss at the end of *Sixteen Candles,* but then it makes me mad things like that don't happen to me. So I end up dissatisfied."

Claire lounged in a cushy rose chintz easy chair. "You never know when it'll happen for you. Maybe... tomorrow."

"Not very likely." Cassia gestured at her frail legs. It was an effort for her to move them toward the side of the bed. A couple of the decorative floral pillows fell to the floor.

Claire suppressed the urge to jump up and help. She'd noticed the spirited redhead preferred to do what she could on her own but wasn't self-conscious about asking for help when she needed it.

"I know a woman from work who's in a wheel-chair," Claire said. "She just got married to a won-derful guy. There *are* good men out there—for anyone willing to look." She thought of her fruitless search. "It just takes a while to weed through them."

"At least you're in there weeding." Cassia rubbed her arms. "I'm stuck at the garden gate, watching everyone else get their hands dirty."

"Someday you'll find a special guy—"

"I don't want a *special* guy. That's a term I hear too often already." Cassia summoned a cheerful smile. "I want a cool guy, like the ones in the movies. Even Duckie will do! Anyone, just to get some experience. It's horrid being a twenty-three-year-old untouched vir-gin who looks as breakable as glass. Guys are fright-ened away even before I can show them what a spar-kling conversationalist and bawdy wench I am." She snorted. "Ha!"

"Men aren't known for their deep insight." Claire

reconsidered, her thoughts shooting to Noah. "Most men. There are exceptions."

"Pooh. That's the problem. I'm never gonna find an *exceptional* man."

Claire nibbled a handful of popcorn from the bottom of the bowl. Cassia's room had been converted from a back parlor. It was spacious and airy, furnished with a double bed and two armchairs done up in coordinating pastel stripes and florals. There was a desk for Cassia's computer and accessories, brimming bookshelves and a full entertainment system. She even had a mini fridge and a microwave, which had supplied them with cans of diet soda and piping hot popcorn for their brat pack movie fest.

"Well," Claire said, wiping her greasy fingertips with a crinkled napkin, "do you have any prospects? You're a darling girl—there must be guys who've noticed."

"I was practically dateless in high school. Except for a couple of group outings and an awful thing set up by my *mother*." Cassia shuddered. "I went to my prom with a couple of girlfriends. We called ourselves the Leftovers."

"You could have starred in a John Hughes movie with a name like that." The whirring VCR came to a stop.

"Then at least I'd have gotten more than a few laughs out of it." Cassia seemed delighted with the thought. "I always had a secret notion that I could have been a good actress, if I'd had the chance."

Claire got up. She put the pillows on the bed and

ejected the videotape. "What about now that you're in college? There must be somebody interesting." Cassia had said she was taking classes part-time at Northern Michigan University, studying literature and secondary education.

"A few, but mostly it's me looking at them." Pink roses blossomed in Cassia's pale face. Her outspokenness usually deflected attention from the underlying reticence, but Claire had noticed the girl wasn't as flippant as she pretended.

Cassia lifted her brows, making a mischievous face beneath her cloud of wild red curls. "What can I say? I like to watch."

"What about if you start out as friends—"

"Nope. Can't do it. I don't want the boy next door. I want Mr. Tall, Dark and Dashing." Cassia laughed at herself. "I'm not asking too much, am I?" She put out her hand. "Would you help me stand so I can get into my chair? I have a hard time getting up and down."

Claire put away the videotape then helped Cassia up. "If you don't mind me asking…"

"Muscular dystrophy," she answered without hesitation. "I began showing signs of the disease as a kid, but I've been fortunate—the progress of my symptoms has been slow."

But they wouldn't stop progressing entirely, Claire understood, even more impressed by Cassia's fighting spirit.

"I shouldn't complain about my lack of men when I've been so lucky lately, getting to move into Bay

House and be on my own for the first time." Cassia stepped toward her chair, holding tight to Claire's arms. "If you stay long enough, you'll meet my mother, the bulldozer. She makes Emmie look like a powder puff. I've been her sole project for twenty-three years, and she's having a hard time letting go."

"You know, we're complete opposites. I'm from a big family, and my mother was so absorbed in running a business that she pretty much left us kids to our own devices." Claire held Cassia's forearms—her bones seemed as light as a bird's and, yes, as fragile as glass—while the girl turned and lowered herself into the chair. "*I* was the one who had a hard time letting go when I went to college."

"Not me." Cassia panted lightly, lifting her feet onto the foot pedals. "I couldn't wait to get away. But it took a few years of relentless nagging to convince my parents I could survive on my own." She looked around the room. "Sort of on my own…"

"Not very many people are completely independent. Except for—well…"

"Noah Saari?" Cassia's eyes lit up. "I was wondering when we'd get around to him!"

Claire laughed. "I haven't noticed you being timid about bringing up the subject."

"You think I'm meddlesome and nosy?"

"Yes!"

"Damn, my disguise as a pitiful cripple isn't working as well as it used to." Cassia waved away Claire's flash of surprise. "Don't get PC on me, please. We were just getting to the good stuff."

"Whatever you say. But I don't think of you as a—"

"Good, 'cause neither do I!'' Cassia shook her head fondly. "Is that settled? I'd prefer talking about guys. They're inarticulate and single-minded and so dense about women, but they sure are fascinating, aren't they?"

Claire pushed aside a pillow and sat at the end of the bed. "Where would we be without them?"

"Living in peace and harmony, but what good would do that do? All the faucets would be dripping, and there'd be no one to stomp on the bugs."

"I can fix a faucet. Men do have other uses."

Cassia flung out her arms. "Here I am, fellas. Use me!"

Claire laughed. "You've got to stop being so shy."

"I'm all talk—away from men. When a good one is around, I blush and stammer something awful. I can barely get a word out."

"All you need is experience. You'd learn to relax."

Cassia gave her a sly look. "Maybe someday. But let's get back to Noah. I want to know what *really* happened. The stuff you couldn't tell Emmie and Toivo."

"Especially Toivo."

"Aha! Then there is something to tell?"

Claire looked into her lap. "I stayed overnight at his cabin. He tended to my injury. It was impossible not to…get to know each other."

Cassia leaned in. "Did he kiss you?"

"Yes."

"Woo-hoo! Was it good?"

"It was amazing."

"Did his beard scratch?"

Claire nipped one side of her lip. "It tickled. I never kissed a man with a beard before." She closed her eyes for a moment. "He woke me up to see the northern lights. There was something magical about watching them together. We stood outside for a long time, looking up, and I got a little dizzy and he put his arms around me…"

"That is so, so romantic." Cassia sighed. "We all got out of bed to see them, too, but watching the lights with Emmie and Toivo and a bunch of guests who couldn't quit oohing and aahing isn't the same thing. Oh, I wish—" She broke off with a sigh. "You are so lucky!"

Claire blinked at Cassia's dazzled expression. "Don't tell anyone."

"Of course not. But what's going to happen now? Do you think you'll see him again?"

"I don't know. This morning we were kind of awkward with each other. Noah was sweet and all, getting me home, but he—well, I just don't know. He seemed kind of eager to put some distance between us."

"You weren't?"

"Well, yes. I was, too. It was as if the whole thing had been a fantasy. Reality does intrude at some point. I started remembering what I was in town to do and that I'd be leaving in a week or so. There's no point…."

"What about Valentina's marriage prophecy?" Cassia singsonged, "Sleep all night in the bridal room, Turn of year, thee shall have a groom."

"You don't honestly believe that."

Cassia shrugged. "I've seen it happen. Or at least heard of it. Three different Whitaker women swore it came true after they slept in the room when this was still only a family house. Emmie's sister was one of them."

"Her sister! You're kidding. Has there been any recent evidence?"

Cassia frowned. "Emmie rarely lets anyone into Valentina's room, so no weddings lately."

"Convenient. What about Emmie herself? She's never been married. Why doesn't she try it out?"

Cassia lowered her voice, thrilled to be telling secrets. "I think she's too scared to try."

Claire shrugged. Cassia was a little too thrilled to be telling secrets. "I'm not a big believer in superstition and curses. Or legends." She laughed. "I'll buy into Valentina's powers when I'm standing at the altar."

"Okay." Cassia smiled like a cat with cream on its whiskers.

Claire jounced on the bed. "Don't look at me like that."

"Do you think it was a coincidence that you met Noah Saari?"

"I met Terry Lindstrom, too."

"You did? You're not interested in *him*, are you?"

"Nope," Claire said quickly. "What's his deal?"

"He's a jerk. Everyone gives him allowance because

he's a Lindstrom and his brother died, but—he's still a jerk.''

''Oh. I'm sorry to hear that.'' Claire frowned. Maybe she'd mistaken his grief for a crummy personality, but she didn't think so.

''You should stick to Noah. He must like you, Claire, 'cause he doesn't associate with just anyone, you know. You're probably the only person who's been at his cabin since he moved there.''

''What about his parents?''

''Maybe them,'' Cassia conceded. ''But ever since his dad retired from the post office, the Saaris spend their winters in Arizona or New Mexico, somewhere like that. I don't think they're even back yet.''

Claire was reminded of Florence, Nebraska, where every secret was open, and reputations were practically set at birth. She'd been the quiet girl from the boisterous family on the wrong side of the tracks. Not particularly expected to rise above her ''gas station'' in life.

''There must be other people he's close to,'' she mused.

''Maybe, but he's really cut himself off. His closest friends were the three Lindstrom brothers, Terry, Rick and Pete, but after what happened—'' Cassia shook her head. ''Now they're enemies.''

Claire's mouth went dry. ''What happened?''

''Noah didn't say anything while you were with him?''

''Not a word.''

Cassia paused thoughtfully. ''Noah was a firefighter out west, in Montana, I think. What they call a smoke jumper—the ones who parachute into danger zones to fight remote fires. His dad liked to report on his heroics at the coffee shop. Well, a couple of years ago there was that big fire in a national park, so big it spread across two states. It was all over the news.''

''I remember.''

''Noah was there. So was Rick Lindstrom. He'd followed Noah out west just a few months before the big fire. And, well, he was one of a bunch of firefighters who got caught by the wildfire. Noah parachuted in to help turn it back, and he managed to get some of them out. But not Rick.''

Claire was suddenly queasy, the butter flavoring from the popcorn not sitting well in the pit of her stomach. ''You and Toivo said that Noah was considered a hero when he came back to town?''

''Yes. By everyone but the Lindstroms. Terry especially. He and Noah used to be buddies, but now he blames Noah for his brother's death.''

''That's not fair.''

''I know, but...'' Cassia shrugged. ''Rick was about six years older than me. I remember him as being this really good-looking guy who never had to work for what he got. Kinda spoiled, but he had charisma, not like the third Lindstrom boy, Pete. Yuck. My enemy.'' Cassia stuck out her tongue before continuing.

''Anyway, Rick had a fancy car and tons of girlfriends, but I guess he wanted more adventure or whatever, like Noah. He looked up to Noah, who was a few years older. After the tragedy, Terry kept saying that Noah should have been looking out for Rick and that his brother wouldn't have been killed if Noah hadn't let him on the ground crew in the first place.''

Claire kept quiet while she mulled the story over. It might not be the entire truth—small town gossip rarely was—but enough of it fit that she believed the main points. She remembered Noah's abrupt ''Nobody's hero'' and wondered if he blamed himself for his friend's death.

''Noah really didn't say a word about *any* of this?'' Cassia asked.

''No. Nothing. Even when…'' Now that she knew the story, Claire was more impressed by how calm and efficient he'd been when smoke had filled the cabin. ''No, nothing,'' she repeated softly.

Cassia blinked. ''And you didn't see…''

''Scars?'' Claire focused, shaking off her memories of Noah. So much had been left unsaid, unexplored, but maybe it was better that way. ''There were no disfiguring scars.'' *Unless his beard hid them.* ''At least *that* particular rumor can be laid to rest.''

''I knew Myron Mykkanen wasn't to be trusted.''

''Maybe Noah was still recovering from his burns when he came back, and the severity became exaggerated over time. Then the rumors continued unchecked because Noah had made himself so scarce.''

''Yeah,'' Cassia agreed. ''But still. Myron's the kind of guy who catches a prize trout every time he goes fishing.''

''We'll have to start a counterrumor.''

''Through Toivo,'' Cassia said. She eyed Claire speculatively. ''But why do you care?''

When Claire fumbled for words, Cassia interrupted. "It's not like you're going to *marry* the guy or anything, right?" Her laugh made merry fun of Claire's serious disavowals. "Right? Isn't that right, Claire? Huh, Claire? Claire, you're not answering me!"

ONE, he never should have kissed her.

Two, he shouldn't have brought her to the cabin. Now it was empty without her. Of course, he couldn't have left her on the bluff injured, but it would have been a lot easier if he'd somehow got her to her car right away. Then he could have retrieved her purse and brought it to Bay House himself.

Which would have meant appearing in town. Maybe running into Terry, who lived next door to the Whitakers.

Not the greatest idea, either.

You're going to have to do it sometime, Noah told himself, squinting at his reflection. He hardly recognized his face in the minuscule mirror. How long had it been since he'd bothered to look? He couldn't remember. Even when he'd trimmed his beard after the first encounter with Claire—it was a bad sign when a woman mistook you for a bear—he'd done it mostly by feel, not look, snipping off tufts until the beard was short enough to be a beard and not a hairy bib.

He'd filled the basin with hot water. The razor had been tucked away in his shaving kit, along with a can of shaving cream and an old bottle of cologne. He'd thrown that away, wondering why he'd ever wanted to smell like a rich man's polo pony. Probably a gift from

Lizabee. Once every few months, she used to get an idea—he'd called it a Lizabee in her bonnet—that they should have a real date and get dressed up to go out to a fancy restaurant. He'd say he liked her the way she was, drinking beer from the bottle, chowing on fast food, cracking crispy critter jokes in a sweatshirt and ratty jeans, but she'd be determined. Sometimes a woman wanted to feel like a woman, she said. Whatever that meant.

Apparently Rick had known.

Noah scowled at the stranger in the mirror. Three, he shouldn't have talked so much. Talking, even when it was only about inconsequential matters, made him human again. Being human meant he had to think and feel, which opened the floodgate to all the old emotions.

The guilt and grief came first. No wonder he'd dreamed. And again last night. The smoke, the voices, the sound and heat of the fire burning at his heels. He never saw the flames in the dreams. Maybe because the screams were terrifying enough. Especially when they were screams that sounded like his name.

Several drops of blood had plopped into the water and spread, dissipating like smoke. He'd closed his hand around the razor; the blade had sliced into thumb and forefinger. He set it aside and plunged his hand into the basin, watching the swirl of blood. Enough to discolor the water.

He wrapped his hand in the towel he'd set out, swearing ripely. Damn, he wasn't even civilized.

Couldn't shave, couldn't converse, couldn't even kiss a woman without it turning him inside out.

Back to one. He shouldn't have kissed her. Never, never, never.

A COUPLE OF DAYS later, Claire was in deeper than she ought to have been. She knew it wasn't wise to get involved, but the people at Bay House were so naturally friendly and good-natured, she found herself responding as she would to her friends back home. The place reminded her of home, in a way—crowded with people of diverse character and opinion, none of them shy about sharing insults and laughter, all talking at once, coming and going, needing help, asking questions, giving advice. Except in this instance it was Emmie who was the mother figure. Claire was the not-so-innocent bystander.

Bay House was a character in itself. Emmie was justly proud of her cooking skills, but it was obvious she had too much kitchen work to stay on top of everything that needed doing in the rest of the house. As a result, dust and disrepair prevailed. The maid seemed to always be on a mission in the attic or the basement; so far, Claire had only heard the woman, clumping and thumping and muttering gripes as she dropped newspapers by the guests' doors each morning. Whereas Roxy Whitaker was forever underfoot, working on leaky pipes in the kitchen, stopping a flood in an upstairs toilet, patching the crumbling ceiling or unsuccessfully resticking loose wallpaper.

Roxy wasn't as approachable as the rest of them. She

was a little abrupt and prickly, but she warmed up when Claire hung around talking home repairs. Ostensibly. Although Claire felt like an undercover spy, her intention was to get a handle on the state of the inner workings of the house. While Roxy seemed knowledgeable enough, she admitted that she was mainly self-taught. Emmie called in a professional for the major disasters, like the time the fuse box had been shooting sparks.

After asking a few discreet questions, Claire had learned that although the Whitakers were once one of the area's wealthiest families, their finances had taken a downturn during the Depression. Running Bay House as a B-and-B was the only way Emmie and Toivo could keep it going. There wasn't enough money for the complete overhaul the grand old house desperately needed.

Good news for Bel Vista, if Claire deemed the house a suitable prospect. She wasn't sure yet. Most of the B-and-Bs in the corporation's small luxury division were larger and in affluent locales. Alouette, which Claire had been exploring, was rich in scenic vistas and colorful history but certainly wasn't a hotbed of trendiness or wealth. No ritzy gift shops masquerading as quaint; no Starbucks; not many million-dollar yachts in the marina.

Personally, Claire liked the town better for its lack of pretension. The typical Bel Vista traveler was another breed, however, whose likes and dislikes she'd have to calculate into the profit-loss projections.

Yadda, yadda, yadda. There were more pressing matters. Like—

Roxy called her name. "Claire? Wanna grab the ladder?"

Claire pushed aside her cell phone, pen and paper and emerged from the greenery of the foyer, which was normally an unobtrusive place to make notes and keep an eye on guest and staff activity.

The Whitakers' niece was setting up a rickety wood ladder in the center of the space. The bib pocket of her overalls bulged with a new package of lightbulbs. She started climbing before Claire could react, making the ladder sway.

"Yipes." Claire grabbed on to steady it.

"There are eighteen bulbs in this freakin' thing," Roxy said of the chandelier, an elaborate monstrosity with loops of crystal beads and a hundred dangling doodads. "I wait until at least a third of them are burned out before I change them."

"So that's why the foyer's always dim." Claire looked up as Roxy climbed to the very top of the ladder and still had to stretch to reach the chandelier. Half the flame-shaped bulbs were out, unattractively blackened.

"That and the depressing wallpaper," Roxy said. "I don't know if the fairies started out a putrid yellow and gray, but they sure are now."

"You could strip the paper and paint the walls a nice, light color. Remove half the plants and furnishings and there'd be—" Claire stopped herself. She was not to get involved. "Sorry. None of my business."

"No, you're right." The chandelier tinkled as Roxy

reached over to unscrew another bulb. She glanced down. "Are you a decorator or something?"

"Or something."

"What then?"

"I'm, ah—" A chirping from the jungle saved her. "That's my cell phone." She let go of the ladder. It swayed dangerously, and she grabbed hold again. "Never mind. Let it ring."

"I'll get it." Cassia wheeled from her room, a backpack slung across her chair.

"That's okay," Claire said. It could be her boss, Drake the Snake, checking up on her again. "I'm sure it's not that important—"

Cassia had located the cell. She used her knuckle to press the talk button. "Hello? This is Claire Levander's cell phone."

Claire winced. *Please don't be Drake.*

Giggle. "No, I'm not actually a cell phone. My name's Cassia."

Another giggle. "Not kasha. Cassia Keegan." She spelled her name. "But you can nibble on me, if you really want!"

Claire goggled. Even Roxy stopped to listen.

"Not too sweet," Cassia responded. "I'd say… spicy."

She listened to the caller, so absorbed she'd forgotten the onlookers. "Hmm, how did you know?" Her voice was flippant, flirtatious. "It's red. And before you ask, yes, red *is* my real color." She squealed. "Of course I won't prove it!"

She finally looked at Claire, her eyes widening, then

smiled and said, "Nope, they're hazel. Green-eyed red-
heads are so standard issue, don't you think?"

Not Drake, Claire decided. He turned on the charm
only for important people or those he needed favors
from. She knew only two men who'd flirt with an anon-
ymous voice over the phone, and they were both her
brothers.

"You have no idea," Cassia said. "I'm full of surprises."

"Is it Max or is it Jesse?" Claire asked.

Cassia lowered her voice. She was practically purring, never mind her declaration that men made her
stammer. "Are you Max…or are you Jesse?"

As she listened, a blush mottled her cheeks. She
mouthed, "Jesse," to Claire, then ducked her head and
murmured an answer so softly the eavesdroppers
missed out.

Claire frowned. Jesse. The man had far too much
testosterone. He could be lethal to an innocent like Cassia. "Tell him I'll call back."

Cassia ended the call after a few more bantering re-
sponses. She wheeled closer and handed the phone to
Claire. Her face was suffused with pleasure. "That was
one of your brothers?" She flapped a hand at her
flushed cheeks. "Be still my beating heart."

"You don't want to mess with Jesse, Cassia. He's a
Navy sailor—here today and gone tomorrow without a
word of explanation. Too much to handle, for even
an—"

"Able-bodied woman?" For an instant, Cassia's

eyes flashed with hurt. Then she blinked and was smiling again as if it didn't matter.

Claire's throat tightened. "No. I was going to say he's too much for even an experienced woman. Jesse has a way with the ladies, as they say."

"Sorry," Cassia mumbled. "Low self-esteem. I jump to conclusions." She brightened purposefully, determined not to put a damper on the discussion. "His voice was totally sexy. Is he handsome?"

"Yeah. In a big, mean and dangerous sort of way. He's got the animal magnetism thing going on."

Cassia and Roxy exchanged glances. Together, they said, "Woof!" and then burst into laughter. Claire clutched the rocking ladder.

"My other single brother, Max, is more your type, I'd think," she said when they'd subsided. "Closer to your age, too. He's still in college, getting his master's in education. Smart and handsome and really nice. You'd have a lot in common."

"I'm not picky." Cassia grinned. "Got any pictures?"

Claire was promising to drag out her wallet at the next opportunity when the doorbell rang. Emmie's voice called from the kitchen. "That must be the new guest. He's early. And here I've got my hands in a ball of bread dough! Would one of you girls please get the door?"

"I'll do it," Claire said. But the ladder wobbled when she let go.

"I'll climb down," Roxy said, used lightbulbs dropping from her pockets. One shattered on the ladder; the other hit the carpet and rolled behind a potted palm.

''For goodness' sake,'' Cassia said, sounding like Emmie as she sailed by, ducking low beneath the palm fronds. ''Allow me.''

The doorbell pealed again. Cassia grasped the knob, but pulling open the heavy front door was a difficult task for her weakened hands.

Roxy yelled, ''Come in!''

Cassia had managed to open the door. She rolled her chair backward, swinging the door wide as she went.

Claire gaped at the figure on the doorstep. The face was different, but the rest of him…wow! She could hardly believe what she was seeing.

''Noah.''

She must have let go of the ladder and walked toward the door, because she heard Cassia's faint echo somewhere behind her. ''Noah!''

And then even Roxy's. ''Noah?''

''Noah,'' Claire said, concluding the refrain. ''Is that… You shaved. No…beard?''

It took her a moment to grasp the obvious. Noah had shaved his beard. He'd put on nice clothes, too—belted trousers and a regular button-down shirt, with a tie. But it was his face that held her attention. It was a good face, even handsome. Without the beard, he looked years younger. His eyes were alight, and his tentative smile was…well, it made her breath catch. His hair was cut, too, looking a shade darker with the sun-bleached ends trimmed off.

Noah the hermit had shaved his beard.
And he'd come to town.
Claire looked at the bouquet of flowers in his hand.
Good glory gracious! Had he done it all for *her?*

CHAPTER EIGHT

NOAH FELT like a doofus. A big, naked freak of a doofus.

He'd known people would stare, and that hadn't been any big deal. Staring was nothing compared to accusations that could slice your heart out. But this...

Three women gaping at him, their merriment abruptly cut short.

This was the reason he never followed impulses.

Claire was shocked to see him on her doorstep and didn't bother to hide it. The petite redhead in the wheelchair was all eyes—scaredy-cat eyes. The pony-tailed girl was descending the ladder, one hand clutched to the front of her overalls. The ladder swayed. Something dropped out of the woman's pocket, and she lurched to catch it.

Noah thrust the flowers at Claire as he flew by. His arms went out as the woman said ''Damn!'' and lost her balance completely. Instead of falling into his arms, she managed to twist like a cat in midair and land on her feet.

He found himself with an armful of ladder. Abruptly, it folded up on itself, and he staggered beneath the ungainly weight for a few seconds before finally setting it in place with a sharp *clap*.

"Hey, there, big boy, don't bust my ladder," the tomboy said. "Can't you see it's an antique?"

"Roxy!" That was Claire. "Noah was trying to save you from a broken neck."

Roxy brushed at her dingy overalls. "I'm not that breakable."

Noah backed off, crunching glass underfoot.

"Watch out. You're grinding the lightbulbs into the carpet."

Claire took his arm. "Let's go into the parlor." She shot a glare at Roxy. "See if *you* get an introduction!"

The tomboy laughed, unbothered.

"That's Roxy Whitaker," Claire told Noah under her breath. "Don't mind her. She's got etiquette problems."

The young lady in the wheelchair hadn't moved from near the open doorway. She was still staring at Noah, her mouth hanging open in amazement. Or maybe hostility—for all he knew, the Lindstroms had pressed their connections and everyone up and down Bayside Road considered him the enemy. This wasn't the best location for his reintroduction into polite society.

Claire, at least, had recovered and was trying to act as if his visit was perfectly normal. "Cassia, this is Noah Saari. Noah, Cassia Keegan. A Bay House boarder." She squeezed his arm encouragingly.

Cassia's gaze crawled up his body and across his face. He knew she was looking for the scars, but he withstood the scrutiny with scarcely a blink. Outward scars didn't concern him all that much. It was what

some people suspected him of—including himself—
that had kept him away.

"Cassia?" Claire said, an audible nudge.

She gave her head a little shake. "Oh. I'm, uh—"
She leaned toward Noah, holding her hand out. "Nice
to meet you, Noah. You startled me! But I'm so glad
you're here. I really am." Her smile was wide and
friendly and unabashedly curious. "Claire told me
about you, and of course I already knew—"

Noah clasped her delicate hand.

"—about your heroics," she said, surprising him.
Even touching him.

A van drove to Bay House, honking its horn. Cassia
glanced out the open door. "Crap. That's my mother.
What lousy timing." She pressed a toggle button on
the arm of her chair and swung neatly around. Outside,
a woman with flaming red hair was stepping out of the
van. She slid open a side door, then turned to wave at
Cassia as a wheelchair lift lowered from inside the van.

"I have to go to class." Cassia dragged on a jacket
that had been across her lap.

"Can we help you?" Noah offered.

"Nope, we've got the loading and unloading down
to a science. Someday I plan to hire on at Fed Ex as a
package-handling expert."

"I'll get going, too," Roxy said, coming forward.
She put her hands on the back of Cassia's chair.

Cassia arched her brows at Claire. "Sorry I have to
leave so quickly, but I guess I won't be missed too
awful much." She aimed a salute at Noah. "Nice to
meetcha." She grinned. "Yeah, I always appreciate

meeting someone who's even more of a hermit than me!''

The two younger women departed. Claire waved them off, then shut the door, turning to Noah with a sheepish smile. ''That's Cassia. She can be rather outspoken. Which seems to be a trend in Bay House. I wonder if it's something in the water.''

''You don't have to be nervous, Claire.''

''I'm not nervous. I'm flustered.''

''All right.''

She took a deep breath as her nose dropped into the bouquet. ''Thank you for the flowers.''

''They're just wildflowers. I picked them on the walk over. My mom always said not to arrive empty-handed.'' He knew he was gawking, but he couldn't take his eyes off Claire. She was dressed smartly, every hair in place. But he remembered how she'd been, soft and sleepy in his arms, her hair in disarray, her defenses down.

''Did you come to pick up your swampers?'' she asked, blinking rapidly.

''No. I came by to see how your ankle's doing. Fully recovered?''

She walked in a fast circle, then did a dance step, waving the scraggly wildflowers in the air. ''Almost good as new. I still can't rock climb, but then I couldn't before, either.''

She looked past his shoulder. ''Here's Emmie.''

Noah turned. He remembered Emmie Whitaker well. He, Terry, Rick and tag-along Petie used to hang around Bay House, offering to do the raking or shoveling, knowing they'd get paid in homebaked cookies, cake or Finnish *riieska*. Emmie was a no-nonsense woman, strict but always fair and generous. He could count on her not leaping to conclusions about his part in Rick Lindstrom's death.

"Noah Saari, as I live and breathe!" Emmie gave him a big hug. "It's been years—so many I don't want to count." She stepped back, flipping her long gray braid over one shoulder, looking him up and down with her usual directness. "Well, you haven't changed a whole lot. Gained some muscle, filled out even more." She searched his face. "Got yourself a few lines around the eyes and mouth. Oh, me. We're all getting up there." She put her hands to her hair, smoothing it in an utterly female gesture. "I must look like an old woman to you now."

"You're as chipper as I remember. And just as cheeky."

"I still haven't found a diet that works." She crinkled her eyes, waiting for the expected compliment.

"You know you look good. Besides, your lumberjack cookies are worth a few extra pounds."

Pleased, Emmie turned to Claire. "What are we doing, standing around the door? Take your young man into the parlor like a proper guest, Claire. But give me those flowers first. I'll be in with a tray in two shakes. I may even have some of Noah's favorite cookies tucked away in the larder. And maybe a few of the chocolate chip, too. I remember that sweet tooth of yours!"

"Lumberjack cookies?" Claire said curiously after Emmie had bustled away.

"Cookies big enough to satisfy a man's appetite, built not to crumble in his hand. Good for dunking, too." He gave Claire a look. "I like my women the same way."

She smiled bashfully. "And the dunking?"

"We'll see if you're up to the challenge when you come for a sauna."

They had entered the front parlor, which was unchanged from the last time Noah had visited. Had to be five years ago, maybe more. Certainly before he'd gone west for good and taken up smoke jumping.

The heavy drapes were open, but yellowed lace sheers filtered the sunlight. Fine oak floors were covered with English Wilton carpets, brought over by boat when the first Whitaker built Bay House, along with an entire household of antiques—wardrobes, Hepplewhite tables, stiff, tufted sofas. Not so much as a stick of it had been moved in all that time, although as Noah remembered it, Mae Koski, the Finnish housekeeper who'd married Ogden Whitaker III, had added a few of the homier touches—rag rugs in the bedrooms, cookies in the larder. Emmie wasn't a decorator. She was a caretaker—polishing and tending, watching over the house, determined not to change it. Noah wondered briefly how Roxy Whitaker felt about being the heiress of so much family history. She didn't seem the type.

"How long are you planning to stay?" he asked Claire as they sat together on a settee.

She lifted her shoulders. "My plans are open-ended.

Probably a few more days.'' Her nose wrinkled. ''Didn't I tell you that?''

''I don't recall.''

''I think I did.'' Or maybe it had been Terry Lindstrom she'd told. Noah probably wouldn't want to know about that encounter.

''I've been hoping you'd decide to stay longer.''

''I do have a job to—get back to.''

Why the hesitation? ''Right, the job with Bel Vista. You never did tell me exactly what you do there.''

She didn't dodge the question, but answered with an import that made his ears perk up. ''I am an executive in the small luxury inn division.''

Click. The piece he'd been lacking fell into place. At the cabin, she'd been a little evasive about why she'd come to Alouette. Now he was sure she was here on business. So the questions she'd asked about the area, its history, environment and people were not for her personal edification. She was evaluating, not enjoying.

He frowned. ''Your company is interested in Bay House?''

''That's to be determined.''

''By who? You?''

Emmie's footsteps were heading their way. Claire tilted her head, tucking a short hank of hair behind one ear. A small pearl earring winked at him. ''Could we talk about this another time?'' she murmured, flickering her lashes at the innkeeper as she came though the doorway.

Noah jumped up to help Emmie with the tray. It was

loaded with more than a snack—there was everything from hefty sandwiches to slabs of pound cake, along with a dozen assorted cookies. "You're joining us, aren't you, Em?" he asked, counting only two coffee cups.

"Not this time." Emmie's blue eyes twinkled, telling him she hadn't lost a speck of vitality. "But you come by the kitchen before you leave. And don't be a stranger. It's no good for a young man like yourself to be living all alone the way you have." She shushed his reply and swept from the room, sliding the pocket doors shut behind her.

The doors were heavy oak, but even so, Toivo's voice sounded clearly from the foyer, asking who was in the parlor. "Noah Saari's come to court Claire," Emmie said in an urgent whisper. "You get away from that door, Toivo. I don't want you butting in with your nonsense. Leave the young people alone."

There was no way to pretend they hadn't both heard. Claire let out a soft moan as she pinched the bridge of her nose. She glanced apologetically at Noah. "I'm afraid Emmie has some old-fashioned ideas."

"There's something to be said for old-fashioned ideas."

Claire fidgeted, pinning her gaze on the refreshment tray. "In certain circumstances, I would agree." She was being as oblique as he. "Shall I pour the coffee?"

When he didn't answer, she set down the pot. "Don't worry. I'll set her straight."

He cleared his throat. "What if Emmie has it right?"

Claire's head came up, eyes widening.

"I'm wearing a tie, for Pete's sake."

She gave a choking laugh. "I wondered about that."

"Sunday best," he said. "And it's not even Sunday."

"Are you suggesting…" She kept blinking. "Do you really mean to…"

"Let's say I'm expressing a gentlemanly interest by making this visit. If you would like me to return, a small sign of encouragement would do the trick."

Claire didn't move. The only sound in the room was the measured ticking of the Sheffield clock on the mantel. "I don't know what to say," she finally whispered. "This isn't anything I'd expected to happen and—" She stopped. When she looked at him, her mouth was set so tightly her chin had dimpled. "You're putting me on, aren't you?"

Insult made her eyes snap with blue electricity. Noah was baffled by the sudden switch.

"It's a joke," she said. "They put you up to this because of that stupid wedding prophecy, didn't they? Roxy, Cassia, Toivo— It had to be one of them!"

"The wedding prophecy?"

"Noah, how could you?"

"You wouldn't mean that foolish story about Valentina, would you?"

"Of course. Toivo gave me Valentina's room, and now they all seem to think I'll be overrun with suitors." Claire snorted indelicately. "Not very likely!"

"I don't know anything about what they're thinking," Noah said.

''Sure you don't. It's obvious that you and Emmie are old buddies.''

On impulse—*another* one—Noah touched the back of Claire's neck. She clamped her lips shut again, eyes wounded, the color of a bruise. His fingers closed around her nape. He was startled by the tension that wound through her. She was tremendously affected considering she'd taken his interest for a joke.

''Look, I know about Valentina Whitaker.'' He kept his voice quiet and calm. ''But that doesn't have anything to do with my coming here today. *Everyone* who grew up in this town knows about the Whitaker wedding legend.''

Claire's eyes met his. ''Cassia's been teasing me ever since Toivo put me in the bridal suite. So when you showed up with flowers...'' She swallowed, growing doubtful. ''But you're not here to tease me, are you? You're serious.'' About *courting* her.

''Serious enough to put on a tie.''

''And shave your beard.'' The tension had dissipated, and her voice was as silky as raindrops. Wonderingly, she touched the back of her hand to his cheek. Her knuckles brushed over the new, baby-soft skin.

His fingers moved upward, threading through her hair. She made a small sound, lifting her lips toward his. He hadn't thought this all the way through. Nor had he planned on kissing her in the parlor with Toivo Whitaker's eye pressed to the keyhole, but when opportunity presented itself...

He kissed her. No fireworks, no dancing light filling

the sky, but she was warm and curvaceously female and, oh, sweet Mary, it felt good to touch her.

Her fingertips brushed his smooth-shaven cheeks, over and over again, even after they'd drawn apart. "No prickles or tickles this time," she said, laughing softly as she nudged his face with her nose. She skimmed her mouth over his, breathing an invitation. Her lower lip was as full and ripe as a berry. He sucked lightly at it, running his tongue along the underside until she moaned and her lips parted wide and the kiss became a serious, heated thing.

Noah didn't know how long it was before he made himself stop. Long enough for both of them to lose their breath. Claire panted, looking at him with a cautious joy in her eyes.

Enough to make him wonder what he'd started. Enough that he couldn't wait to find out.

But he shouldn't have kissed her. Not unless he was prepared to do it again and again and again.

Claire Levander wasn't a one-kiss-and-out kind of woman.

THE NEXT MORNING, Claire opened an eye, saw Valentina's stern disapproval and flipped over, mashing her face into the pillow. Aside from the portrait, she could get used to this. Even though she was accustomed to travel, she rarely got to stay in one place long enough to feel really comfortable. Bay House was different. She was coming to think of the bridal suite as *her* room.

Thwap. The thin local newspaper hit the door. Claire

held her breath, waiting for the thudding footsteps and the mumbled complaints that always followed. This morning, there was nothing.

She sat up.

The doorknob was turning. Very slowly. So slowly that when Claire stared at it she wasn't sure it was turning at all. Until the small *snick* sounded as the lock held. Emmie had decided she trusted Claire enough to turn over the old-fashioned latchkey. Last night, she'd left it in the keyhole, tassel dangling. It was a habit she'd developed after the morning she'd wakened with the eerie feeling Shari Shirley's eye was pressed to the keyhole. She'd heard muffled breathing, and it wasn't coming from Valentina.

What was the housemaid up to this time?

Claire got out of bed and put on her robe, avoiding the creaky spot in the floor. She crept closer, planning to fling open the door.

She put her ear against it. There it was—the heavy breathing she'd come to associate with the unseen Shari.

Gonna catch her this time. Claire closed her fingers around the latchkey. The lock always stuck a bit; she'd have to turn the key fast and fling the door open at just the right moment.

Twist, turn, fling—and…nothing!

Except…

Claire jumped into the hall in time to glimpse someone disappearing around the corner where a door opened onto the back stairs that ran from the kitchen to the attic. *Clumpety, thumpety, bump.* Shari Shirley had escaped to the attic.

The door at the top of the steps banged shut. "Good morning to you, too," Claire said, staring at the water-stained ceiling as her visitor made a racket overhead. Par for the course. She picked up the newspaper and returned to her room, glancing over the headlines as she swung the door shut behind her.

There was a loud bump from above.

Claire felt the whoosh of displaced air as a huge chunk of plaster fell from the ceiling onto the bed. She leaped back from the foot of the four-poster, then ran and pressed herself against the door, afraid the entire ceiling would come down around her ears. Plaster dust hung in the air.

After a few moments, Claire risked opening the door. "Emmie! Toivo!"

The Whitakers were hurrying upstairs. "What in the world?" Emmie said when she saw the wreckage.

Toivo walked into the bedroom and hunched over the pile of broken plaster. He peered upward. "Holy wah!"

"Me, oh, my." Emmie examined Claire. "Were you hurt, Claire, honey?"

"No. I'd just gotten out of bed."

"Lucky for you," Toivo said.

Emmie marched to the French doors, her shoes gritting in the plaster dust. She threw them open—for the air, Claire thought, until the innkeeper stepped onto the balcony. She leaned over the railing, her raspberry polyester pants pulling tight across her derriere. "Yoo-hoo! Roxy, Noah—never mind those bricks. We've got us a real emergency up here."

Noah? Claire thought.

He'd finished yesterday's unexpected visit by spending a half hour in the kitchen with Emmie and Toivo, catching up. Nothing had been resolved between him and Claire, unless she counted the sure fact that he was a good kisser and, by extension, so was she. She couldn't quite believe the mention of courting had been serious, but he had made it clear she'd see him again soon.

She hadn't expected it to be quite this soon.

Bricks?

"What's Noah doing here?" she asked Emmie, but before the older woman answered, he and Roxy rushed into the bedroom. They could have been brother and sister—both of them tall and strong, with dark blond hair and a workmanlike way of dressing. Claire pulled the lapels of her pale blue terry cloth robe together.

"Whew." Roxy picked a chunk of plaster off the bed. "What happened?"

Claire looked at Noah, who was hovering beside her with a concerned expression, then at the rest of them, awaiting an explanation for the obvious. "I'd just wakened. I heard Shari at the door dropping off the paper. I went to, um, get it…and that's when the plaster fell."

The ceiling creaked. Everyone looked up. Where the large patch of plaster had broken away, thin strips of lath showed, some of them jagged and broken. They could see the ancient darkened floor joists and several spots and filaments of light from above. Claire walked closer, squinting at a disembodied eyeball staring through a gap in the ceiling. "Shari Shirley," she said under her breath when the eye disappeared. The light shifted from above as the joists creaked and a door banged as the maid moved into another room.

Claire turned to the others. "Someone needs to go upstairs and take a look."

"I'll go," Roxy said.

Toivo hurried after her. "Me, too." Overhead, footsteps creaked, and a door shut.

"Water damage," Emmie said, ignoring the maid's maneuverings. "Our pipes leak like sieves. Oh, look at Valentina's wedding ring quilt. It's covered in plaster dust."

Luckily the quilt and the crocheted spread had been neatly folded at the foot of the bed and were not damaged. Emmie gathered them to shake out off the balcony.

Over the wreckage that covered the bed, Noah looked at Claire.

Claire looked at Noah. "What brings you here so early?"

"Maintenance issues. Frost heave has turned the brick path into a danger zone. Someone's going to trip and crack his skull open. The Whitakers can't afford a lawsuit."

"Isn't that Roxy's job?"

"She can't do everything on her own."

"So you're going to help out?"

"Emmie promised me a fresh batch of lumberjack cookies."

Claire's eyes narrowed suspiciously. "This has nothing to do with—"

"Me courting you?"

She blinked. "I was going to say—" She glanced at Emmie, flapping the quilt in the wind, and dropped her voice. "Are you trying to interfere with my evaluation of the inn?"

Noah's eyes glinted. "Want to explain that?"

She wasn't used to his face yet. Even though she'd touched and kissed every inch of it and was getting hot just remembering. She licked her lips and said, "Later," as Toivo called from above.

A pudgy pink finger wormed its way through a crack in the attic floor and waggled at them. "We got us some loose flowerboards up here."

"Water seepage, yup," Roxy said faintly. "Wood's warped."

Claire wasn't convinced. "They should be looking for signs of intentional damage. I've heard someone up there, and I'm pretty certain it's the housemaid. She's probably been drilling holes in the floor so she can keep an eye on Valentina's room. No joke."

"Why would she need to do that?"

Claire shrugged. "You'd have to ask Emmie. But I'd guess it has something to do with—" She pointed.

Noah turned to look at the portrait of Valentina Whitaker. "The jilted bride herself." He stroked his chin contemplatively. "I haven't seen that picture since I was eight years old and snuck up here on a dare." He glanced over his shoulder at Claire. "Not the ideal bedtime companion, is she?"

Emmie came inside with her arms full of bedding. "Valentina didn't make the roof come down."

Claire agreed. "But Shari Shirley might have. You said she was determined to get into this room, isn't that right?"

Emmie was dismissive. "Pshaw. Shari's shenanigans are harmless."

Claire threw a significant look at the slab of crumbled plaster on the pillow where her head had lain only minutes ago.

"Besides, getting in and staying overnight are two different things," Emmie said. A furtive sound from the hallway made her raise her voice. "Shari can try, but she's never sleeping in the bridal suite as long as I'm in charge of Bay House."

"Skrumpshettlebitch," came the muffled, muttered complaint.

A COUPLE OF HOURS later, the household had settled down. There was presently only one guest besides Claire, a medical supply salesman from Minneapolis who was planning to be gone all day. Emmie was in the kitchen baking. After clearing the plaster and moving the bed away from the damaged ceiling, Roxy and Noah had returned to their brickwork. Toivo, as usual, had disappeared before he could be roped into sharing the cleanup; Claire had learned that he spent most of his time with his cronies in the coffee shop. Bill Maki was working day shift at his job in a local iron mine— good thing, according to Cassia, because he'd have been scared out of his boots to know Shari was lurking near his attic bedroom.

Thank heaven for Cassia. She was the only one who gave credence to Claire's theory that Shari had been up to no good in her quest to invade the bridal suite. Before leaving for a lit class, Cassia had confided that Shari was Emmie's cousin's daughter's best friend and therefore granted a family dispensation for her poor job performance.

Claire had decided to dismiss the incident. Shari Shirley wasn't her problem, although she sure was curious to get a look at the mystery woman. The falling-down plaster and the leaky pipes were what she should be concerned about, for her report.

After her talk with Cassia and a leisurely stroll through the house, taking notes on suspicious cracks and water stains, she wandered to the kitchen. Emmie handed her a plastic bottle of water. ''For Noah.''

Not so subtle. Especially when she nudged Claire out the back door and called for Roxy to come into the house and check the pilot light on the gas stove. Claire added *gas* to her mental checklist.

''Robert's arriving this afternoon, and I have a lot of cooking to do,'' Emmie said as the screen door swung shut.

''Fandamntastic,'' Roxy griped.

Avoiding the deconstructed path and the piles of broken, mossy bricks, Claire walked to Noah and gave him the water bottle. He unscrewed the cap and took a long drink, his Adam's apple sliding up and down his throat as he swallowed. In a collarless sweatshirt, the flat, shiny scars on the side of his throat were more obvious, but no one had commented.

"Do you know who Robert is?" Claire asked, distracting herself from the sight of Noah's strong brown arms. The sleeves of his sweatshirt were frayed where they had been hacked off above his biceps.

"Nope." He wiped his mouth with the back of his hand. Offered her the bottle.

She took a dainty drink, experiencing a funny little sensation at the intimacy of sharing the bottle. Silly. They shared the same air, too.

She gave the water bottle to him. "Hope you don't have cooties."

He grinned. "If I did, you'd have already caught them."

She rolled her eyes, and he surprised her by swinging in and planting a friendly kiss on her. The sensation became a frisson. "What was that for?"

"Wouldn't want you to think I came back only for Emmie's cookies."

She was shy about looking at him right then, so she let her gaze roam over the garden. It had been neglected, but there were many signs of what it would look like now that it was bursting with the optimism of springtime—bushy lilacs not quite in bloom, sweet white narcissus, the distinctive leaves of a grouping of long-established delphiniums, grape hyacinths poking up among last year's weeds. To one side was the carriage house garage she'd noticed on her arrival—a quaint building in matching sandstone, run over with the vines of vintage roses.

She cleared her throat. "I didn't expect to see you so soon, Noah."

"Yeah, well…" He set the water bottle on a stack of bricks and picked up a tool that looked something like a garden hoe. Muscles flexing, he pried a row of uneven bricks out of the earth. Beetles scurried through the moist soil, seeking refuge in the shaggy grass. "We don't have enough time to play around."

"Enough time for *what?*" she blurted.

He smiled, more to himself than at her. "Courting."

She flapped her hands in frustration. "Look, just because Emmie went and said that—"

"It's not Emmie."

"Valentina's bridal prophecy, then." Claire caught sight of her hands flying around like frantic bats and pulled them in, stabbing her fists into the pockets of her black pants. Her emotions were out of control. She toppled a brick with the toe of her boot. "Sheesh. I'm beginning to understand why they sometimes call it a curse."

"It's not the curse, either." Noah was frustratingly calm. He went on overturning and stacking bricks, more than content to wait for her to ask.

She wouldn't. Because he couldn't possibly be serious.

Suitors bent on courting didn't search out women like her. Some women were born to be romantic heroines and some just plain weren't. Which wasn't to say that the latter kind didn't meet men they would marry and live perfectly happy lives. There just wasn't a grand drama to it. They weren't swept away on the tumultuous tides of their heart's desires.

Hermits, jilted brides, curses, tragic fires...

You couldn't get much more dramatic than that.

"What is it then?" she heard herself saying. *Dammit.*

Noah plunged the implement into the overturned earth. "Simple. I'm a forthright man, Claire. I know what's wrong and for sure I know what's right. I know what I want when I see it." He peeled off the dirty gloves and stuck them in the back pocket of his jeans. He stepped over and stood square in front of her, fixing her with his deepest stare. "I've been alone so long, it took me a few days to recognize this for what it is, and I guess to accept it, but life is too short to let a good thing go.

"I want you, Claire. That's as plain as I can put it."

She couldn't speak. Her brain was imploding, her heart was in a vise, and a river of fire ran through the center of her. This was gosh-darn cataclysmic!

And she forgot every bit of it when Noah put his arms around her and kissed her. This was no friendly kiss, no hermit-comes-a-courtin' kiss. It was passion and heat and animal magnetism. It was basic, like Noah. Simple, straightforward lust.

And she wanted it. Wanted him. Oh, yes, she certainly did.

But she pushed him away. Then stood stock-still and gaped at him in dumbstruck disbelief. "It can't be that simple." Her lips felt red and raw—*burned.*

He breathed hard though his nose. "Why not?"

"Because we're not—" She searched for the right word. "We're not primitives. We have pasts and doubts and complications. It can't be that easy!"

"Don't make this complicated, Claire. What happened between us the other night is a rare thing."

"Yes…" She was bursting inside, wanting to throw aside every concern and think only of the magic of falling in love beneath the northern lights.

Noah stood still, waiting for her to decide, even though she could sense the volcanic urges that filled him. His cheeks were ruddy with heat. And his hands— those big hands that could be so gentle and loving— were knotted with tension.

She couldn't do it.

"Listen, Noah. I'm not an impulsive woman. I make plans, I think things through. I evaluate the prospects and decide with a clear head which option has the highest chance of success." *Here comes the hard part.*

"You and me…" She shook her head. "How can that work?"

But Noah wasn't defeated so easily.

"Because we'll talk it out," he said. "I'll tell you everything you want to know." He grabbed her hand and towed her through the scrabbled garden toward the spruce trees at the back of the yard. Toward the cliff. "Come on."

"Where are you taking me?"

"Bride's Leap," he said.

CHAPTER NINE

THE VIEW from the bluff was incredible.

Far out in the bay, the cream brick lighthouse stood lonely and remote on its stony peninsula. White specks fluttered around it—gulls, flapping back and forth between the water and the rocks. It wasn't a particularly windy day, but Lake Superior was so vast that what wind there was picked up over the endless expanse of water, creating low rolling waves that broke over the craggy rocks in spumes of foam. Where there was flat rock or pebbles, the waves smoothed out with a soft swoosh. The sound was even more hypnotic up close— so relaxing that Claire wanted to sink onto a rock near the edge of the cliff and close her eyes.

She did, finding a niche in the fissured stone. The sun was warm, and she lifted her face to it, sniffing the fresh breeze, the redolent evergreens. There was still a tension in her, but it was giving way fast.

Noah moved easily among the rocks. She watched him, filled with longing. The idea of him wanting her, so openly, was a new and amazing thought. All her previous relationships had been orderly and civilized— an introduction, a meeting over drinks, tentative approval leading to a dinner date and so on and so forth. She'd never been overcome with passion.

Maybe it was time. Even if it didn't last. How could it? She'd worked hard to leave behind small-town life. Even lately, when she'd been having second thoughts about her choice, the idea of changing her entire life was too much to accept. Small changes—slowing down, taking better care of herself, reconnecting with her family and abandoned social life—were enough.

Noah pointed to a jutting finger of rock, where the golden-red sandstone had been worn into a deep, smooth curve by water erosion. ''They say that's where she jumped.''

Claire flicked her bangs out of her eyes. ''I'm not sure I believe it.''

''No?'' He came back to her, going down on his heels nearby.

''Does it make sense to you? The Valentina Whitaker in that portrait doesn't look like the type who'd fling herself off a cliff in the name of love. She would want to stay around to exact revenge.''

''Humiliation is a powerful stigma to live with, and it would have been particularly hard in those days. A jilted bride would need a lot of fortitude to stand up to the shame.''

''I'll bet Valentina's will was iron.''

''Then what? Was she pushed?''

''I hadn't thought about it.''

''Her intended groom was supposedly on a train, eloping with his true love. Who else would have a motive?''

''I have no idea. Maybe Valentina was crazed. She

ran out here to curse at the world—I can see her doing *that*—then slipped and fell.''

''I suppose it's possible. The history's murky by now. Emmie has never liked talking about it, and Toivo...'' Noah shrugged.

A chill tapped along Claire's spine. ''It's a gruesome ending, whatever happened.''

Noah gazed over the water, dangling his hands between his widespread, muscular thighs. Men paid trainers for his kind of thighs.

Noah had more important things on his mind, but he kept his tone light. ''Happy endings don't always show up when you expect them.''

Claire wasn't fooled by his ease. He was a banked fire, she thought, hot as ever at the core.

Was she kindling? Or was she the blanket that would smother his tragic past into a nice, comfortable middle age?

Foolishness. That's what her mother would say. Clarice Levander was a tough broad who didn't have time for fanciful imaginings. The only soft spot she'd ever showed was when she'd refused to stick her baby daughter with the name Clarice and had insisted on switching a few letters around. Claire had loved that story as a child, even though it was always her father who'd told it, teasing his wife out of her exhaustion with a smile and a bit of whimsy.

''I've always thought that 'happy endings' is a misnomer. If you're happy, you don't end. You go on.''

''That would be the way to do it,'' Noah grittily agreed.

"I'm sorry."

His head came around. "For what?"

"Making you...remember. Being too practical not to believe in us, at least the possibility of us, without knowing more."

"You want to know what you're getting into. I can respect that."

She reached out to him, laying her hand on his shoulder.

He took it, moving to sit beside her. "I know you've heard the talk. Considering some of it came from Toivo, you're probably wondering what's true."

"Cassia was right in there, too. She thinks you're a romantic, tortured hero."

"And what do you think, Claire?"

She regarded him steadily. "There's got to be a compelling reason you've cut yourself off from civilization."

He grimaced, lines carving into his cheeks. His skin was still smooth; he must have shaved again that morning. "Not really. I've always been this way. I blame my dad. He was a postman for most of his life, but he loved the outdoors. My bedtime stories were all adventure tales. Chapter by chapter, he read through the classics by Hemingway and Robert Louis Stevenson. Nonfiction, too—Muir, Lewis and Clark, all the great American adventurers. When I was old enough, he took me hunting and fishing every chance. I was spoiled for school—couldn't take being inside, sitting at a desk. I was restless. Imagined myself having great adventures of my own."

"So that's why you had all those rugged jobs and moved around so much."

"Yeah. I tried pretty near everything."

"And then you were a firefighter."

"A smoke jumper, to be specific."

Claire inhaled, knowing they were heading into dangerous territory. "A risk taker."

"Sure, there's that. A lot of the guys were adrenaline junkies, no doubt about it." Noah rubbed his jaw, looking momentarily surprised to find it beardless. There was an indent in his chin, like a thumbprint.

"You weren't?"

"I liked the thrill well enough, but mostly it was the chance to save the forest from being ravaged. And the hard, physical work, the teamwork. I'm a tactile kind of guy. Couldn't survive as a desk jockey, stuffed into a suit and tie."

She smiled. "I've noticed that about you." And was baffled by how she'd ever thought she could be meaningfully attracted to the polished, urbane sort who believed that Hugo Boss was, well, *boss*. There was something so much more elemental and instinctual about her desire for Noah.

He didn't speak for a long while. She stayed quiet, too, letting the rhythm of the waves wash over them. Finally he looked at her, a sheen in his eyes, and she knew it was okay to ask.

"What happened?" she whispered.

He took his time. "I met a woman and fell in love with her. Liza Beth Skinner, but everyone called her Lizabee. She was something. Bossy and tough, but she knew how to be sweet and kind, too. She cared about people. Everyone went to her for help and advice, but she wasn't a soft touch. She could kick the ass of the biggest, meanest firefighter and be respected for it. Lizabee was one of the best crew bosses a firefighter could ask for.''

''You worked with her?'' Aha. This was one part of his story the gossipmongers hadn't gotten hold of.

''No, not really. Lizabee bossed a ground crew—the hotshots. We did work side by side for my first couple of years as a firefighter. Then I took the smoke jumping training.''

''She sounds like an admirable woman. I'm glad you had…someone you loved.''

One corner of Noah's mouth quirked. ''Not a shred of jealousy in you, huh?''

She shrugged, even though it wasn't true. ''I can't compete with someone who has those qualities. You know why I'm here and that I haven't told the Whitakers. It's not an admirable position to be in.''

''I trust that you'll be fair.''

Her stomach jumped. ''You do?'' *How,* she wanted to ask. *How do you trust your instincts with such certainty when I'm sitting here asking you to prove yourself to me?*

''Sure. I can see what kind of woman you are.''

''I see what kind of man you are, Noah. I do.'' She swallowed. ''But I want to know what made you.''

''What made me into a hermit?''

''That, too.''

He moved restlessly, raking his hands through his

hair. Finally he got up and walked along the cliff side to Bride's Leap. Claire watched as he stood there, staring at the lake for a long moment, small and vulnerable at that distance in a way he could never be up close.

No, that wasn't true. How well she knew size didn't save you from hurt and pain—especially on the inside, where it mattered most.

She waited for him to come back, but when he turned and started toward her, she couldn't sit still any longer. She went to meet him, scrambling among the rocks in her city-girl boots, hoping she wouldn't slip and fall in stark contrast to the capable superwoman, Lizabee.

Who had also loved Noah.

Claire couldn't fault her.

The realization that she was deep in love and therefore deep in trouble had barely registered before Noah caught her in his arms and brought his mouth down on hers with a fierceness that drummed romantic notions right out of her head. She remembered this wasn't about courting. It was about need, so hot it burned away their other concerns.

Noah wants it that way, she thought, but his lips were so hungry and his tongue was so daring, thrusting into her mouth until her need pulsed as rhythmically as the waves, that she gave in to it. *Swoosh, swoosh, swoosh.* She was drowning in a flood of pure male pheromones.

He pulled her closer, and she felt all of him, hard against her body. Arms, chest, thighs...*erection.* Not an inch of tenderness, where he had been so gentle and considerate before. A good part of her wanted to let loose and glory in the unrestrained sexuality, but…

She shoved her hands against his chest. Dragged her mouth away. "Hold on, there, cabin boy. Let's take this a little slower."

Emotions churning, she patted him a couple of times on the chest. Rock hard and heaving. She'd known there was an earthquake inside him. The question was if they—and this alarming, astounding attraction— could survive the upheaval.

He didn't look pleased that she'd pushed him away. "'Cabin boy?' Where'd you come up with that?"

"I never knew a man who lived in a log cabin before."

His brows drew together. "What does my cabin have to do with anything?"

"I don't know, but I'm trying to figure you out. And kissing the stuffing out of me is a nice distraction— especially twice—but it won't last forever."

"Let's hope it doesn't, because I'm in pain." He winced a little, sliding his hands into the pockets of his jeans.

Her gaze dropped to the prominent bulge beneath his zipper and then rebounded fast, shooting across the water. *Oh, my.* She turned away and breathed deep, reaching up and sliding her hands over her hair, clasping them at the back of her neck. She counted to ten. Trying not to think about how it would feel to be at his cabin, naked in his arms, naked beneath him, making love with the scent of wood smoke and cedar in the air and a million stars in the sky, the moon dropping silver coins into the lake.

"Lizabee," Noah said. His voice was soft, but suddenly it was the only sound in the world. "Lizabee—she busted my heart wide open."

Claire whirled. "Oh, Noah. I'm so sorry."

He shrugged his massive shoulders. "I don't want sympathy. Not from you, Claire. You're not a part of all that. You're something new. Something different." Recovered, he hooked his thumbs in his belt loops and looked at her with care instead of ferocity. "Someone special."

She walked over and leaned her forehead against his shoulder, touching only his arms, her palms coasting over the firm, warm muscle and hair-roughened skin. "You healed," she said, not sure if it was a question.

"Over time. It was easier for me, doing it in solitude. I've always liked animals more than people, anyway."

Claire grew bold. She lifted her head, reaching all the way up his arm to his shoulder, lightly touching her fingertips to the scars at his throat. "Then it wasn't because of the scars that you stayed away so long?"

"The scars were never that bad. I hadn't intended to become a hermit, but when I heard that folks were carrying tales about me, turning me into some kind of backwoods Phantom of the Opera—well, I didn't care. I didn't try to prove otherwise. Let 'em talk, I figured, as long as they left me alone."

"Your parents didn't explain to anyone?"

"Guess not. Oh, my dad probably enjoyed the tall tales. Wouldn't surprise me if he egged it on. And my mom's a modest Finn—she keeps family matters private.''

"It will be a bit of a shock, then, when townspeople see you without a beard.''

"They'd stare either way.''

"Head-to-toe scars, is what I was told.''

Noah dropped his face close to hers, kissed her cheek. "And you dared come to my cabin anyway?''

"You had my purse.''

"I want more.''

She hesitated. He seemed so sure, so ready to risk his mended heart. "You're a brave man.''

He reared back again, stiffening as if she'd insulted him. "Why do you say that?''

"I don't understand. What's wrong with—''

Nobody's hero.

How could she have forgotten?

He'd withdrawn because of the tragedy and scandal, not the scars.

THE CONVERSATION was zigzagging all over the place, but Noah didn't know how to keep it line. He'd wanted to set Claire's mind at ease in a simple, straightforward manner, and instead her thoughts had gone in directions that disturbed him. He didn't want to analyze and absolve the past—he wanted it to be over.

Over and done with, once and for all.

He didn't know for sure what would happen with Claire. She was right. The courting thing had come from Emmie, and he'd used it to his advantage. A flustered Claire was a sight to behold. He could tell she wasn't used to getting knocked for a loop. Or being pursued.

He was a plain dealer. His interest in Claire had come as one hell of a surprise, but he could roll with the punches.

Bay House was a punch. When he'd arrived, looking for Claire, it had hit him hard that while he'd been off in the woods, nursing his wounds, people he cared about had been facing their own troubles. If the Whitakers didn't want to sell—and he was sure they didn't—he'd do whatever he could to help them out, even if that meant showing up seven days a week until the house was back in tip-top shape. He wasn't worried about Claire's reaction. She had a big heart under that efficient career woman exterior. When push came to shove, she'd gracefully acquiesce to the Whitakers' wishes.

Noah grimaced. Her corporation had better follow suit.

"Let's get back to what happened between you and Lizabee," Claire said, veering off when she saw she'd prodded him toward the edge.

He didn't particularly want to. Repeatedly touching a tender spot only brought more pain.

And so he hesitated.

Crack. A gunshot split the air. So close the sound hurt his eardrums.

He wrapped his arms around Claire, hunching over her. *"Get down."* That shot had been too close for comfort.

They dropped among the rocks. Claire folded herself

into a ball, her fingers clutching his arm. She cringed at the sound of movement in the nearby trees. "Was that what I think it was?"

"Shotgun, I think," he said. "Don't be afraid. We're probably okay, but I don't want to take any chances. Hunters can be goddamn stupid about hitting their targets." He squeezed her, keeping his tone light. "And I *have* been known to be mistaken for a bear."

"Was he shooting at *us?*"

"No." Noah raised his head. There was a good expanse of bare rock around them, adorned only by a few hardy scrub pines. But the border of trees between the cliff and the Bayside Road properties was dense in several stretches, penetrable only by a stray bullet.

Three quick shots came in succession. *Pop, pop, pop.*

Claire shuddered, but she was calmer. "That was farther away."

"You're right." Noah rose, shading his eyes. "The shooter's moving toward Bay House, by the sounds of it."

Still kneeling, she peered around the rocks toward the slate mansard roof and witches' peak tower of the inn, all that was visible beyond the treetops. "Bay House?"

"It's probably a target shooter, or a backyard hunter with more caliber than brains." Noah took her hand. "Let's get out of here."

She scrambled after him. "But isn't it illegal, shooting so close to a residential area?"

"You bet it is." Noah bit down so hard his jaw

ached. As soon as they entered the forest, he heard the shouts. Something was very wrong.

"Stay back while I check this out," he told Claire, pushing through the tree branches.

A woman was screeching. "Argh! This thing is attacking me!"

From another direction, a man shouted above the fray. "Outta the way! Let me get a clean shot off."

"No!" the woman howled, as Noah burst into the Whitakers' backyard. It was Roxy, hollering louder than a wounded moose. She was on the ground, tussling with a roly-poly ball of fur.

"Scrap," Claire said, arriving only seconds behind Noah.

Another figure emerged from the trees, rifle held high while he crashed through the rose and lilac bushes in a flurry of leaves and broken twigs. "One clean shot, that's all I need. That animal ripped out two of my new fruit trees."

"Put the gun down, Terry." Noah strode across the garden and grabbed Scrap by the scruff. He hauled him off Roxy, who'd been getting her face washed by the cub's sandpaper tongue. Aside from minor scratches on her arms, she appeared to be unhurt.

Claire rushed in. "You're okay, Roxy. It's only Scrap, Noah's bear cub. He's just playful."

Roxy was sprawled on the grass, disheveled and out of breath. "I came out to see what the shot was, and this...*fur bomb* barreled through the bushes, straight at me."

Noah had lifted the hefty cub in his arms. Scrap was

squirming and grunting with pleasure. "I'm sure he was more scared than you."

Roxy jumped up. "He was squealing." She glared at the man with the rifle, who hung behind and was watching them balefully. "Did you shoot at the cub, Terry? You could have killed it. Or me! Or any other innocent bystander."

Terry Lindstrom again. Claire studied the neighbor with a fresh eye now that she knew how he related to Noah. Terry looked the worse for wear today, chin unshaved, hair uncombed, wearing jeans and a wrinkled polo shirt. She had to remind herself that he was about Noah's age; Terry's unpleasant expression made him seem older. Aside from the reddened face and downturned mouth, there was a deep, steeping anger in his eyes—the kind that couldn't be entirely masked even in the best of circumstances. In this case, he made no pretense of trying.

Noah's quiet voice was underlined with certain menace. He could be intimidating when he had to. "Unload the rifle and put it down, Terry."

Terry lowered his head like a bull to meet Noah's eyes. He was breathing heavily, and a shock of blond hair had fallen across his glistening forehead. The rifle was held across his body. At the request, his grip on it tightened. He wasn't ready to back down.

"We don't want an accident." Noah was trying to hold on to Scrap and control the situation at the same time. Claire moved closer, uncertain which was more likely to get away from him. "I'm giving you the benefit of the doubt. Maybe you fired into the air to chase the cub away. Don't be stupid and make a wrong move now."

Terry's silence was packed with tension and a malignant ill will. He eyes flicked over Claire, taking in the hand she'd placed on Noah's arm. Her skin prickled. There was something about the way his eyes glinted....

After a long moment, Terry lifted the rifle—slightly but unmistakably. Noah took one step, then set his stance, seeming to grow bigger and harder before her eyes. "Take Scrap, Claire," he said, not shifting his stare from the other man.

Claire didn't reach for the bear. She stepped in front of Noah, instead. Roxy came forward, too, her hands on her hips, looking ready to rip someone's head off.

Terry's mouth twisted into a jeer. "That's right." He cracked the rifle chamber open and let the remaining rounds fall onto the ground. "We wouldn't want to have an accident. We wouldn't want an *innocent* bystander to get killed."

Roxy's mouth thinned. "Is that a threat?"

"Take it how you want."

"Get out of here, Terry. Next time I'll be reporting you to the sheriff."

"Next time, I won't be putting a scare into you. If I see that man's face around here again—" Terry jabbed a seething glance over the women's heads "—I'll shoot to kill. I told him to stay away and I meant it."

Claire's inhale felt like the thrust of a knife. Terry

wasn't merely an arrogant blowhard. His threat was serious.

"You're such a fool, Terry." Roxy followed him when he slung the rifle over his shoulder and strode off the way he'd come, through the overgrown border between properties. "From what I've heard, your brother's death wasn't Noah's fault. Do you think a bullet is going to bring Rick back?"

"Let him go," Noah said tiredly. He bent to set Scrap down. "Just let him go."

Who? Claire wondered. *Terry or Rick?*

"Keep that wild animal off my property!" Terry yelled before he disappeared into the foliage. "Both of them!"

Claire reached for Noah. "I was so scared."

He slid a hand along her back, patting her comfortingly, but she could tell his thoughts weren't really with her. "Don't worry. Terry's filled with anger—it'll burn out."

"When?" Roxy said, joining them. "Hasn't it been two years now? I'd like to know what makes Terry Lindstrom think he rules the world. You're welcome at Bay House any time you want, Noah. Even if you bring *that* along." Looking repulsed, she gestured at Scrap, who was scratching at the earth of the torn-up brick path, his pink tongue swooping up the occasional plump grub or centipede.

"Sorry," Noah said. "Scrap must have escaped from his pen and followed my scent. I'd better get him out of here."

Claire was flabbergasted. "Isn't anyone going to call the cops? We had a shooting, for pity's sake!"

Noah shrugged. "I don't want the trouble."

"Maybe we should," Roxy said.

"Of course we should. He threatened to kill Noah!"

Noah was adamant. "No."

Roxy looked at Claire. "You've got to learn this about Yoopers, Claire—they're independent cusses. They'd rather solve their own problems than call cops or hire lawyers."

"Sounds like you fit right in." Claire was reluctant to let the matter go. She didn't want it swept under the rug, especially when there was still a threat of violence.

"Well, I'm half and half. I spent a lot of summers here, growing up. Aunt Em and Uncle Toivo always had room for one more."

Claire eyed Noah. He seemed ill at ease, wanting for all the world to hightail it to his cabin. Away from all this open emotion and turmoil, she supposed. She ought to give him a break. Let him go.

Even if that pulled at her heart with worry and longing and, she had to admit, curiosity over unfinished business.

Before she spoke, a cherry-colored sports car pulled into the parking area off the carriage house, its horn tooting in staccato burps.

"Oh, great," Roxy said, brushing bits of grass off the seat of her overalls. "It's Rob."

Noah and Claire exchanged a baffled glance. *What now?*

CHAPTER TEN

"MAMA MAE laid a fine table," Emmie said proudly, overlooking the guests from the head of the long oval dining table. Havilland china and old silver had been laid over a hand-embroidered cloth. On cue, Toivo carried in the platter of pot roast, his elfin face beaming, cheeks shiny from steam. "I can only do my best to follow her example," Emmie continued, bowing her head with modesty.

The modesty was not entirely genuine. In Emmie's pleased smile, Claire saw an expectation of praise, but she couldn't deny the innkeeper her due. Not even crumbling plaster, hideous wallpaper and squeaky floorboards could distract from the rare excellence of an honest-to-goodness home-cooked meal.

Accolades were heaped upon Emmie's head. She tut-tutted them away. While Toivo carved, the side dishes were sent around the table. Noah spooned the mashed potato and rutabaga casserole onto his plate and Cassia's—handling the weighty serving dish was too much for her—and then passed it to Claire. Beet salad came next, followed by glazed carrots and a green mixture she couldn't identify. By the time Claire had added a hot biscuit and several thick slices of roast, her plate was overflowing.

"Gravy?" Noah asked, holding up the gravy boat.

"Oh, why not? Ladle it on." *I'll start the diet to-morrow.*

A minute later, having tasted the heavenly gravy and potatoes, she said "I need an exercise plan, because I'm not giving up this food."

"You can hike double time to my cabin anytime you want," Noah murmured. Beneath the tablecloth, he touched her thigh. A fleeting stroke, but enough contact to make her relegate dinner to second place on the list of favorite sensory indulgences.

"I don't have your stamina," she replied. They were safe enough. With eight chattering, chewing adults at the table, no one else was listening. Except perhaps Cassia, who had openly professed a proprietary interest in the progress of Claire's romance.

Noah tore a biscuit in half. "You have no idea."

She arched a brow. "Oh, I have *some* idea."

After the unneighborly shooting incident, Noah had taken Scrap to the cabin but had been persuaded to return. Emmie wouldn't hear of him missing the supper she'd planned to welcome Robert Whitaker to Bay House. Rob had turned out to be Roxy's half brother, who'd driven north from downstate. Just why remained something of a mystery. Roxy wasn't overjoyed with the visit. And Rob only smiled.

"You must let me drive you back," Claire said to Noah. "How many miles is it? At least five from here. You've walked that three times today."

"Actually, I like to walk. There's no better way to explore the countryside."

Claire leaned forward to address Cassia, sitting on Noah's other side. "A perfect chance to finagle me back to his cabin, and he doesn't recognize it. He'd rather sightsee." She shook her head. "The man's clearly out of practice."

Cassia inclined her head to speak past Noah. Her smile was impish. "They tell me it's like riding a bike."

"Then they haven't been doing it right," Claire said in a low whisper. Cassia tittered.

"Behave yourselves, girls," admonished Noah. He was blushing.

"What are you youngsters whispering about?" Emmie said from one end of the table.

All three answered at once.

"Hiking," said Noah.

"Biking," Cassia said.

Claire's answer prevailed. "The nocturnal proclivities of the mighty Sasquatch."

Across the table, three pairs of eyes widened. Roxy, Robert and Bill had fallen silent—or remained so, in the latter's case.

Only Toivo understood. He nodded and said, "Ah, you mean sex," as he forked up a dripping beet and popped it into his mouth.

Emmie pursed her lips. "Hush. We don't speak that way at the dinner table. And use your napkin, you sloppy old son of a gun. There's beet juice on your chin."

Claire nipped her lip. "Sorry, Emmie."

Cassia's smile was undeterred. "We'll behave."

Noah said nothing, but he touched Claire under the tablecloth again, laying his entire palm on her thigh and squeezing. She had to clench her jaw to prevent a this-close-to-orgasmic moan.

As soon as Emmie was occupied with passing the cut-glass butter dish, Claire surreptitiously lowered her fork and jabbed the tines into the back of Noah's hand. He hastily retreated.

"Hey," he said out of the side of his mouth. "Keep your prongs to yourself."

She covered her response with a napkin. "You, too."

"I only have one." He stared straight ahead. "But sometimes one is enough."

She stuffed half the napkin in her mouth, trying to hold back a hysterical laugh. Instead she started to choke. Noah thumped her on the back.

Emmie eyed them with suspicion. "Try a sip of water, Claire." She turned her attention to the guest of honor. "Robert, it's so good to have another one of Val's children at Bay House. How is my dear, dear, sweet sister? Still living in California? I'm afraid I can't keep up with her from one Christmas card to the next." Her smile was fixed.

"Val's in Big Sur now. After the last divorce, she said she wanted to simplify her life."

Roxy pushed a carrot around her plate. "Yeah, life's so real and simple in a million-dollar beach house."

Toivo screwed up his face. "Now what was that husband's name?"

Roxy shrugged. "Does it matter?"

"That's why I'm here," Rob said, smiling big enough to prove he could ignore his half sister's surliness. He and Roxy shared a family resemblance physically, both being tall and sandy-haired with athletic builds. Rob's face was boyish, with full cheeks and a dimpled chin; Roxy's was more refined. Where she was genuine—if genuinely a grouch—his smile was so frequent and steady, the happy-to-meetcha personality seemed as forced as a used car salesman's. Which, it turned out, he was.

Emmie looked askance. "What do you mean, Robert?"

"Val asked me to come up and check out how the business is doing."

Like me. Claire looked guiltily at Noah. He made a face that was easy to read. *You made your bed, kid.*

"The business?" Emmie was seriously mystified.

"The bed-and-breakfast." Rob managed to keep smiling at his aunt even while he spoke. "Have you forgotten it's supposed to be a profitable business? Heh, heh."

Emmie dismissed that concern with a wave of her hand. "Val has never expressed an interest before. She couldn't wait to move out of Alouette. Took off for California the day she turned eighteen and has been back no more than a half-dozen times since," Emmie told the table.

"What a coincidence," Roxy said, dripping sarcasm. "She has the exact same number of ex-husbands and assorted children."

"Yes," Rob said, still smiling, "but Val does still own a third of Bay House."

All sound stopped.

Glances flew around the table, darting from person to person through the suddenly strained atmosphere.

With a clatter, Toivo dropped a butter knife onto his plate. "Ar-har. That she does."

Emmie's chin quivered. She clamped her lips shut and breathed through her nose in quick puffs.

Rob continued blithely. "Val wants to divest herself of worldly goods. They entangle her aura." His dimple deepened. "Or was it her karma? Anyway, she asked me to arrange something for her share of Bay House."

Emmie gave an explosive snort. *"Something?"*

Even Bill, the only one of them who'd resumed eating, looked taken aback by the unusual shrillness of her voice.

"Well, say, there's nothing to worry about, Aunt Emmie. Val wouldn't do you wrong. She's perfectly willing to be reasonable. You and Toivo have first right of refusal on her share." Rob looked from one to the other, nodding and grinning, grinning and nodding, until finally he couldn't maintain the facade. The smile peeled away. Without it, the twinkle in his eye looked more like a glint of avarice.

A snake shedding its skin, Claire thought.

Outrage had boosted Emmie a few inches above her seat. Her hands were fisted on the table. "I cannot believe that even Valentina would sell out. Father must be rolling in his grave."

"Whaddaya say?" Toivo blinked. "Val's diverting?"

"Divesting," Rob said through his teeth.

Roxy remained detached and cynical. She pinged a finger against her water glass. "I suspect that diverting's right on the money. She probably needs cash for the luxury karmic tour of India. Cleanse your chakras on a thousand bucks a day."

Emmie collapsed onto her chair. "How does Val expect us to come up with the purchase price? We're barely profitable, and she knows it! She never did bother answering my letters, but I heard from her right quick when there were no dividends to pay out." Emmie swept the napkin out of her lap and dabbed at her eyes. "Oh, my. Oh, my. Please don't mind me. I'm overcome. I'll be all right in a minute."

Cassia, seated at Emmie's right hand, reached out with one arm to comfort the older woman. "Oh, Emmie. It'll be okay. We'll think of a way."

"We'll fight for you and Toivo, Aunt Em." Roxy glared at Rob. "You can count on it."

"We could put together a syndicate," Bill said, breaking his silence. He kept glancing shyly at Emmie, his long bony face pulled even longer with dismay.

"That's a good idea," Noah said, nodding.

Rob was stymied, not pleasantly. "What are you—"

Roxy interrupted. "We're spoiling your big plan, that's what."

"I didn't come here with a plan!"

"You always do. I'll bet you have a buyer already lined up, huh?"

Emmie's head came up. The napkin dropped out of her fingers to her lap. "Oh, no," she breathed. After the moment of shock, she made another attempt at gathering herself together, but her eyes remained the glassy blue of marbles. "Robert Whitaker, what exactly is going on? Before you answer, you might remember that I used to take you in every summer, young man."

Rob tried an obligatory smile. Emmie scowled. He looked around the table for support. Not an eyelash flickered. Not a lip unfurled. Finally, he gave in with a sigh and grudgingly confessed, "There's no buyer yet, but I've been shopping it around, looking for the best price. Val said I'd get a percentage if I brokered the deal."

Toivo bobbed to his feet. "I'll broker your head."

Rob threw up his hands. "I said you have right of first refusal!"

"At top price." Emmie shook her head. "We already took out a line of credit for operating expenses and the new wiring. We'll never raise enough cash to buy Val's share."

Claire was miserable. The situation couldn't be more ideal for Bel Vista, but all she felt was shame. Emmie had trustingly revealed her most private finances. Claire didn't want to hear another word.

"What about Bill's idea?" Noah said.

Claire's hands tightened on the knot she'd made of the linen napkin. Even Noah—who *knew* what a bind she was in, dammit—was assuming she could be trusted with all this information.

How bad would it look if she stood up and excused herself from the room?

"Syndication?" Toivo asked. "Bay House ain't a TV show."

"In this case, a syndicate is a group of people who pool their money for an investment," Noah explained.

"I'd do it, but I'm more or less broke," Roxy said. "Emmie gives me room and board for my services."

"I have some savings," Cassia volunteered.

Noah nodded. "And me."

Bill raised a bony finger in agreement.

Claire cleared her throat. "I hate to put a damper on this, but you're probably not aware of this property's value. You'd need somewhere in the neighborhood of—" She named a price that prompted gasps. Even Noah looked surprised.

Roxy whistled. "But we'd need only a third of the price, isn't that right?" She made a tsking sound. "But I guess we don't have even that much."

"Um, no," Claire said. "That would be the price of a one-third share, approximately. You understand I'm estimating. It could be even more, if there are…other offers."

"Why do you know all that?" Rob asked accusingly. Two spots of red had flared in his face, making Claire wonder if he'd hoped to somehow take advantage of his aunt and uncle. "You're just a guest. Not a member of the family."

Roxy scoffed. "You're calling yourself family, you troll?"

Claire answered quietly. "I have some experience

with these things." She prepared herself for full confession.

Emmie didn't pick up the thread. "Claire's right, I'm afraid. Bay House is worth a great deal, even in its present shape. I do thank you all for the offer—"

"We could look for other investors," Roxy said.

Rob opened his mouth to speak, but there was a scuffling sound under the table, and he snapped his lips shut again, his eyes bulging. It was Roxy who continued, adding acidly, "Investors we can *trust*."

"No, dear. I wouldn't want that. My father wanted us to keep the house in the family, and that's where it will stay." Emmie mustered a brave smile. "Toivo and I will think of a way for that to happen, won't we, you batty old buffoon?"

Toivo nodded at Emmie from the opposite end of the table, but he looked so naive and hapless that Claire had to stifle a groan. This was bad. What was she going to tell Drake? He'd already called three times asking for her report. She'd have to come up with an excuse to delay it until she could figure out a way to do the right thing.

Whatever that might be.

She really wanted to look at Noah, see his reaction, so much so that she forced herself not to. There lay trouble. More of it. She focused on Emmie, who had stood.

"Please accept my apologies for the lack of hospitality," the innkeeper said with a stiff formality. "But this dinner is over." Emmie held on to her stalwart expression for a second or two, but then her face began to pucker. She walked swiftly out of the room.

Toivo muttered, "Exqueeze me," and went after her.

Bill made a small sound in his throat. Apparently embarrassed by that, he leaned over to pick up Emmie's napkin, his color rising.

The remaining dinner guests looked at each other uneasily.

Roxy thumped a fist on the table, making the china rattle. "Man, this better not also be the end of Bay House."

WHAT ARE YOU going to do, Claire?

She could have sworn Noah had said it out loud, but he hadn't. He hadn't moved a muscle, only stayed leaning against her rental car, his arms crossed over his chest as he stared into the forest that surrounded them like a silent, darkened cathedral.

What are you going to do, Claire?

So the question was inside her head. Repeating endlessly.

She sighed and reached forward, resting her elbows on her knees. She'd given Noah a ride to the point on the logging road where he'd pick up the trail to his cabin, but they'd been reluctant to say goodbye. To say anything, really. She was sitting on the hood, and he was standing beside her, and all they'd done for the past five minutes was look at each other and give useless little shrugs.

What are you going to do, Claire?

She tilted her head. It wasn't late, but darkness came earlier in the woods, where the foliage blocked out the remaining dollops of sunlight. Overhead, the sky was painted indigo between the swaying treetops. The silence and wildness no longer seemed as overwhelming. They were almost…embracing. She was beginning to love the north woods.

What are you going to do, Claire?

She spoke at last. "My company would pay a good price. Invested properly, Emmie and Toivo would be set for the rest of their lives. They—Emmie—wouldn't have to work so hard."

Noah turned his head and looked at her.

"I know." The words were almost a groan. "I know. They don't want to give up the family's legacy. But there might be no other choice."

"They can try for a second mortgage."

"They'd have to show an income."

"I'll move in. That's another boarder, paying full price twenty-four seven."

Claire's heart gave a hard thump. "You'd really do that?"

Noah nodded. "It would be easier for me while Roxy and I handle the renovations." That had been the one course of action they'd settled on after the dinner had come to an abrupt end. Roxy, Cassia, Noah and Claire had convened in the kitchen, throwing out ideas to save Bay House while they washed the dishes and put away the leftovers. The two women hadn't noticed Claire's discomfort.

"What about your animals?"

Noah rubbed the side of his jaw. "The fox is ready to go, as soon as I take out the stitches. The owl, soon enough. Same with Reader and Rocky. Scrap's a problem, though."

"You could bring him along."

"No. Too many people around. Wouldn't be good for him."

Silence.

"Would it be good for you?" she asked.

He eyed her. "What do you mean?"

"Giving up your cabin."

"My mother would be thrilled. She thinks I've been hiding from the world long enough." Noah took Claire's hand. "She's going to like you."

She matched his fingertips with her own. The huge yearning, the ache for more, had opened inside her again. "Are you forgetting that I'm leaving soon?"

He was, amazingly, not concerned by that. "We have to think of a solution for that problem, too."

"You're positively intrepid." The warmth of him drew her like a magnet; she leaned into him, let it absorb her. "That was a scary situation, this morning. With the neighbor."

Noah didn't speak. But he put his arm around her and nestled her closer. Claire closed her eyes, letting time and worry go. If she could stay like this, exactly like this…

Eventually the need in her to fix, to caretake, rose again. *What are you going to do, Claire?*

"What happened, Noah?" *How can I make it better?*

CARRIE ALEXANDER 227

"Why does Terry Lindstrom hate you so much?" She wanted to hear it in his own words.

Noah cleared his throat before he answered. "He thinks I let his brother die. On purpose. Murder, of a sort."

She sat up, shocked. "Murder? Oh, no…"

"Terry and I were once best friends. Rick was his younger brother, kind of a crazy kid. Rick was home and at loose ends when I came back for a visit and, well, he decided smoke jumping sounded exciting and dangerous and, hell, even glamorous. I told him he was way off base, but he ended up following me to Montana. He got a job on Lizabee's ground crew and was talking about applying for skydiving training as soon as he could."

Noah would have moved away then, but she held his hand and wouldn't let him go. He gave in with a heavy sigh, the muscles in his abdomen relaxing then gradually clenching again as he went on. "Even though Rick was in good shape physically, he was still too soft. Accustomed to the finer things. He probably wouldn't have lasted the season, but he never got the chance to quit—" Noah stopped when his breath hitched in his chest.

Claire wanted it all to come out at last. "The big fire."

"Yeah."

"Rick was killed."

"Lizabee's crew got trapped in a tight valley. The fire turned on them, and there was only one way out, straight up to the ridge. A bunch of us smoke jumpers had been called in when the situation got hairy. I was there when Lizabee made it out, but Rick had been left behind. I started down into the valley to find him. But the smoke was too thick. I couldn't see, even though I heard him calling to me...." Noah touched his neck. "A burning tree fell right in front of me. I had to turn back, Claire. I tried to reach Rick. I swear I tried—"

Noah's voice was strangled. He doubled over. Dry sobs clutched in his chest, but he didn't cry. She wound her arms around his broad body, holding his head against her breast, murmuring the meaningless words that were comforting nonetheless. "It's okay, it's okay."

Noah shuddered and pushed her away. "No, it isn't."

"But anyone can see that *you* weren't at fault! How Terry can blame you—"

"Because he knows. Somehow. I didn't tell him, but he knows...."

Claire's mouth went dry. "Knows what?"

Noah's eyes were lit with a hard, burning emotion, so similar to the look in Terry's eyes that morning she gasped. It was scorn. Scorn for himself.

"He knows that I hated Rick. That I'd wished for him to be...gone."

"Why?"

"Because Lizabee was cheating on me—with Rick Lindstrom."

A COUPLE OF DAYS passed. In spite of Terry's threats, Noah showed up at Bay House early every morning and worked at whatever task Emmie thought needed doing. He tried to keep to himself, but the Whitakers and Cassia wouldn't let him. By the second day, Toivo had convinced him to join the local volunteer firefighters—a motley crew in desperate need of guidance. How Toivo did that, Claire couldn't imagine, because Noah had closed up around her after revealing his secret guilt. But Toivo was apparently too enthusiastic— or purposely dense—to allow for reluctance or regrets. As far as he was concerned, Noah's valuable expertise shouldn't be wasted.

Claire was at loose ends. Drake called every day on her cell phone, trying to hurry her along because he wanted to send her on another assignment. Dreading the thought, she finally told him she was officially on vacation and would stay in Alouette for as long as she pleased. He would have to wait for her report until she got back, she told him, making Bay House sound as unlikely a prospect as possible. She was still hoping for a solution that would involve betraying neither her company nor her new friends.

On the morning Noah was to have his first meeting with the firefighters' group at a popular downtown diner, she gave him a lift to town, meaning to do some shopping. She went to a women's dress shop and a sporting goods store and bought herself practical gear—extra socks, jeans, a couple of simple, cheap tops she wouldn't mind messing up, a pair of solid hiking boots and a weatherproof jacket lined with a thin layer of fleece.

Coming out of the sporting goods store, she checked

her watch. An hour had passed, but there was no sign of the firefighters' meeting breaking up—she could see them still gathered around a big table by the diner's front window, chomping doughnuts. A waitress filled coffee cups, suffering their joshing with a weary tolerance.

Claire was about to cross the street when a sleek black car that had been moving slowly suddenly sped up with a menacing *vroom* of the engine. The car zipped past her within a foot, blowing her hair back. She stopped short, her heart in her mouth.

Close call! She couldn't be sure, but she thought she'd recognized the driver—Terry Lindstrom, eyes slitted as he hunched over the wheel.

Deciding that was coincidence—he had no reason to run her down, surely—she scurried across the road, carefully looking for traffic before stepping off the curb. And here she'd thought downtown Alouette was always slow and quiet.

''Hiya, there. Almost got your toes run over! You've got to look both ways before you cross the street.''

She saw the smile first, then recognized the face. Rob Whitaker. Roxy had given him the boot after the dinner debacle, but apparently he'd found a hotel room and was staying in the area. He was in the same suit, same smile, same hucksterish spirit. Yahoo.

''Rob, hello.''

''Glad I ran into you, Claire,'' he said. ''I hear you're in the hotel business—''

She interrupted, suspicious. ''Where did you hear that?''

"I have my ways." He chuckled. "I was hoping we could confab. Put our heads together and work out a deal." He saw her immediate skepticism. "One that's advantageous to the Whitakers, of course. Aunt and Unc are my first concern."

"I'm sure." She started to walk.

Rob joined her. He seemed determined to work the opportunity. "So you work for Bel Vista? That's a big operation. Are they interested in acquiring Bay House?"

"I don't know...." She paused and admitted it. "Yes, I suppose they might be."

He rubbed his hands together. "Fantastic!"

"Not necessarily." She stopped, determined to get rid of him. "I'm merely here on vacation, and from what I've seen so far, Bay House is not a viable option. It's falling down. Bel Vista is looking for only the most luxurious of properties." In this case, a white lie was forgivable.

Wheels turned in Rob's eyes. "Well, they're working on it. We can sit back and let that lumberjack guy do all the work, and when the house is back in working order—"

"No, thank you," she snapped. "Let me put this to you straight. Even if I was interested, I'd approach Emmie and Toivo with an offer—not you." She nodded, dismissing him. "Thank you for your time." She strode away.

Rob's smile had fallen, but he called after her. "Don't forget—I've got a third share. And my price just went up!"

Claire didn't look back, grateful to be rid of him. She only hoped Noah hadn't seen them from the diner across the way—he'd be bound to jump to conclusions. She supposed if she'd been operating purely as a businesswoman, she wouldn't have been so quick to dismiss Rob's offer.

Her step faltered. Was she losing her perspective? Rob was no worse than others she'd dealt with. She might have been more amenable, at least until she'd made up her mind what to do. It wasn't smart to make enemies of the shareholders of a valuable property.

Troubled, she wandered slowly along the street, gazing into windows. A twig chair caught her eye and she glanced at the store's sign. North Country Crafts, it read. Handcrafted Items, U.P. Made.

A bell rang over the shop door as she pushed inside. The store was small but pleasant, with light pine wood floors and shelves made of driftwood and unpeeled birch trees. Several customers were scattered throughout. The one employee at hand was busy at the cash register, allowing Claire to look over the chair uninterrupted. A tag dangled from the arm. A significant price was hand printed on one side; the other was stamped with a label that said Handmade from Natural Products by Cabin Boy & Co.

Claire's nearly giddy laugh drew stares.

She smothered it, turning quickly to examine other products. She moved among the birch-bark baskets, quilts and pottery, searching for Noah's work. At the back of the store, she found an entire display of it— twig chairs, the willow branches bundled and bent into arches; solid benches made of natural logs; polished wood coffee tables in free-form shapes. There was one of the carved wood chandeliers, suspended from the ceiling. She checked the tag. If Noah's work was selling, his income certainly would be comfortable enough to support a more luxurious lifestyle.

But then, he was at the cabin out of choice, not necessity, wasn't he?

"Great stuff, isn't it?" A young woman had appeared at Claire's elbow. "We sell a lot of it during the summer season, so if you've got your eye on a particular piece, snap it up now. We get new product in only a couple of times a year."

"It's beautiful work."

"All handcrafted locally."

"I saw the tag." Claire glanced at the clerk. "Cabin Boy and company?"

The clerk smiled. "That's the name we're supposed to give, but just between you and me, I can tell you a little bit about the artisan. It's a fascinating tale."

"Oh, really?"

"Cabin Boy is really just one man—a bachelor who lives way out in the woods in a tiny log cabin. He's a hermit. No one ever sees him. I've been working here part-time for nearly a year and all I know is his name." She looked around the shop, hushing her voice to whisper. "Noah Saari."

"Ah," Claire said, nodding. "How interesting."

"It's scary, really. I've heard he's so big he's almost a giant, and crazy as a bull moose, with a big, bushy beard, a face that was just about melted off in a fire and feet so big no boots will fit them. He wanders the woods at night with an ax and a shovel. He'll chop up anyone who comes near. If somehow you got close enough to look into his eyes, they say you'd be burned right up because they're as red-hot as hell. He's mad, of course.'' The clerk laughed. ''Not that I believe it! But that's what people say.''

''Horrible,'' Claire said. Her mouth twitched. ''But nice furniture.''

The clerk laughed again. ''Yeah. Are you interested?''

''Seriously.''

''Great!'' Her eyes lighted.

''But not in the furniture. At least not today.'' Claire walked toward the exit with the clerk trailing her.

''Be sure to come back before you leave town.''

Claire stopped by a jewelry display. She picked up a pair of dangly earrings, each one made of three delicate gold hoops strung with tiny beads and chips of aquamarine sea glass. Shoulder brushers that would jingle when she walked. They were pretty but impractical. Too frivolous for her to wear to work.

She put them back.

''Tell me,'' she said to the clerk as several men emerged from the café across the street, ''do the tourists believe that story about the crazy hermit who practically shoots fire with his eyes?''

She giggled. ''Some of them.''

''Part of the story is true, you know. But not all of it.''

"How would you know?" Her eyes widened. "Which parts?"

Noah was at the window. He tapped on the glass and gave Claire a wave. She waved back before turning to the clerk and lowering her voice to a ghost-story hush. "Because I've *seen* him. In fact, there he is now." She pointed.

The clerk looked at Noah with skepticism. He was far too well groomed to qualify as a backwoods monster. "That guy's hot, all right, but he's no lunatic. You're pulling my leg."

"He cleans up nice." Claire went to the door. "His feet are big. But I make him wear shoes now. And as for the eyes…"

Noah was looking at them. His eyes went to Claire, and she shivered at the visual caress.

"That part is true." Claire had forgotten about the clerk; she was staring at Noah and speaking only to herself. "I burn every time he looks at me."

CHAPTER ELEVEN

SEVERAL HOURS later, Claire was singing as she came out of the bathroom, toweling her hair. She stopped in front of the portrait of Valentina Whitaker. Whether it was stardust, the legend or the magical mystery of the right chemistry at the right time, she was more in love with Noah every day. "If this keeps up, I might even grow to like you, Val, old gal."

Valentina, Ice Queen Supreme, still wasn't batting an eyelash. Claire glanced over the collection of family photos on the wall. Black-and-whites, all of them. The couple that had to be Ogden and Mae Whitaker were stiffly posed in their wedding portrait. Ogden had a brushy mustache, a button nose like his son, Toivo, and a bowler hat. His young wife was pretty, a blonde with clear eyes and wide cheekbones, clutching a bouquet to her tiny corseted waist. Claire had to assume they hadn't been as stern and humorless as they looked in the photograph; the heir of the family fortune didn't marry a poor Finnish parlor maid unless there was a good dose of rebellion and passion running through his veins.

Claire went to the bed, where she'd laid out a pretty dress with touches of lace at the collar and sleeves, a style she rarely wore but had purchased on a whim out of boredom with her drab suits and well-cut trousers. Noah would be at dinner again, so after helping him plaster and paint all afternoon while wearing her new— and newly grungy—work clothes, she was going to dazzle him with femininity. He'd never seen her in a dress. Or out of one, she thought with an excited shiver. Her ankle had shrunk to its normal size, so she could wear the matching rose-colored pumps.

There'd been something inspiring about working together in ''her'' bedroom, even with Emmie and Roxy running in and out all afternoon. They'd borrowed a CD player from Cassia and laughingly battled over what to play. Neither of them went for Cassia's new stuff—Shakira and Moby and other one-name singers—and Noah only laughed at her attraction to the soundtrack from *The Breakfast Club,* but they'd finally settled on a classic. James Taylor. She should have known. Noah was definitely a James Taylor kind of guy, even though he swore he'd been more of a heavy metal rocker in his formative teenage years. *That* she couldn't imagine.

After she'd serenaded Noah with ''Handyman'' while he patched the ceiling, they talked about sports, books and movies. She confessed her addiction to Molly Ringwald movies. Noah thought that was mighty strange, but he asked questions until her motivation came clear—she'd been so busy mothering her siblings that she'd never had a proper teenage experience of her own, so those movies were a vicarious reliving. The insight was illuminating. Claire wondered why she hadn't thought of it before.

As she slipped the light, silky dress over her head, she mused over what else she might learn about herself through Noah. Or was it Noah at all? Maybe it was this place—the wild woods, the overwhelming lake, Bay House itself. Even Valentina.

Claire laughed and blew the tragic bride a kiss as she flew out the door.

"Claire!" Cassia called from downstairs. "You have a gift!"

"A gift?" Claire arrived breathless.

"Noah left it."

"He's gone?"

"He said he'd see you tomorrow, something about a fox, but he left you this present." Cassia bobbed up and down with delight. "Open it, open it!"

A small box had been set on the newel post of the staircase. It was wrapped in silver with a froth of blue curling ribbon. Claire picked it up and sat on the steps, placing the box on her knees. She sighed.

Cassia maneuvered closer until one of her rubber wheels bumped into the bottom step. "What's wrong? If a man gave me a present like that, I'd be jumping over the moon. Don't you think it's romantic?"

"I was looking forward to dinner, that's all. But this is very nice." She pulled one of the spiraled ribbons.

"He *is* courting you. I didn't totally believe in Valentina's wedding prophecy, until now." Cassia's gaze flicked from her wheelchair, up the steps to the bridal suite. She gave a little shrug and returned her attention to Claire. "Go on and open it already!"

Claire laughed and tore the paper off. "Oh, wow." She lifted an earring from the cotton batting inside the box. The thin golden hoops chimed. "I was admiring these earrings in a shop downtown. He must have gone in and talked to the salesclerk."

Cassia oohed over the earring. "They'll be perfect with your dress."

Claire slipped the plain gold studs from her ears and put the beaded earrings on. They tinkled when she moved her head, swinging against her jaw and neck, a constant reminder that she was a woman with emotions and delicate sensibilities, not just a corporate drone.

"You look so pretty," Cassia said. "Too bad Noah's not here to admire you." She smiled mischievously. "Why don't you see that he does?"

Claire ducked her head. The earrings slid across her cheeks. "I can't—"

"Sure you can."

She looked up. "I can?"

"You did it once."

"That's true...."

"Besides, you've got Valentina behind you. No one disappoints Valentina without there being dire consequences."

Claire laughed, shaking her head. The earrings chimed, saying *yes* to every *no*.

"C'mon, Claire!" Cassia was laughing, too, her eyes round with excitement. "Do it for all the Molly Ringwalds and Ally Sheedys and, well, *pffft,* the Cassia Keegans of the world.''

That did it. Claire hopped up, dropping the gift wrappings in Cassia's lap as she turned and ran up the stairs.

''Where are you going?'' Cassia called.

''To change into practical shoes. I'm not spraining an ankle this time!''

''SHH, FELLA. Don't be afraid.'' Noah opened the cage. The fox was hunched in the corner, its ears gone flat against its head, white-tipped brush of a tail clamped to scrawny hindquarters. ''Here you go.'' He placed the dish inside. ''One last meal for the road. Raw liver and sunflower seed oil. I even caught you a couple of grasshoppers. Yum, yum.''

The fox lifted its narrow muzzle and bared sharp little teeth. Earlier, Noah had covered it with a blanket and held it down to remove the stitches from its belly. The fox hadn't been appreciative.

He closed the door and latched it, quietly moving away to tend to Scrap and Reader and Minx, the shy screech owl. Rocky the raccoon had been set free but was sure to be back for a visit. After finishing, Noah walked toward the fox's cage, which was at the edge of the woods, away from the other animals. Sunlight hung softly in the air, slowly rolling back as deep shadows from the woods crept across the grass. The blades trembled with whispers.

That was when he looked up and saw Claire coming toward him across the sweet green field, wearing something pink and filmy that skimmed her curves. He focused on her eyes, her smile, the proud tilt of her chin, long before he noticed the earrings, swinging with each stride. His heart lifted. Then he saw her feet—clad in sturdy hiking boots. His laugh rose even higher.

"There she is," he told the fox. "There's my girl."

Claws scrabbled against wood and straw as the fox withdrew.

Noah went forward into the amber sunlight.

He swooped Claire into his arms and swung her around. Laughter and tears glittered in her eyes; they danced blue like waves on the lake. She spoke, but he didn't hear. He knew only that having her there in his arms was enough. Letting her slide down his front, he cupped her face in his hands—brushing her cheeks, catching the earrings—and kissed her.

She leaned against him. "Oh, Noah."

He stroked inside her mouth, sucked at her soft lips, her warm tongue. Every inch of her was luscious.

She rubbed against him. "Oh, Noah…"

"You're wearing the earrings." He flicked one of them with his fingertip.

"They're beautiful."

"You're beautiful."

"You make me believe that."

"Has nothing to do with me."

She slid a fingertip over his nose. "Has *everything* to do with you." Her gaze dropped to his mouth as she traced it with her finger. Soon her tongue followed, and then they were kissing again.

When it got to be too much, he threw his head back, exalting. He felt as solid and strong as an oak planted deep in the earth, opening to the sky. Claire was soft and smooth, liquid to his solid. Wild honeycomb, filling the hollow inside.

"Why did you leave Bay House?" she asked, rolling her head against his chest. "Emmie told me you were staying for dinner."

He buried his nose in her hair. Breathed her in. "Had to take care of the animals."

She drew a deep breath matched to his. "Take care…"

"Take care?"

Her lips found his ear. The whisper tickled. "Take care of me."

"I plan to. Can you wait five minutes?"

"Maybe. Why?"

"We're releasing the fox."

"Oh." Her head bobbed in surprise. "Did you say *we?*"

"I think that would be fine."

They walked, arms entwined, into the woods. The fox's cage was on a platform, so Noah covered it with a blanket and carefully moved it to the ground. He pushed the blanket up on one side, revealing the door. "Care to do the honors?"

Claire's eyes were round beneath her ruffled bangs. She nodded and stepped beside him, then bent low over the cage, her dress sweeping the pine needles. Her hand trembled as she undid the latch. She hesitated, glancing at him questioningly.

"It's all right. He won't leap out. Nudge the door

wider, then we'll move a ways back to give him room.''

The hinges squeaked as she pushed the door open. A flurry of movement in the shadowed cage made her leap away. Noah took her hand, drawing her farther back, almost behind a tree.

They waited, watching the open cage. Yellow eyes shone from inside.

''Nothing's happening,'' Claire whispered. She gripped Noah's hand tight enough to impede blood flow.

''He's scared. Give him time.''

''Is he healed?''

''Well enough.''

''Maybe it's too soon....''

''No. Shh. He's poking his nose out.''

The fox's muzzle appeared around the side of the cage, sniffing the air. Dainty feet, trimmed in white, stepped onto the dirt. The red fur gleamed.

''He's a beauty.''

''Watch. There he goes.''

The skinny fox slunk out of the cage, paused for one second, then sped silently away, slipping beneath the ferns without disturbing a stem or frond.

''So fast,'' Claire said, awed.

''Wait. Look there.'' Noah pointed.

One stray sunbeam had reached between the tall pines to illuminate a patch of bare ground. The fox paused there for a moment, its thick coat burnished by the dusty light. Its head came up, the neck telescoping, showing off an elegant ruff. The triangular ears pointed, flickered. Then the long bushy tail gave a wide swipe of the air, and suddenly the fox was gone in a blink of an eye, almost as if it had disappeared.

"Off to set the night on fire," Noah said.

Claire sighed. "You never told me. What was the fox's name?"

A pause. "Rory." Noah smiled. "For the aurora borealis."

"Oh, how perfect." Claire's gaze lifted, first to his, then up and up, past the tree trunks, the heavy branches laden with cones, past the spider-thin branches, the new green tips—all the way to the indigo sky.

Her eyes were filled with wonder. "I love you, Noah Saari."

"How ARE WE going to do this?"

Noah's brows arched. "Like riding a bicycle, remember?"

"Not that." She plucked her lace collar. "This."

"It would be my pleasure."

"I—" She shook her head. "I don't know. I should be feeling like we're all God's creatures and nudity is a beautiful and natural state of being, et cetera, but...I can't help it. I still feel awkward and shy."

Noah considered, his gaze touching her face with both softness and warmth. How did he do that? She could feel his eyes like a caress. And it was always so good.

"If you could see yourself through my eyes..." His voice was hushed, prayerful.

"Sometimes I think I do."

"We could race," he said unexpectedly. The rustic log bed frame squeaked as he shifted a few inches closer. They were kneeling face-to-face on his bed in the loft within touching distance, though they weren't touching. Except by glance.

"That way it would be over before you got self-conscious." He smiled, turning whimsical again. "And I'd see you naked all the sooner."

Her mouth opened. She wheezed with a silent laugh, her hands pressed to her cheeks. "Noah!"

"Ready, set, go!"

He started by ripping at his laces and prying his boots off. A sock went flying over the balcony railing. He tore at the buttons of his shirt. "I'm winning."

After the moment of shock, Claire threw caution— and her modesty—to the wind. If there was ever a man she felt safe about being naked with, it was Noah. He'd never once made her feel she should be spending more time at the gym, working on her glutes. That didn't mean she wasn't nervous, but...

She toed off her boots, then pulled off her socks. Whipped the dress overhead. The slip went next.

Noah's chest was bare. He was sliding down his jeans.

Distracted by rippling muscle, she thumbed open the clasp on her bra and slipped out of it without thinking. She'd gone bare-legged, so all that remained was a pair of rosebud-dotted bikini underpants.

Noah—well, he was finished and kneeling before her. He was naked. One hundred percent pure, naked, flagrantly aroused male.

She froze with her thumbs hooked in her elastic waistband. Somewhere far away she could hear her heartbeat.

"I win," he said.

She licked her lips. Her voice came from the end of a long tunnel. "I guess so."

"You know what what I win?" His eyes, that tangible, stroking, petting gaze, lowered slowly over her blushing body. Her breasts felt heavy and warm. The nipples lifted, tightened, tingled. Her belly jumped. The warmth sank lower, thick and sweet, swelling...

"This is what I win." He put his hands over hers and gently lowered her underpants. His hands slid around her hips to her bottom, baring it and pulling her toward him at the same time. She felt the heat of his body and the cool air behind and then his hands, spreading, squeezing, fingers sliding everywhere in exploration, across her breasts, making her head swirl then tilt back and swing around, his hard shaft bumping against her belly. All of it was good, so very, very good...

Their mouths connected. Their bodies merged, lowering to the bed in a tangle of limbs. Intense, electric heat sang between them. The fears were blasted out of her head by the strength of that heat.

"I love you, Noah."

"I love you, Claire."

His fingers and then his lips were on her breasts. She squirmed, rolling her shoulders at the pleasure. His arms caged her as he moved over her, keeping most of his weight on his elbows, but she rose to meet him, wanting the bulk and heat of him, the muscle, gloriously hard. So male.

She found herself reacting with daring abandon. Pressing her face against his hairy chest, flicking his nipples with her tongue and teeth. Reaching for him, not shy, marveling at the impressive length and girth of his erection and how her body opened, undulating, asking him to fill her.

Noah tried to go slow, to cherish her, but she wouldn't have it. Not this time. "I want you now," she said, and after a long moment of staring into her eyes, he nodded.

He took a moment to roll on a condom, then moved down, pressing her thighs apart, trailing kisses over them, his hands running across the curve of belly, traveling lower, until his touch was scorchingly intimate. She sucked in a breath, riveted. He stroked her with a finger, with his tongue—oh, heaven, his *tongue*.

"Noah. Please…"

He reared up like a beast, wild mane and broad shoulders, the massive, muscled body, beautiful in his raw need. A little scary, even. Out of an instinct to protect herself, she slid an inch or two higher, the pillows bunching behind her.

His eyes were dark, almost black, and intent on only her as he moved heavily between her thighs again, a millimeter from driving himself inside her. "You're afraid? Say so and I'll stop."

That was a lie. He couldn't stop any more than she wanted him to. Nice of him to think so, but…

She tossed her head. "You stop and I'll never forgive you."

That was all the green light he needed. She let out a cry—an animal cry—as he entered her in one swift thrust filled with power and aggression and fierce, burning love. It was a claiming, a mating, and they both knew it. They welcomed it. In that hot, ecstatic moment, they welcomed it without restraint.

"Yes! *Take me!*" she shouted, hardly believing she'd say such a thing. It was being here, in a cabin in the woods, completely alone and far from civilization. There was only freedom. Nature. *Noah.*

She met each thrust, each lunge. The bed rocked with their rhythm. A wonder it didn't break. She tried to bring her knees up, but her legs were like water, weak with tiny tremors that spread, incrementally at first, but then the pleasure was rushing through her and every muscle quaked, inside and out, spasming with a wondrous climax. She wrapped her arms around Noah's shoulders and clung, so overwhelmed that she was almost sobbing. He reassured her with his hands and his mouth and his voice, holding her, kissing her, saying her name as he buried himself deep and let go. Incredibly, another thrust, even deeper. Let go. A choked cry. *Let go.*

There was an instant of abrupt silence. Claire opened her eyes. Noah was propped on his arms, biceps bulging, still inside her where slick flesh fused with throbbing pulse. He looked into her eyes, speaking without a word, a moment of such clarity, such soul, that she would remember it forever.

She inhaled. Noah exhaled, hugely. He collapsed, pulling away to avoid crushing her, but dragging her with him so she was nestled at his side. His chest heaved. She stroked a palm over it, finding the thunder of his heartbeat.

His head was lying flat on the bed, but he lifted it and looked at her through slitted eyelids. "Did I take care of you?"

"Oh, yes." He had to ask?

His head dropped. One arm flopped off the bed. "Man."

"Man's the word, all right." She went up on an elbow and looked over his sprawled body. *Man* was definitely the word.

"Let me tuck you in." She reached for the blankets that had been unceremoniously wadded at the end of the bed. Even that small movement was enough for her to know she'd be sore in the morning. Well, it had been a strenuous performance. No wonder Noah was exhausted.

Whereas she was exhilarated. *Oh, woman!*

"Is it cold or is it just me?" she asked, smoothing the blankets over Noah. The cool air met her perspiration, making her shiver.

"Yeah, it's chilly." He stirred. "I banked the fire before I went to Bay House. I'll go down and add a few logs. In a minute." One eye cracked. "Cozy up to me and you'll stay warm."

"Mmm." She burrowed beneath the blankets. "*I'll* take care of the fire. In a minute. I can't believe you still need a fire in May.'' He must be hungry, too. They'd had no dinner.

His voice was lazy. ''Winter lasts six months up here.''

''And how long is summer?''

''July Fourth.''

She smiled. Kissed his chest. ''Think that's going to scare me off?''

''I sure hope not.''

The air grew heavily expectant, as thick a layer as the blankets. It might have been only Claire's imagination, but she didn't know how to respond, so she crawled from beneath the warm covers. Avoiding the ''That was great, but what does it mean?'' talk was key, but now came the *really* awkward part—climbing naked out of bed.

Aha. She snagged Noah's plaid flannel shirt and slipped into it. The wood floor was cold. She went looking for her socks but could only find one of hers and one of Noah's. She bent to pull them on, then popped up. ''I'm borro—''

Well, imagine that. Her fierce, marauding beast was sound asleep!

''THINK OF IT as an experience,'' Noah said.

''A nude experience.''

''You can keep your towel. But then it won't be authentic. In Finland, people of all ages share the sauna without a stitch on. It's no big deal.''

''Sort of different when we've just—'' Claire made a face. ''You know.''

"I know you're beautiful. You don't need the towel."

She laughed, rolling her eyes even though there was pleasure in her face. "Suck up."

His response was a wicked smile.

"Stop that," she said, dropping her towel and opening the door to the inner room of the sauna. "Agh!" She danced out, her arms clasped in front of her breasts. "It's like a blast furnace in there."

"That's the purpose. If you've got *sisu,* you can stand up to it." He took her by the elbow and led her into the steamy sauna, scooping up her towel along the way. "Sit on the lowest bench." There were three levels. He spread the towel for her and patted her spot. "For beginners."

He added a log to the firebox of the stove and ladled water over the rocks that had been baking for an hour. They sizzled, sending up a curtain of steam to shroud the small room in an incredible heat.

Noah discarded his towel and stretched out flat on the top bench, taking shallow breaths of the humid air. He saw Claire looking and winked. "The sauna isn't sexual. It's a tradition. Social, maybe even spiritual—"

"You forgot dehydrating."

"When you get too hot, step out for a few minutes to cool off."

Claire swiped a hand over her face. "How hot is too hot? I'm sweating like a pig."

"When black spots begin dancing before your eyes, it's time to get out."

"That's not what's dancing before *my* eyes," she

muttered, shooting a saucy glance at him. Her eyes were on a level with the top bench, but she turned away when he rose to an elbow. Steam hung between them like a veil, softening the edges of the cedar benches and paneling.

Claire sat upright, braced on her arms. She had draped the towel loosely around her hips, and it was dipping low enough in back to reveal the ivory swell of a world-class derriere. Her back was straight and strong, sheened with perspiration. She'd caught her hair in a clip or something, but strands had come loose and were glued to her neck in runnels of sweat. The pink tip of her left breast came into view when she sucked in a lungful of air.

"Shallow breaths," he said.

"I can't breathe at all."

"Wimp," he teased. "Go on and take a break. Sponge yourself off from the bucket of cold water."

She gathered her towel and hotfooted it to the door, stopping only to splash another ladle of water onto the hot stones. "There ya go," she called through the cloud of scorching steam.

"Two minutes," he said.

Surprisingly, she did come back. "You still here? I thought you might have melted by now."

"Only parboiled."

She took a seat on the second bench and within minutes was squeezing a wet washcloth over her face and neck. She checked over her shoulder. "Are you asleep?"

"Just watching you."

"Now, Noah, let's have none of that. You said so."

He flipped over. Ouch. "I might have been wrong."

"It's already hot enough," she sighed as he looped an arm around her and pulled her toward his lips. She was wearing the towel around her hips like a sarong. Her breasts gleamed, round and rosy. He cupped one. Licked at her soft mouth. "Too hot," she said, breathing against his cheek. He tilted her head, found her tongue—like warm velvet. The kiss was wet, salty, searing.

Their bare skin burned where they touched. "Now comes the beating," he said, lazily thumbing her nipple.

"The beating?"

"With the *vihta*," he said. "The birch switch. See the bundle of branches I put in the bowl of water? You use the *vihta* to beat your skin—it stimulates blood circulation."

Her eyes were slumberous. She smiled dreamily. "I don't think we're having a problem in that area. Besides, it sounds perverse. I'll pass."

"But you wanted the authentic experience. Don't tell me you won't try the lake, either."

That woke her up. "Oh, no, I never agreed to that! Not the lake."

He swung his legs off the bench. "I'll throw you over my shoulder if I have to."

"You wouldn't dare."

He laughed as he climbed to the floor and reached for her. Claire was batting at him, giggling, trying to keep him at bay. He picked her up and tossed her over his shoulder, then ran from the sauna, banging open one door after the other, his blood charging hot through his veins.

The night air was starkly cold in contrast. The lake glittered in the moonlight, a calm midnight blue. He plunged straight into it, splashing to his waist. Yikes!

"Noah!" Claire wailed.

He slapped her bare ass. She screeched and struggled. He swung her into his arms, and he was about to toss her into the water when he saw the serious alarm on her face. He grasped her to his chest instead and dipped them into the lake, turning in an arc, letting the cold silken water envelop their heated skin in shocking sensation.

Claire grabbed his shoulders. "Oh—oh—*oh!*"

"Breathe," he said.

"I can't. It's too—" She panted. "I'm numb."

He swooped her through the water. "This is nothing. You should try it in winter. My father has been known to chop a hole in the ice so he can take a dip."

She hooted. "Crazy!"

Noah staggered out of the lake with her still in his arms. Inside the sauna's anteroom, she let go and slithered down his body, as limp as a spaghetti noodle. He wrapped them both in a big towel and rubbed it vigorously over her glowing skin. "Don'tcha feel great?"

"My heart is pumping, that's for sure. Brr-rrr."

"Take a sauna a day and you'll live to be a hundred."

"But who'd want to?" She hugged him close, still shivering, her laugh ending in chattering teeth. "Thank you, thank you, Noah, sir. After this experience, I'll never look at a tame hotel sauna the same way again.''

He got quiet. Her words bothered him. How did you tell a modern career woman that you wanted her to give up her entire life so she could share yours? That you'd devote yourself to making sure that you were worth it? He'd have offered to meet her at least halfway if living in the city had been even a remote possibility for him. But it wasn't. And she'd never given a sign that she might stay.

The opposite, in fact. She'd said several times that she intended to go soon.

''Noah?'' Claire tilted her head to look into his eyes. He dabbed an edge of the towel on her glistening face. ''Something wrong?''

Wrong? Not really. The problem was that she was too damn *right*.

''Nope,'' he said, pushing away the thought that Lizabee had been right, too. A perfect match, everyone said. Too damn bad the match had started a flame that burned them all.

''Just thinking about that report you're making for your boss,'' he lied.

Claire clutched the towel around her, her hands fisted beneath her chin. ''I've decided that all I can do is tell the truth. I haven't worked the numbers yet, but from experience I can say it's unlikely I'll be recommending Bay House to Bel Vista. The location's too remote, too many repairs are needed, there aren't enough rooms to generate sufficient income…''

''That's good, isn't it? For the Whitakers?''

She sighed. "Not necessarily. They're in a vulnerable position. At least a purchase offer from Bel Vista would have given them another option—a lucrative one."

"You're worried about what Rob's planning? I saw you talking to him this morning."

"You did?"

"Yeah."

She blinked. Loosened her hold on the towel, letting it drape over her arms. The sway of her breasts drew his gaze. "And you didn't think we were, um, colluding?"

"'Course not. I trust you."

"You trust me?"

"I've said that."

Her eyes were as soft and pretty as the petals of a pansy. "You're an amazing man, Noah Saari."

He grinned, setting his hands on her hips. "I'd have to be, wouldn't I, to keep you happy?" There was only a minor twinge inside him at the irony of the words. Whatever had gone wrong between him and Lizabee had nothing to do with Claire. Nothing.

"C'mere." He sat abruptly on the wood bench where their clothes were piled. His legs were rubbery. Delayed reaction from the shock of going from the hot sauna to the icy lake.

She looked at his naked lap. He was semiaroused. Her brows rose into her spiked bangs. "Where? There?"

His palm coasted across her rounded stomach, fingertips tickling her rib cage. Her eyes darkened as he reached inside the towel. "I could get used to this kind of social event," she said, letting him coax her into his lap. She made a small humming sound, dragging the towel around both of them as her arms looped his shoulders.

"A society of two." She nuzzled into his neck, mindless of the scars that had caused so many rumors. Or maybe not. She pressed biting kisses onto his throat, the slope of his shoulder, following the path of smooth pink skin. He tensed, waiting for a comment that didn't come. The towel dropped. She caressed him with gentle fingers, pressing into muscle, kneading, her breath shortening as the heat increased, even though they'd left the outside door hanging wide open.

Her thighs spread, tightened. He lowered his face to her breasts. She whispered sweetly, her hips rocking. The air smelled of damp cedar and hot stones and female flesh. He guided himself into her, the first stroke of liquid heat sending his brain reeling. She lifted slightly, then slowly sank inch by inch.

"You..." she breathed, taking all of him. "And me..."

Noah shuddered.

Was that enough for her?

CHAPTER TWELVE

NOAH WAS mumbling in his sleep. Half-awake, Claire snugged close to his backside, reaching an arm around him. She petted his chest, soothing him, beginning to drift away when there was a scratching at her cheek.

"Mmph." She twisted her head free of the edge of the blanket.

Next came a pressure—*warm?*—then a delicate, raspy *pat-pat-pat.* Her brain was waking up. She frowned, batted at the annoyance and got a handful of...fur.

"Ee-yah!" She bolted upright, flinging the covers away and scrambling backward into the pillows.

Noah came instantly awake. "What?"

"There—there—look—" Claire pointed with a trembling finger. "Oh, God. There's an animal in the bed!" She hunched against the headboard, squeezing her eyes shut. "Get rid of it."

A lump was moving under the blankets she'd flung aside. Noah got out of bed and cautiously peeled back the covers.

A raccoon sat up and looked at them with bright black eyes.

"It's only Rocky," Noah said. "Now that the

splint's off, Rocky's back to her old tricks.'' The raccoon agreed, wiggling its nose at them before waddling toward Claire.

She vaulted from the bed. "It woke me up. It was touching my face!" She shuddered. "Oh, yick. Oh, yick. Oh—" she took a deep breath "—yick."

Noah lifted his head. "I smell smoke."

"I've got news for you." Claire was keeping an eye on the raccoon as it climbed the headboard like a tree trunk. "The cabin always smells like smoke."

Noah leaned over the bed to look out the small window in the peak of the loft. "Smoke. Dammit—the workshop's on fire." In a flash, he disappeared down the ladder, jumping the last rungs to land with a thump on the floor below.

Claire leaned over the railing, her mouth hanging open.

"Bring the blankets," he shouted as he opened the screen door and ran out, stark naked.

"Blankets, right." She dragged them off the bed, glancing out the window alongside the raccoon. Orange flames flickered through the tree branches. Her stomach dropped all the way to her bare toes. She pushed away the raw panic that bit into her usual levelheaded efficiency.

"Stay calm, Claire. Put on some clothes." Her dress wouldn't do. She whipped open a bureau drawer and grabbed the first thing at hand—a pair of waffle-weave long johns to wear under Noah's plaid shirt. She pulled his clothes on, then scooped his jeans off the floor, wadding them up with the blankets and sheets. She threw the bundle out of the loft and climbed down. The raccoon's sharp little face poked over the edge, watching with interest.

"Stay here, Rocky," Claire said, thinking with horror of Scrap and the possum and screech owl, trapped in cages next to the workshop. Noah would get them first thing.

She spun around the main room of the cabin, trying to think what to take. Buckets? She grabbed one from under the sink, then ripped another blanket off the couch and ran outdoors.

The sky was lightening with dawn, making it easier to see as she circled the cabin. The trees between it and the workshop were an eerie sight—witchy shapes illuminated from behind by the bright flames and wispy smoke. A dark figure ran through the haze just ahead of her. For an instant she thought it was Noah, but then the man stopped at the edge of the wood, and the light from the rising flames struck his sweating face.

Terry Lindstrom.

His features were contorted, his bloodshot eyes wild.

Claire skidded to a stop, cold with shock. "Noah?" she whispered, her voice a dry crackle. Fear reared inside her. Please, God. Had Noah run into Terry? What had Terry done?

She dropped the clump of blankets. A scream tore out of her throat. "Where's Noah? What did you do to Noah?"

"Claire!"

"Noah!" Her knees almost buckled at the sound of his voice.

He raced toward her on the path that led to the workshop, empty tin buckets clanging in his hands. "I'm here. Take the blankets to the lake and soak them. We can—"

"*Noah.*" She gripped his arm. "Did you see…"

He swung around in time to catch sight of Terry, who was running across the open field away from the cabin.

Noah barely spared his enemy a glance. "Never mind that," he said. He pulled on his jeans. "We might still be able to put out the fire."

"The animals?"

"I got them out in time. Scrap took off through the woods, but he'll be back. Let's go."

The next minutes were a blur to Claire. Noah beat the flames with wet blankets while she filled buckets at the lake. He came to help, and together they hauled water, scooping and splashing and heaving until she was weak with exhaustion. They managed to dampen the flames on one side of the workshop, but the fire had circled to the other walls. The blaze shot to the roof, hungrily devouring the dry planks and shingles.

Noah stopped and swiped his arm across his grimy face. His shoulders slumped. "We might as well give up. The workshop's a total loss."

Tears welled in Claire's eyes. "No! All your work—"

A sharp explosion shook the night. Flames burst higher, reaching for them with a deadly roar. Thick gray smoke billowed from the blackened workshop. Noah dragged her away, both of them coughing violently. ''Stay back. Cans of varnish and paint—they're exploding.''

Claire tasted acrid smoke. Her throat was raw. She turned, sick at the sight, and pressed her face against Noah's shoulder.

He steadied her. ''We have to keep the fire from spreading or the trees will go up.'' One of them was already burning—a small pine, its green boughs recoiling into a tangle of charred black lace.

''How?''

''We'll wet everything down, including the cabin. I'll cut as much of a fire line as I can.'' He swore. ''My tools were all in the workshop.''

''Noah—my cell phone! If it works, I can call for help.''

''Try it,'' he said grimly, moving off again. She saw his feet were bloodied and black with soot, then looked down and saw her own were, too. Her palms were scraped red. For a moment, her head whirled, and she thought she might faint, but the sound of Noah splashing into the lake to fill the buckets broke through her shock and got her moving again.

She found shoes for both of them first, and wet down a bandanna for Noah to tie over his mouth. The cell phone crackled badly when she called 911, so she raced partway up the hill until the signal was clear enough to get a message through.

Next, she and Noah used a sheet of plastic to rig up a sluice from the hand pump in the kitchen and out the window, saving them from hauling the buckets so far. Claire pumped, keeping the water flowing. She lost track of time, but it seemed ages before she heard the gunning of engines approaching the cabin. Soon headlights were shining through the windows and sounds of activity surrounded the site of the fire.

Someone came inside to relieve her. Hands led her away from the pump; she looked up and saw Toivo's round face, smiling, nodding, speaking. She waved him away. "Go help Noah," she croaked, not recognizing her voice.

A surprising number of the volunteer firefighters had made it to the cabin on motorcycles and ATVs. Many of them were middle-aged men with bald heads and beer bellies, and they scrambled around in a flurry of disorganization. Claire had never seen a more beautiful sight.

Noah took charge, and soon the fire was contained. Eventually a burly older man with a badge arrived. Noah went over to talk with him, standing beside the charred black skeleton of the workshop as the firefighters worked to douse the remaining flames.

By then, the sky was suffused with morning light, the horizon over the forested ridge tinged faintly with dusty pink. The stinging smoke around the cabin had dissipated, drawn upward. Claire wandered into the yard and saw Noah—bare-chested, dressed only in jeans and unlaced boots, his body and face streaked with ash and blood and perspiration. The sight hit her with a wallop, and she folded up on the spot, too weak to stand any longer. One of the firefighters rushed to her, but she assured him she was fine. She only wanted to sit.

Noah looked at her. She shook her head. But he said a few words to the sheriff, clasped his hand and went to Claire, striding past the gaping men with his eyes ablaze.

She swallowed the lump in her throat as he leaned over her, drawing her to her feet with his hands on her elbows. "Are you all right?"

"Oh, Noah. Don't worry about me."

He smiled and wiped black grime from her cheek.

She touched her face—no, it was tears mixed with ash. "Go back—finish up—"

"Everything's under control. Let's go inside."

She sniffed. "I feel like we're in the last reel of a movie. Side by side, the brave frontier couple watches their homestead go up in flames." She twined her arm with his, sent him a shuddery smile. "I'm so sorry. All your beautiful work—lost."

"I don't care about that. We saved the cabin and most of the trees. We stopped what could have become a forest fire."

"*We* did? You did."

He smoothed hair from her face. Kissed her forehead. "And you did."

"Did you tell the sheriff about Terry?" she asked, muffling her voice from the interested onlookers. The firefighters—Bill, Toivo, Myron Mykkannen and a bunch of others she didn't know—were passing out the beers that had come from a cooler brought along by a latecomer. Forget fire trucks or proper hoses—they had beer. It was hilarious. If she hadn't been so strung out, she might even have laughed.

Noah avoided the question. He took her arm. "C'mon. Let's just go inside."

She went, but not without saying, "Noah, you have to tell him. If you don't, I will."

NOAH'S LIDS DROOPED. For an instant he was back in Montana, pushing through the intense heat and smoke of the wildfire, so thick it was like battling a living thing—a malevolent entity that wanted to consume him alive. He heard the voices, then lost them in the crackle, the roar. *Noah. Help...*

"Noah? Want to help me out here?"

"Shh. He's sleeping. I'll do it." Lizabee's hands moved across his legs. Warm and gentle. Competent.

He came awake with a start. Claire was trying to shift his feet to the coffee table without waking him. They were bandaged, mummified. One of the firefighters, a young guy named Brandon or Bradley, something like that, was packing up a toolbox kit of first aid supplies.

Claire rubbed a corner of a damp towel across Noah's chest, swabbing away the fire residue. "You must be cold. I'd give you a blanket, except all of ours—yours—are sopping wet or burned through."

"I'm fine." He was, especially when she turned her eyes on him and smiled reassuringly.

"That's it, then," Brandon or Bradley said. "A couple guys are staying to watch the embers, but—"

"They can go," Noah interrupted. "I'll take care of that."

"Sure, if you say. Ma'am?" Brandon-Bradley

looked at Claire. "If you need a ride into town, I can take you on the back of my—"

Claire's turn to interrupt. "No, thank you. I'm staying here."

Noah blinked. "Claire, why don't you go on? You'd probably like a shower and clean clothes." He blinked again, noticing for the first time that she wore his over-size flannel shirt—now ripped and stained with soot— and a pair of his long johns, bagging in the behind and the knees, the excess length wadded at her ankles. She'd pulled a pair of clean socks over her bandaged feet.

"I can wash in the sink. Or the lake," she said, lifting a brow. "And I'm sure I can find something to wear." She paused, cocking her head at him. "But if *you* want me to leave…"

Did he?

His mouth opened. "No," he said.

Fighting a fire with her had scared him to death— even a small fire like this one—but he didn't want her to go simply because of old worries and guilt that he damn well should be over by now. Lizabee had hurt him bad, but it was an old wound. No more important than the scars on his neck. If he wasn't over it, the past two years of his life had been a waste.

"Tell the guys thanks," he said wearily as Brandon-Bradley left the cabin. Soon the putter of ATVs died, and they were left alone in silence. The air stunk of sulfur and chemicals. When he tried to swallow, the scraped raw feeling in his throat was all too familiar.

"Noah." Claire ran a washcloth over his forehead. "You're spent. You should try to sleep."

He laid his head against the back of the couch.

"Put that stuff down and c'mere beside me." She spread the wet towels over the backs of the chairs, then got one of his big, heavy coats from the closet and joined him on the sofa. She draped the coat over him like a blanket. He lifted it, pulling her in close to him, tucking her beneath his arm where she fit so perfectly—a strong woman who knew how to be soft. "Did you get your cuts bandaged?"

Claire gave a murmuring sigh as she curled her legs on the couch. "Don't you remember? You made Bryce take care of me first."

Bryce. Who the hell had a name like that? "Sorry. Guess I was kind of out of it."

"Understandably."

They sat in silence for a long while until Noah started to doze off again. He snapped his head forward. Better not to get too comfortable. Every detail of those last days in Montana was simmering at the surface of his subconscious, waiting to sabotage him as soon as he drifted off. He didn't want Claire to see him like that. He sure as hell didn't want her to hear him calling Lizabee's name.

"Did you talk to the sheriff?" he asked, a surefire way to keep himself awake.

Claire nodded. "And I found out that you'd already told him about Terry. I thought you might not, out of some—" She searched for words while he waited, knowing she was right. "I don't know. Out of a mistaken guilt, I guess."

"Can't say I didn't consider it. But setting a fire, endangering lives—that's too serious to let go."

She breathed deep, then coughed. "Was it revenge?"

"I expect so. For his brother's death."

Her voice got bitter. "I hope they pick him up soon and put him in jail and *keep* him there."

He patted her arm. "Cut him some slack. Terry's still grieving."

"And you're not?" She was miffed for him, protective of him; that made him love her all the more.

"Not like that. Not any longer." He brushed away the recurring dreams like a bothersome housefly.

"Maybe if you talked to him?"

"I tried that when I first came back."

"And?"

"He wasn't having it."

"You could try again. He doesn't look very good to me—physically or mentally. He might need psychological help. I think he'd been drinking that day he shot at Scrap."

Noah was glad to have a reason to change the subject. "Where *is* Scrap? Have you seen him?"

"A couple of the firefighters spotted him in the woods, halfway up a tree, peeking at the activity. I can go and call for him—"

"No, don't bother. You're tired, too. Scrap's okay on his own. He never runs off too far. He'll show up when he sees that everyone's gone."

"What about the owl and the possum? You didn't have to let them go, did you?"

"No, I moved the cages into the woods, far out of the way. I'm sure the smell of smoke and fire got them into a panic, but they'll be fine, too." He produced a rusty chuckle. "As long as Scrap's not agitating them too much."

Claire was quiet again. He could tell she was thinking about the fire but didn't want to fret about it and get him stirred up. He squeezed her. "Thanks for being such a trooper."

"Ow," she said. "My shoulders are sore. I didn't know it was so strenuous, pumping water."

"Welcome to the U.P. Life's tough here."

"Life's tough everywhere."

He closed his eyes, slumping a little lower on his spine. "You seem to have it pretty good. Great job, fancy clothes…"

"Stress, anxiety, loneliness…"

He was cautious about the pinprick of possibility that flared in him at her quiet words. No sense getting his hopes up. "Is that so?"

"It's like they say. Be careful what you wish for." She put a hand on his ribs. "When I was growing up in Nebraska—and my hometown isn't all that different from Alouette except for being flat and brown instead of hilly and green—I used to dream about life in the city. I saw myself with a high-powered career, a spacious apartment that was always clean and quiet, a fab wardrobe. There'd be men who'd send me flowers and take me to expensive restaurants. I'd go to museums.

Glamorous parties. I'd travel." Her voice dropped an octave. "Most importantly, I'd be responsible for no one but myself."

"And you got it all."

"Yes. At a price." She tilted her head back, and he saw that her mouth was smiling but her eyes were sad. "Stress, anxiety, loneliness," she repeated.

"I'd just about resolved to change my life when Drake, my boss, sent me to Alouette. It was supposed to be a working vacation. I'd check into Bay House, give it a once-over, then loll around for a few days before returning to work rejuvenated." She chuckled. "Didn't quite turn out that way."

"Why not?" he asked. "You're still planning on going back, same as ever, aren't you?"

She sat up, turning to look at him. "Not same as ever, Noah." She frowned. "I've changed. Part of it's meeting you, but another part's—" Her eyes lightened as she went over the past few days. "Finding this cabin. Seeing the northern lights. Scrap. Cassia, Emmie, Toivo…Roxy, even. *Rob,* even." She stuck her chin out at Noah. "Do you think I ever want to become the type of person who'd make a deal with him? Drake the Snake would. And if I stay with Bel Vista, I might, too." She shivered, tucking her chin in again and cozying up to him. "Terrible thought."

Beneath the coat, he picked up her hand. "And what were you planning to do?"

"I hadn't gotten that far in my thinking."

"I'm regretting all the times I tried to scare you off. All the comments about how rough life is here."

"Are you?" He could hear the smile in her voice.

"In actuality, life's a bed of roses in the U.P. The sun never stops shining. The water is always warm. Fairies bring you breakfast in the morning. Elves shovel the snow."

"Too late, too late. Every morning at Bay House, Shari Shirley, the mystery maid, flings a newspaper at the bedroom door and curses my morning under her breath."

"Only because she's jealous."

"Oh? Of what?"

"You staying in the bridal suite and getting well and properly cursed. Cassia informed me that I've got till the end of the year to come through for you."

"Cassia has a big mouth."

Noah laughed softly. Claire clasped his hand beneath the coat, idly running her fingertips over his knuckles. He breathed deeply, trying to ease the tightness in his chest. Smoke inhalation, he told himself. But there were words in him waiting to come out. Still, he didn't—couldn't—wasn't sure—

Hell. He was downright afraid.

More scared of spilling his guts and baring his heart to another woman than he was of facing a raging wildfire.

Claire's voice came, deceptively soft, before he could find his. "You've told me about the fire, about Rick. Now tell me what happened with Lizabee."

He tilted his head back, squeezing his face into a knot. "No, Claire. Not now." *Not ever.*

"You shouldn't let it fester. You'll become like Terry."

Blood pounded at his temples. "It's ugly."

"People can be ugly. They can be wrong and mean. They can hurt you. And still you love them." She swallowed audibly. "Noah, I need to know if you still love Lizabee."

"God, no," he said, shocked she'd been worrying over that.

"Are you sure? The way you talked about her that first time..."

"Okay, maybe I still care about her. But I don't love her, not in a romantic way. How could I after—" He choked on the memory of learning that Lizabee had chosen another guy over him. Damn, why was Claire pushing this?

She held on to his hand. Tight. "She cheated on you, Noah. That's different than—oh, growing apart or fighting and breaking up. I'm assuming you found out about it right before the fire, which means you probably never got to resolve your feelings. Rick died. You couldn't be mad at him anymore."

"Yeah."

"And Lizabee must have been as torn up about Rick's death as you. So you couldn't confront her. You couldn't rage."

He sighed. "Yeah. So?"

"So...maybe you need to see Lizabee again. Do you know where she is?"

"I'm not sure. But I heard she stayed in fire fighting for a while, then quit. Supposedly she moved on to another state and started all over again. She was always good at separating her emotions from her job.''

"Cold-blooded," Claire murmured.

"No, she wasn't. She was—" He stopped, considered. He'd always admired Lizabee's toughness, but had it sprung from a lack of emotion? She'd been a good woman, friendly and kind enough, but she hadn't been giving or understanding, like Claire. Where Claire could stand up for herself and battle with the best of them, but still be soft in private, Lizabee had rarely showed her vulnerable side. Not even in bed. She used to preen when her crew members said she was "just like a man." It was a compliment to her.

"Claire?"

She moved her head to look into his face, her chin pressed firmly into his chest. "Yes?"

"What would you say if I said you'd fought that fire just like a man?"

She screwed up her face, puzzled. "I suppose… hmm. Guess it depends. If the man I was being compared with was you, I'd be flattered. But if it was a general comment, well, I guess I might say that I'd rather be praised for doing it just like a woman. *Praised,* because I certainly would take that as a compliment.''

He studied her hopeful eyes and plucky smile. Man, but she was something else!

He grinned at her. "That's what I thought you'd say.''

"But was it the right answer?"

In response, he leaned down and kissed her, not even

minding the slightly smoky taste of her mouth. She was tough and strong and soft and luscious. She was everything a man could want, wrapped up in one curvy, womanly package. He'd be a fool if he let some heavy unloaded baggage and a little unfinished business with Lizabee stand in his way.

CLAIRE GOT BACK to Bay House late that afternoon. She'd been ready to spend another night with Noah, but he'd insisted, obviously having figured that she was secretly dying for a hot shower and clean clothes in the proper size. Besides, he said he wanted to go into town himself to see the sheriff.

They had dozed off for a while, wrapped in each other's arms on the couch, then been wakened by Scrap, who was grunting with impatience and rattling the screen door. They'd gone out to look over the charred remains of the workshop in the light of day. That had been devastating to Noah, but he'd put a brave face on, swearing that the loss was minimal compared to what might have been. Maybe that was so. He knew about losses more vital than material possessions.

He'd been quiet on the trip into town. She wondered if it had been a mistake, urging him to make peace with the ghosts—or demons—from his past. Maybe she was only a temporary comfort to him. When he was whole again, she might be of less use.

"Don't do that to yourself," she muttered, entering the foyer of Bay House. "I yam what I yam. Noah likes that. Shoot, he even says he *loves* that."

As soon as Claire closed the door, Cassia's chair

zoomed into the hallway. "Claire! I've been waiting for you." Her wheelchair hummed at high speed, sailing over the carpet bumps. "Toivo told us all about it, but I wanted to get it straight from you. Is it true that Sheriff Bob arrested Terry for arson? Did you and Noah really fight the fire in the nude?"

Claire was stunned. "Whoa! Wait a minute! Who told you that?"

Cassia was all eyes beneath the fluff of red hair caught in a messy topknot. "Which part?"

"We had clothes." Claire was glad she'd left her dress in the car, though, and had worn another shirt of Noah's and a pair of cutoff sweatpants cinched in and knotted at her waist—even if she did look like a mess in them. "I wore a shirt and, um, leggings, and Noah had jeans on." She rolled her eyes at the thought of what wild rumors the volunteer firefighters would be spreading. "But what's this about Terry being arrested?"

"That came from Bill, so I guess it's more reliable. I thought you and Noah would have been told. The town is buzzing with the news."

Claire passed a hand over her face. "We're rather cut off at the cabin."

"You had your cell phone, didn't you? I heard it was you who called in the fire."

"That's right." Claire checked her purse. In all the hubbub, she'd forgotten about her phone. She wasn't even sure where it was at the moment. She couldn't remember tossing it aside, but she must have. She hoped one of the firefighters hadn't crushed it with a careless boot.

"How bad was it? Some people are saying that Noah's cabin was half-burned, but Toivo—"

The pocket doors of the front parlor rolled open, cutting off Cassia's curiosity. Emmie stood in the doorway, dressed as usual in her apron and colorful pants but looking different, for some reason. Toivo was hovering behind her, crumpled and sad. They were both staring at Claire.

She supposed they also had questions about the fire, but the vibe seemed wrong.

"Miss Levander," Emmie said, and then Claire *knew* it was wrong. "Would you care to join us? It seems we have something to discuss."

For a long moment, Claire was frozen.

Cassia, too. She stared at Emmie, blinking in consternation.

"Emmie?" Claire's voice squeaked. "Have I done something—" A crazy thought came to her. Suppose Emmie was insulted at her guest being caught in a compromising position at a bachelor's cabin in the woods? Maybe Claire had crossed the line of proper small-town B-and-B houseguest behavior?

"It's about the offer on Bay House," Toivo said.

Oh. "Well, I did run into Rob yesterday—" *Was it only yesterday?* "And we did talk for a brief while, but it wasn't—I didn't—"

"Miss Levander," Emmie said stiffly, her lips pinched. She nodded at the parlor. "In private, if you please."

Claire moved forward on wooden legs. "What happened?"

"Did you lose your self phone?" Toivo said. "'Cause this fella from Chicago called up Emmie when he couldn't get through to you proper—"

Emmie unpinched her mouth long enough to say, "Be quiet, you blithering baboon."

Claire stepped into the parlor. Her last sight of Cassia was the young woman watching, stupefied, as the doors rolled shut between them.

CHAPTER THIRTEEN

THE SHERIFF'S office was in the bottom level of the brick courthouse building. On the floors above, inlaid marble tile, marquetry paneling, brass sconces and crystal chandeliers spoke of a more elegant era when municipal buildings had been paid for by wealthy citizens instead of additional taxes. The fancy details had become slightly shabby over the years, but the grandeur remained.

The sheriff's department, however, was a gloomy den. Almost no natural light penetrated the narrow horizontal windows. Though clean, the walls and floor were a symphony of industrial colors—gray, putty, taupe. The color scheme didn't do good things to Sheriff Bob's complexion.

Sheriff Bob couldn't have cared less. In his campaign posters, he was always posed against a field of the old red, white and blue. And his slogan was always the same—a vote for Sheriff Bob is a vote for American values.

Noah wasn't complaining. The slogan had worked for as long as he could remember—thirty years, at least. Sheriff Bob was an Alouette institution, along with pasty suppers at the Lutheran church, Finn versus

Swede snowball battles and neighborly espionage over top secret blueberry patches and fishing holes.

A youth with droopy pants, jingling chains and multiple tattoos and piercings was led through the corridor, scuffling at air and swearing a blue streak at the deputy accompanying him. Some things did change, even in Alouette.

Noah turned to the receptionist, a stocky young woman with her own tattoo—a dolphin peeping out of her blouse over her left breast. His gaze shot to her face. She smirked. "Can I help ya?"

"Sheriff's expecting me. Noah Saari."

"For Pete's sake…" Her mouth hung open, displaying two fillings and a wad of purple chewing gum. Noah blinked as her eyes crawled over his face; like the rest of them, she seemed disappointed that he wasn't hideously disfigured.

"Noah," Sheriff Bob said, coming out of his office, "glad you could make it into town. You check the burn site before you left? We don't want that fire flaring up again. The crew is pooped! If you have a problem, you come to Sheriff Bob—I'll take care of you. We treat our hometown heroes right, don't we, Kitty? You remember my daughter, Kitty, hey, Noah? Sure you do. She was a couple of years behind you in school—"

"Gad, Dad. 'Smore like ten."

Sheriff Bob chuckled. "Time sure flies, doesn't it?" Like the rest of his questions, no answer was required. The portly sheriff came around the counter, swaggering in his holster and equipment belt. He jingled a key ring. "We picked up Terry this morning. Follow me. I'll tell you, old man Lindstrom was on the horn with me something fierce all afternoon about keeping his son in jail, but I told him Sheriff Bob's brand of justice is justice for all, and just 'cause he has deep pockets don't mean the system's going to move any faster. You know what I'm saying? We got a hearing scheduled for tomorrow, so it's a good thing you made it into town before then. I'm not guaranteeing that Terry's gonna talk to you any more than he's talked to me, a course—''

The sheriff went on, but Noah had tuned him out. They'd walked past various offices and into the lockup area. Several jail cells were illuminated by too-bright fluorescent lights, but they still seemed dismal and gray. The kid with the tattoos sat dully in one cell. Terry sat in another.

He glanced up. His hangdog look turned to belligerence when he saw Noah. ''Fine thing.'' He spat the words. ''That murdering bastard's running around free while I'm locked up. You call that justice, Sheriff Bob?''

The words were the same as always, but Terry's demeanor was sullen now rather than vicious. Noah began to hope that the extreme act of setting the fire had finally broken the back of his old friend's anger.

''Don't go off now, Terry. You'll be out soon enough.'' Sheriff Bob unlocked the cell. ''Providing you don't lose your head and add on a few other charges like assault and battery. You think of your momma, boy, and how she cherishes the family reputation.''

Terry muttered unintelligibly.

"Give us a yell when you want to come out," Sheriff Bob told Noah, ushering him inside the cell.

Terry flinched. "I never said you could let him in here." He stood, puffing himself up, but Sheriff Bob pressed a hand to Terry's shoulder until he sat down.

"You want to talk to Noah, Terry. Could be that if you get things settled between you, the arson charges will be knocked down to a misdemeanor." Sheriff Bob sighed and swung out of the cell, his gut leading the way. "Lord knows that would save me a whole lot of grief from your old man." Keys jingling, leather shoes squeaking, he walked away through the harshly lighted corridor.

Terry and Noah stared at each other.

"You don't look good," Noah blurted to break the tension.

Terry layered on the sarcasm. "You don't say? Gee, thanks, Mr. GQ."

"Yeah." Noah ducked to sit on the lower level of the bunk bed opposite Terry's. On the wall between them was a stainless steel toilet and sink unit. The smell was pungent, undisguised by the sharp tang of cleaning chemicals.

"Long way from Bayside Road," Noah commented.

"Go ahead and throw it in my face."

"I don't need to, Terry. You're a grown man, you can see for yourself what a stupid thing you've done."

Terry sneered an epithet, but the attitude was clearly wearing on him. It took a lot of fuel to keep up an anger so hot. Sitting alone in a depressing jail cell wasn't providing it.

Terry dragged his hands through his hair. It was shaggy, something the old Terry wouldn't have allowed. He'd once mocked Noah's rugged outdoorsy appearance. Women wanted a man who looked prosperous and presentable, he'd claimed. Both Rick and Terry had been well-groomed and proud of it, but then they had the money to back it up.

Terry was changed. His previously athletic build had softened, his muscles covered by a spongy layer of fat. His clothes were wrinkled and dirty, his posture slumped, but it was his face that told the tale. Sallow skin, reddened cheeks, bloodshot eyes, deep grooves around the mouth. A tortured man who seemed to have been using alcohol and anger to assuage his grief.

Terry turned his bleary eyes on Noah. "Some of us get caught, and some of us don't."

Noah leaned his elbows on his knees, determined to reach the Terry he'd once known. "We used to be friends. Why would you choose to believe the worst of a friend?"

Terry wouldn't meet his eyes. "I warned you, didn't I? I told you not to get Rick involved in your risky stunts."

"Rick made his own decisions."

"He was an impressionable kid!"

Only four years younger, Noah thought. Not a brash teenager who believed himself immortal. "I never encouraged him."

"No, you just showed up, bragging about your exploits, making it sound like a little reckless summer fun…''

Noah shook his head. No use denying that, even though it was more Rick's interpretation of the facts than his own.

Right from the start, Rick had brushed off the serious danger and hard work; he'd focused only on the supposed glamour and rewards. Noah had figured that once Rick had hired onto a ground crew—where the rookies all had to start—and worked a fire or two in the trenches with no more glamorous tools than a shovel and a Pulaski, he'd cotton to reality fast enough.

Trouble was, by that time he'd been interested in Lizabee, even though Noah hadn't known it yet. A besotted man would go through hellacious agonies to impress the object of his affections. So Rick had hung on. Through blisters and burns and pulled muscles, he'd hung on.

Noah had to give him that, even if it had been to impress *his* girlfriend.

He said, ''Rick came to Montana of his own free will,'' not sure if he was telling Terry or himself. The truth was that he did feel responsible. Not for suggesting Rick should come—he'd been against that from the start. But he had been responsible in the way an older brother looks out for his bratty tag-along kid brother…

Suddenly, Noah understood why Terry blamed him. *Because Terry blamed himself even more.*

''It wasn't my fault,'' Noah said, then paused. He took a deep breath. ''And it wasn't yours, either.''

Terry looked at his old friend at last, his face slowly

crumbling. "Who the hell said it was?" Tears streaked down his cheeks, and he swore, dashing almost violently at them. "It was you—you were with him. You were at the fire. You knew Rick wasn't an outdoorsman. You should have been there with him. You should have. You—you…" Terry doubled over.

Noah stayed where he was, gripping the sharp metal edge of the bunk until his hands cramped. Terry wouldn't accept his sympathy…not yet.

"Rick was part of a ground crew," he said, "so I couldn't be with him. I wish I had been, Terry. Every day, I wish I'd been there. By the time the smoke jumpers were called in, there'd been a wind shear in the valley where Liza—where Rick's squad was working. They were trapped by a firestorm. It was a miracle that any of them made it out alive."

"I heard you got your girlfriend out. Why her and not Rick?"

"It wasn't my choice. Lizabee reached me first. But, you know, Rick wasn't the only one who died. There were others, too. One was a good friend, name of Martin Lewiston. I'd been a pounder with him, my first summer working fires. So it wasn't just Rick. I would have given my life if it meant saving any of them. But I didn't have that option."

"You should have saved Rick. I don't give a damn if you wanted to kill him for screwing—"

"That never entered my mind, Terry."

"You should have saved Rick."

Noah opened his hands; they were as stiff as an old man's. "Yeah."

"*I* should have—" Terry choked on the words. He put his head in his hands, shoulders heaving. "I was supposed to always look out for him. I shouldn't have let him go."

Noah's heart was heavy. "Rick did what he wanted. Always."

"He was making time with your girl. Was that why you left him?"

"I'd have gotten him out if I could have, Terry. I swear to you."

A weighty silence descended on them. Noah couldn't say if Terry believed him when there'd always be a question—an infinitesimal doubt—in his conscience. He *had* risked his life trying to go back for Rick and the others. A tree had fallen right in front of him—one of its burning branches had whipped across the side of his head and seared into his flesh. Still, even that might not have stopped him if there'd been any chance at all. But by then the smoke had been so thick he couldn't see. He'd turned to leave, hoping like hell there was still time to outrace the fire. And that's when he'd heard it from the valley below. One voice. Calling his name. One voice filled with an unbearable pain.

He'd made it to the top of the ridge, the fire licking at his heels. Other men hadn't, one of them Martin, a family man, and one of them Rick, the greenest of pounders, the bratty kid who'd been almost like his own little brother.

When Lizabee had come to his hospital room, shaken, blistered and humbled like he'd never seen her, he'd turned away. Told her to leave. And that had been the last time he'd spoken to her. When he'd been released two days later, she'd already packed up and moved on.

Son of a bitch. Claire was right.

He had to confront Lizabee.

Terry shifted on the bunk. Bedsprings creaked. He glanced at Noah, regret in his eyes. "I never meant to burn down your workshop. I, uh, didn't know about the animals being so close by, either. I only wanted to—" he shrugged "—I don't know. To put a scare into you. I saw you with that woman, and I knew I couldn't stand aside and watch you live a happy life, getting married and having kids..." He grimaced. "That's never going to happen for Rick. Dwelling on that for the past few days made me a little nuts."

It wasn't exactly an apology, but it would do.

Noah stood, wondering if Terry would shake his hand. No, too soon for that. "Are you making excuses so I'll drop the charges?"

Terry rose slowly. Without anger to mask his grief, he looked like a broken man. "I'm owning up because I've hit rock bottom," he said through his teeth. "I can't go on like this."

Noah nodded. "You need to rebuild your life, in *honor* of Rick. Starting with restitution."

"Name your price." The capitulation came too quickly. Cash was one thing the Lindstrom brothers had always been free with.

"I don't want money," Noah said.

Terry looked at him warily. "Then what?"

"Have you ever hand-fed rodents to a screech owl?"

WHEN NOAH ARRIVED at Bay House two days later, he was confronted with chaos. Although he'd phoned Claire from the jail to tell her about his plans, she'd seemed distracted and distant. Some part of him had worried, all the way to California and back, that she'd decided to pack up and move on. Even so, he'd gone to the cabin first thing to check on the animals. Terry had been there, looking much improved. Scrap was in fine health, along with the owl and the recovering possum. Rocky was hanging around, living the good life of a hero. The wreckage of the workshop had been cleared into one pile. Terry had begun to nail together a few boards from the fresh pile of lumber he'd had delivered, making a frame for a new structure. Not a professional job, but it was the effort that counted.

They'd greeted each other with reserve, but a tentative path to renewed friendship had been laid. Even Mr. and Mrs. Lindstrom—who'd harbored resentment of Noah—had been pacified when he'd suggested Terry's charges be dropped in return for physical, hands-on restitution.

The front door of Bay House stood wide open. Noah paused at the threshold for a minute or two, studying the activity inside. Music was blaring. Roxy was on the rickety ladder again, shaking the entire contraption with her vigorous motions as she worked at scraping off shreds of clinging wallpaper. Cassia was zipping through the hallway, her lap hidden by a pot of greenery being transported out of the diminishing jungle.

Steam hung in the air. Noah's eyes followed the hissing sound to Toivo, who was dripping with sweat as he wielded a wallpaper steamer against the pattern of dancing nymphs. Emmie had long ago given up on keeping her brother actively employed, so Toivo's toil must be Claire's doing.

She came out of the open dining room on the right, which was in equal disarray. "Ew—dusty," she said, screwing her face up at the bundle of decades-old drapes overflowing her arms. "Will Emmie hate me if I throw these straight into the trash?" She glanced over, saw Noah and sneezed.

"Gezundheit," he said.

"Maybe we can wash the drapes, dye them and make slipcovers or pillows or something out of them," Cassia said, coming down the hallway with an empty lap. "That's what they do on *Trading Spaces,* and their budget's nearly as miserly as ours...." Her voice trailed off when she spotted Noah.

"Noah," Claire said, and sneezed again.

"Where have you been?" Cassia said.

"We could have used a pair of manly arms around here," Roxy called from her perch atop the ladder.

"Heyah, what about me?" said Toivo. He looked happy enough, though, having a good excuse to put down the steamer.

"Where have you *been?*" Cassia demanded, rolling forward onto his toe. She bumped his leg with her foot. "How could you just disappear like that? Don't you know the hero's supposed to stick around for the happy ending?"

"Cassia," warned Claire. She was red in the face,

from either the sneezes or pleasure at his return. He hoped the latter. "It's barely been two days."

"Didn't Claire tell you?" he said.

Cassia frowned. "Claire? Were you holding out on me?"

"I didn't know, for sure," she said faintly, waving a hand beneath the pile of grimy drapes.

I do, Noah thought, elated by the sight of her. *I know exactly how happy this ending will be.*

CLAIRE DUMPED the heavy curtains on the floor. Without them, the dining room was ten times lighter. *Sort of like my heart,* she thought, not caring that she was being all fluttery and girlish about this. Happiness was percolating in her veins.

Noah had come back to her!

"Let's go into the parlor," she said, taking Noah's arm and sending a quick warning glance at Cassia as they passed. "For *privacy.*"

As if privacy was ever available in Bay House.

"What's going on here?" Noah asked.

Cassia, clearly thrilled to her toes, flipped a two-thumbs-up signal as Claire pulled the doors shut.

"You've missed a lot. Decisions have been made."

Noah swooped her up for a big hug. She gave in gladly, turning the thrill of having him back into a squeeze so tight she didn't want to let go.

"I was worried that you'd leave while I was gone," he said, kissing her.

She closed her eyes, savoring the caress of his hungry mouth, his roving hands. "I was almost *asked* to leave. But even if I had, I wouldn't have gone far."

He pulled back. "Asked to leave?"

She nodded, licking the taste of him off her lips.

"That doesn't sound like either of the Whitakers."

"Emmie can be formidable when she's crossed."

"You crossed her? I'm confused."

"The day of the fire," Claire said. "When you went to the jail and saw Terry and I came back here. It turned out that my boss had called, looking for me. Apparently I lost my cell phone at your cabin."

She moved to the settee, dusting off the overalls Roxy had loaned her. "Drake talked to Emmie, demanding to know what was going on. He said enough to get her curious, and once he understood that she was the owner of Bay House, he spilled all the beans. He didn't actually extend an offer, but he made a veiled threat about how if Bel Vista decided it wanted Bay House, they could buy out anyone who stood in their way." She snorted. "Drake's a snake."

"So Emmie believed you were up to no good."

"Well, she wasn't sure, but she had questions."

Noah sat. His brow furrowed. "How does that explain the—" He gestured toward the entry.

Claire's chin lifted. "I wrote two reports." Her pulse was racing, but no matter how Noah reacted, she knew she'd made the right decision. "The first one I sent to Bel Vista, along with a letter of resignation. That report said Bay House would never be sufficiently profitable for them to consider purchasing. And it was true." She chuckled. "That was the best part. I didn't even have to lie. Although I would have, if it meant saving Bay House for the Whitakers.''

"Good for—'' Noah stopped. "Did you say 'a letter of resignation'?''

She had to bite her lip. "I did.''

Noah's eyes widened. "What does that mean?''

"It meant that I was unemployed.'' She made a face. "But also…free.''

"Wait a minute. You said *was*.''

"Uh-huh. Which brings us to the other report. That one was for the Whitakers' bank. I calculated repair budgets, estimated potential profits, drew up a business plan that would make those profits a lot more likely, and most important of all, convinced Emmie that she should be charging for all the freebie meals she provides. Did you know she sends guests off for the day with free picnic hampers? Invites them all to dinner on the house? Hospitality is wonderful, but there comes a time when business must take precedence.''

Noah looked suitably impressed. "And you were able to convince the bank to give the Whitakers a loan,'' he guessed.

"That's right. But there was one unexpected provision.''

"Yeah?''

Claire grinned. "The loan officer suggested that Bay House should have a proper manager. I was worried that Emmie wouldn't want to give up control, but she's savvier than I thought. She knows she has enough on her plate as it is. She's a kitchen artiste, not a dollars-and-cents kind of person. So we made a decision. I had to rework the budget to pay myself a small salary, but—''

''Pay yourself,'' Noah said, smiling.

She nodded. ''It may not be a permanent position, but for at least the next year, I'll be running Bay House.''

''That's…great.''

Suddenly she felt a bit shy, even though her face was nearly split in half by her increasing grin. ''Do you really think so?''

''Twelve months,'' he said, rubbing his jaw. ''Is that long enough for me to convince you to stay permanently?''

''Possibly. Although you only have until the end of the year if Valentina's prophecy is true.''

Noah smiled. ''We wouldn't want to break tradition.''

''No, we wouldn't.'' Claire sobered. ''Providing…''

''Don't give Lizabee another thought,'' he said, guessing what she feared. ''I found her in a little town in Northern California, working as an emergency dispatcher. She admitted that she'd lost her taste for fire fighting after Rick's death, but I think she's got her eye on the local station house. Wouldn't surprise me if she didn't apply for a job there before too long.''

Claire rubbed her hands over her thighs, scrubbing the filth off. Although it wasn't what she *really* wanted to know, she asked, in a quick, low monotone, ''How was Lizabee handling Rick's death?''

Noah reflected. ''Truthfully, better than either me or Terry. But then, she'd only known Rick for a short time. She said she'd been dazzled by his looks and charm, and that she was sorry...."

"Does that make a difference to you? Did you forgive her?" Claire's throat ached more than it had after the fire.

"We didn't break into tears and embrace to the strains of the 'Hallelujah Chorus,' if that's what you're asking. But I was glad to see her doing so well. She has a dog named Fred and a boyfriend named Blackie. I'm not sure which one she prefers." He chuckled, shaking his head with what seemed like no more than fond remembrance. "I was nervous, meeting her. Didn't know what to expect—love, hate, righteous anger, more blame and guilt. But it wasn't that way at all. What it was, mostly, was a relief. For both of us, I think."

Claire stayed cautious, even with euphoria leapfrogging around inside her. "Did you talk about her relationship with Rick?"

"A little."

"Did she explain?" Never would Claire understand how a woman could have deliberately chosen to cast Noah aside. But she'd forever be grateful for Lizabee's idiocy. He was somebody's hero, all right. *He was hers.*

He shrugged. "Lizabee and I had a good thing for a while, but in hindsight I've begun to see that it was never going to last forever. For all her toughness, she's not strong enough inside, where it really counts."

Claire closed her eyes and reached for him, knowing he'd be there. Always.

He took her into his embrace, murmuring all the sweet nothings she'd been hoping to hear, telling her, even if it wasn't in so many words, that she was his and he was hers and that what they had was a thousand times better than any love he'd ever known.

"I have to know one thing, Claire." Noah arms were around her waist, and she had her hands on his chest. "I thought your career in the city was so important to you. A dream come true, you said, even if it wasn't perfect, after all."

She looked into his eyes and saw her future. "Dreams change," she whispered.

He went very still. "And nightmares end."

She touched his cheek with questioning fingertips.

He explained with an air of relief. "I fell asleep on the red-eye from California to Detroit, and I had a dream. It started like all the rest—me jumping out of a plane. Dropping toward a fire, lost in the smoke…"

"Oh, Noah."

She kissed him, and he moaned and gripped her tighter, nuzzling his face into her hair. "But it was different this time. I jumped, but there was no smoke. There was only blue sky, filled with the crepe paper streamers we drop to measure wind drift. A rainbow of them, falling through the clouds. And then there were the acres of green trees below me. Green all around. No fire, no smoke, no voices but yours."

He kissed her forehead, her temple, her cheek, every touch blessed with love. His low timbre, the inherent promise, made her shiver inside. "Your voice, Claire, calling me home to our cabin in the woods…"

IN THE HALL, Emmie pressed her ear to the parlor doors. "I can't imagine what's keeping them so long."

Cassia looked at Roxy, barely managing to restrain her giggle. "*I* can imagine." She fanned her face. "Boy, can I!"

Roxy plunged her hands into the pockets of her overalls. "Well, this cuts it. Valentina strikes again."

Emmie tutted. "You keep quiet about that, Roxy Whitaker—and you too, Cassia Keegan! Or we'll never hear the end of it."

"Sometimes dentistry needs a helping hand." Toivo had his eye to the crack between the doors. The three women looked at each other in confusion until Roxy mouthed, *Destiny*.

Toivo went on. "You're all forgetting that I'm the one who checked Miss Lavender into the bridal suite."

"I knew that wasn't a mistake," Cassia said with glee.

"Toivo, you're incorrigible," Emmie scolded. "I ought to—"

Toivo flapped his hands. "Shh, shh. They're coming."

They all moved back, jittering and jostling. There was no use in pretending they hadn't been waiting, especially when, as the doors rolled open, they came forward again, every face shining with expectancy and excitement. Even Roxy's.

One look at the expressions on Claire and Noah's faces was enough. No announcements were necessary. A joyful cry went up as the Bay House inhabitants crowded around the happy couple.

A thud at the end of the hall drew Emmie's attention. A door banged. Every head turned as heavy footfalls pounded up the back steps.

"Oh, no, you don't!" Emmie took off at a chugging run, her apron ties flapping in the breeze, followed by Toivo, a roly-poly garden gnome in suspenders and emerald-green pants.

"Shari Shirley's at it again," Roxy said with an exasperated sigh as she dodged the ladder on her way to the stairs.

Cassia wheeled after her, tossing her wild red curls. "Why do I always have to miss the fun?"

Noah and Claire, happy victims of the wedding prophecy, merely looked at each other and laughed. If it was Valentina who'd brought them together, long may she reign. One thing was obvious.

At Bay House, there was always room for romance.